CONTENTS

Acknowledgements 7
Maps 9
Introduction 11
MARCUS AURELIUS OLYMPIUS NEMESIANUS 26
The Hunt (*Cynegetica*) 28
The Night Watch of Venus (*Pervigilium Veneris*) 37
DECIMUS MAGNUS AUSONIUS 44
Bissula 47
The Moselle (*Mosella*) 52
The Crucifixion of Cupid (*Cupido Cruciator*) 65
On the Freshly Blooming Roses (*De rosis nascentibus*) 69
CLAUDIUS CLAUDIANUS 72
The Rape of Proserpine (*De raptu Proserpinae*) 75
Epithalamium for Honorius Augustus and Maria, Daughter of Stilicho (*Epithalamium de nuptiis Honorii Augusti*) 107
AURELIUS PRUDENTIUS CLEMENS 118
Prologue (*Praefatio*) 125
The Battle for the Soul of Man (*Psychomachia*) 127
Hymns for the Various Hours and Days (*Cathemerinon*) 153
Epilogue (*Epilogus*) 215
RUTILIUS CLAUDIUS NAMATIANUS 217
Concerning His Return (*De reditu suo*) 221
PAULINUS OF PELLA (*Paulinus Pellaeus*) 242
Thanksgiving (*Eucharisticos*) 244
ANICIUS MANLIUS SEVERINUS BOETHIUS 263
Philosophy's Warning (from *De consolatione philosophiae*, III, 12) 266

COLUMBA 268
In Praise of the Father (*Altus Prosator*) 270
ALCUIN 278
The Dispute between Winter and Spring (*Conflictus Veris et Hiemis*) 280
Glossary and Index of Names 282

ACKNOWLEDGEMENTS

Both the introductory essay attached to the selection from Ausonius and Ausonius's 'The Moselle' (*Mosella*) were published in the *Delta Epsilon Sigma Bulletin*, May 1963, vol. 7, no. 2, pp. 53ff. and 56ff. The essay was published under the title 'The Poet: A Note'.

'Bissula' and 'The Moselle' were published together in *Arion: A Quarterly Journal of Classical Culture*, Summer 1965, vol. 4, no. 2, pp. 221–32.

'Bissula' is reprinted with the permission of *Arion: A Quarterly Journal of Classical Culture.*

MAPS

1. Western Europe showing major rivers 50
2. Detail map showing the Moselle and surrounding area 51
3. Ancient Italy showing sites mentioned in Rutilius Namatianus: *De reditu suo* 220

INTRODUCTION

It is not really possible to deal with what we here call later Latin poetry and at the same time avoid at least reference to what historians have called 'the fall of Rome'. It is often tempting to treat this phenomenon as though it had occurred at a discrete point in time, as though it were an event or turn of events which occurred in an instant. This understanding, however, cannot be supported by the myriad evidence that so easily comes to hand. In A.D. 410 Alaric the Goth entered and sacked the city of Rome. But this military intrusion came at a relatively late date. In the year 146 B.C. Rome established her authority in the Mediterranean area by the conquest of two ancient enemies: Carthage and Corinth. Almost at once Greek slaves began to function as pedagogues so that Latin Rome began to lose its latinity. Still, the introduction of Greek manners and learning had begun at an even earlier date as the infant Rome began to absorb the Greek colonies located on the Italian peninsula.

In other words, Rome did not so much fall as it changed. The great accomplishments of Rome in the ancient world were law and government. That Rome developed a cultural style should be understood in terms of that particular dual accomplishment. The highways, the routes of commerce, the shipping lanes, the constantly expanded ability to maintain effective contact with the edges of the Empire all made Rome increasingly the gathering place for every cultural strain extant within the area of her widespread influence: Europe, the western regions of Asia and the north of Africa. As the problems of administration increased, it became a matter of expediency that Roman citizenship be extended to more and more areas of the Empire. As the rights and privileges as well as the responsibilities of citizenship became more widely held, so too did the national character begin to be larger than the geographical limits of a city by the Tiber.

In time most sophisticated Romans were delighted to realize that their city had indeed become the world. With such a scheme of things Roman citizenship became a political, purely administrative reality rather than a cultural identity founded in a tradition of language and social experience. That the city was on occasion sacked, that leaders rose and fell, that at times the majesty of imperial government was actually cut off from its Empire are all significant facts. But if we identify any one of these as 'the fall of Rome', we must be prepared to argue that nothing else constituted the fall.

If we consider the age of Cicero, for example, as the very high point of all things Roman, we must also encompass the hellenization of Rome which had been occurring for many years prior to that era. In the year 272 B.C. Livius Andronicus had established himself as a teacher and writer in Rome. He quickly realized that an education based entirely on Roman law and its tradition was quite inadequate to what he considered ideal. Livius Andronicus proceeded to prepare a Latin translation of the *Odyssey* as a text for his Roman pupils. Ennius, a contemporary, also worked to bring a Greek influence into the Roman classroom and culture.

In about the year 168 B.C. the grammarian, Crates of Mallos, came to Rome and found himself teaching the young. Crates introduced the hellenistic modes of literary study so that the classics of Roman literature came to be studied with a new bias and interest. This rather spectacular influx of Greek erudition created its own cultural reaction. Certain figures realized that Rome was suddenly endangered by a one-time victim. As the new methodologies gained currency, it was obvious that the old, and carefully conserved, traditions must undergo change. Yet, what was even more distressing to men like Cato the Elder (M. Porcius Cato, 234–149 B.C.) was the fact that in the assimilation of Greek learning and scholarship there was also an adoption of Greek manners and customs. The conflict can be seen – at the risk of over-simplification – in the development of rhetoric in the era of Cato the Elder.

For Cato, the staunchest Roman of them all, the one thing essential to successful oratory was that the speaker had grasped his matter, for then the words would certainly come of themselves. For Cato, the good orator was an upright man whose ability to speak was dependent on his goodness or virtue. Nothing could stand in sharper contrast to the new Greek ideals. In spite of Cato and his *coterie* the Greek notion of culture, or *paideia*, as Werner Jaeger describes it, was fully acceptable in Rome.[1] By Cicero's time the Greek love of a culture based on the methodological study of literature, rhetoric and philosophy, rather than on simple goodness and moral probity, had become so much a part of Roman life that its effect was to be seen in the curriculum of studies laid out for every patrician youngster.

The two worlds could not be kept separate after the political assimilation of the Greek territories. In Polybius, a prisoner brought to Rome, we find an observable and accessible link between Rome and Greece. A man of many abilities, he was a scientist in the most rigorous sense of the word – a man absorbed by the pursuit of learning. He was a historian who displayed outstanding critical acumen, he was a Roman patriot and he was also a most vigorous admirer of that political greatness achieved by Rome. In summary, he was the embodiment of those intellectual and moral forces which formed the new Greco-Roman culture. Philosophically the link between Greek and Roman cultural traditions was cemented by his almost visceral distrust of intellectual scepticism. One sees this confrontation between the two traditions and the terms of ultimate reconciliation in a speech assigned to Scipio in Cicero's *De republica:*

> I give you my opinion, not as one wholly ignorant of Greek customs, nor as though I were anxious to see them preferred to our own, but as a Roman citizen who, thanks to his father's care, has received a good education and has been fond of study since boyhood; and who, nonetheless, owes more to experience and the lessons of home life than to the study of books. (I, xxii, 36)[2]

The final words are most significant: '. . . who, nonetheless, owes more to experience and the lessons of home life than to the study of books'. ('*Usu tamen et domesticis praeceptis multo magis eruditum quam litteris.*')

In this passage the literary figure, Scipio, presents the two influences as they existed in his own life and also indicates the manner in which he, at least, reconciled their apparent opposition. In the two factors –

1. Werner Jaeger, *Paideia: the Ideals of Greek Culture*, translated from the 2nd German edition by Gilbert Highet, 2nd edition, 3 vols., New York, 1945.

2. My translation of the text as found in *M. Tullii Ciceronis: Scripta quae manserunt omnia*, edited by C. F. W. Mueller, Leipzig, 1898, part IV, vol. II, p. 288.

respect for the traditional and a systematic training in the art of being civilized – we find the beginnings of a new element which would finally be identified as Cicero's particular cultural heritage: *humanitas.*

This rather brief discussion of Rome's absorption of a once alien cultural strain is important here because it demonstrates that the notion of 'fall' or 'failure' cannot be used to explicate the changing thing that was Rome. It is not so much my wish to trace the intellectual history of Rome, though the subject is not without its own interest, as to show that the 'rise and fall' of Rome was an affair much larger than the facts of military and political history alone might indicate.

Christianity began to exist in the extreme eastern edge of the Roman Empire. In an area characterized by a political structure, religion and culture that was unusually foreign to all things Roman, a new religion began a swift development. The earliest Christians considered themselves part of the Jewish community in which they had been born and educated. Only gradually, as non-Jews began to follow the teachings of Christ, did Christianity begin to be separated from Judaism.

In the biblical account of Paul's arrest in Jerusalem we find a good insight into the complex political situation out of which many of these poems ultimately grew. A riot had broken out because it had been rumoured that Paul was not only preaching against the Law of Moses but had also desecrated the temple by taking Gentiles within the sacred precincts. The Roman tribune sent men to the temple area, and, when it became impossible to determine the cause of the disturbance, Paul was placed under arrest. In an attempt to extract some kind of confession, the tribune ordered that the prisoner be scourged and tortured. The text of the story is best quoted:

But when they had tied him up with the thongs, Paul said to the centurion who was standing by, 'Is it lawful for you to scourge a man who is a Roman citizen, and uncondemned?' When the centurion heard that, he went to the tribune and said to him, 'What are you about to do? For this man is a Roman citizen.' So the tribune came and said to him, 'Tell me, are you a Roman citizen?' And he said, 'Yes.' The tribune answered, 'I bought this citizenship for a large sum.' Paul said, 'But I was born a citizen.' So those who were about to examine him withdrew from him instantly; and the tribune also was afraid, for he realized that Paul was a Roman citizen and that he had bound him. (Acts, xxii, 25–9)[3]

After a lengthy imprisonment Paul's case was presented to Festus, a new Roman governor in that area. But instead of submitting to trial like any common criminal, Paul reasserted the fact of his citizenship and then proceeded to claim the right reserved to every citizen of Rome – the right to take his case to Caesar.

When he [Festus, the governor of that province] had stayed among them not more than eight or ten days, he went down to Caesarea; and the next day he took his seat on the tribunal and ordered Paul to be brought. And when he had come, the Jews who had gone down from Jerusalem stood about him, bringing against him many serious charges which they could not prove. Paul said in his defence, 'Neither against the law of the Jews, nor against the temple, nor against Caesar have I offended at all.' But Festus, wishing to do the Jews a favour, said to Paul, 'Do you wish to go up to Jerusalem, and there be tried on these charges before me?' But Paul said, 'I am standing before Caesar's tribunal, where I ought to be tried; to the Jews I have done no wrong, as you know very well. If then I am a wrongdoer and have committed anything for which I deserve to die, I do not seek to escape death; but if there is nothing in their charges against me, no one can give me up to them. I appeal to Caesar.' Then Festus, when he had conferred with his council, answered, 'You have appealed to Caesar; to Caesar you shall go.' (Acts, xxv, 6–12)

Yet Festus, after examining the case privately, was forced to conclude that the entire affair lacked substance in Roman law. Because of this lack of substance, the case should have been dismissed and Paul should have been freed at that moment. However, the appeal to Caesar carried greater weight than the decision of a governor and Paul was necessarily shipped to Rome.

As this matter of law seems to turn on rather ridiculous technicalities – the fact that Paul had supposedly broken a Mosaic rather than a Roman law – it is important still to remember that it is precisely this devotion to the *minutiae* of law which brought Paul, the Apostle to the Gentiles, to the very centre of the Roman world. Once again, new patterns of thought were being brought to Rome by the

3. *The Oxford Annotated Bible and Apocrypha: Revised Standard Version*, edited by Herbert G. May and Bruce M. Metzger, New York, 1965.

inexorable demands of law and political expediency. Though a citizen, Paul arrived in captivity just as Livius Andronicus and Polybius before him. By extending Roman law to every corner of the known world, Rome drew to herself the seeds of future change.

In Rome and in contact with the all-pervasive Greco-Roman culture, Christianity began to grow away from its Hebraic and Jewish origins. This hellenized religion was almost certainly not invented by Paul, but in all probability was already extant from the earliest days so that he served only as its most prominent vehicle to Rome. Paul's background, though clearly Jewish, was also most certainly Greek. Living in the prevalent Greek and Jewish communities of the day, unlike his more provincial brethren, he found it quite easy to move within the huge confines of the Roman world.

After Titus had destroyed Jerusalem in A.D. 70, the Christian religion had become well established in all the heavily populated cultural centres of the Empire. Asia Minor, Syria, Egypt, Greece and Italy had all become areas in which there were significant Christian communities. In each area Christianity began to manifest the local cultural pattern, so that in Greece and Italy Christianity became more thoroughly hellenized than before. The earliest Christians in Rome were, like Paul, Greek-speaking Jews. All their writings were in Greek and the correspondence between the leaders of the various communities was also carried on in Greek.

With the political division of the Empire in A.D. 330, the use of Greek in the west began to decline. Though Latin had long been used among the lower classes of Rome, it soon became the language of all. During the fourth century A.D. Rome again became a city in which Latin was the universal language of commerce and society. The Christian community had no choice but to follow the general trend from Greek to Latin. By the end of the fourth century Latin had become the language of the Christian Church just as it had already become the language of the western Empire.

Throughout the early years of Christianity the psalms, with their dominantly Judaic bias, were virtually the only hymnbook. What Latin hymns were written at the time were modelled on Hebrew rather than on classical models. However, as a Latin Christianity began to develop, its models naturally became the Latin poets of the classical age as Roman education had retained its essentially pagan and traditional orientation. Derived as it was from the times of Cicero, Ennius, Polybius and Livius Andronicus, education rested almost entirely on the study of grammar and rhetoric.

Though rhetoric had once been valued as the key to success in political affairs, in the days of the Empire it lost its political effectiveness as the government became less republican. Rhetoric, as F. J. E. Raby puts it, 'did not cease to be admired for all its apparent foolishness.... The acquisition of style was the one thing to be aimed at, and to that end the schools of grammar and rhetoric put forth all their efforts.'[4]

In addition to rhetoric the student studied grammar, which included the careful study of literature. The grammarians taught the rudiments of reading and writing and followed this with a study of accent, pronunciation and diction. At the same time the poets were being read and the grammarian was conveying enough information for the student to decipher the allusions to history, mathematics, philosophy and so on. Poetry, then, was the only subject to be studied: rhetoric concerned itself more with style than with material content.

In accepting Latin, the Church also committed itself, at least for the time, to the methods by which it had traditionally been taught. Though classical studies were condemned by Tertullian, we find both Jerome and Augustine – to mention only two – admitting delight in such study at whatever costs in guilt and fear of ultimate punishment. Augustine's sermons show every indication of a careful and consciously used rhetorical theory.

It should be noted that there had been in the ancient world a persistently close relation between poetry and rhetoric. Aristotle provides us with what is probably the best reason for this relationship.

> It was naturally the poets who first set the movement going; for words represent things, and they had also the human voice at their disposal, which of all our organs can best represent other things. Thus the arts of recitation and acting were formed, and others as well. Now it was because poets seemed to win fame through their fine language when their thoughts were simple enough, that the language of oratorical prose at first took a poetical colour, e.g. that of Gorgias. Even

4. F. J. E. Raby, *A History of Christian-Latin Poetry from the Beginnings to the Close of the Middle Ages*, 2nd edition, Oxford, 1953, p. 4 f.

now most uneducated people think that poetical language makes the finest discourses. That is not true: the language of prose is distinct from that of poetry. (*Ars rhetorica*, III, i; 1404a: 20–7)[5]

Gorgias, to whom Aristotle refers, was the founder of that new prose style which made such a great impact in antiquity. This new verbal elegance was characterized by a use of what had formerly been identified as 'poetic' words combined with an extravagant and almost staggering use of metaphor. All the tricks of language – antithesis, word play, cadenced expression and even rhyme – became devices which a skilful rhetorician might well exploit.

Much later Latin poetry clearly shows this confusion of rhetorical with poetical mode. Indeed it is tempting to point to specific authors, poems and passages and state that there at least the poet took his matter and his style from the mannerisms of the rhetoricians rather than from those of the poets.

To cite a single example of such expression, one need only turn to the *Psychomachia* or *The Battle for the Soul of Man* of Prudentius. As C. S. Lewis rather trenchantly observes, 'fighting is an activity that is not proper to most of the virtues. Courage can fight, and perhaps we can make a shift with Faith. But how is Patience to rage in battle? How is Mercy to strike down her foes, or Humility to triumph over them when fallen?'[6] Throughout the battle the epic formulas are always present as norms of martial conduct. But the virtues are in no way martial figures. When we find them, like Patience, donning armour and simply riding out the storm of the attack, we may well be impressed to know that virtue is always its own best defence. Still, we cannot help wondering at such a peculiar battle.

The source for the prime metaphor, however, is not only classical literature. The rhetoric of struggle and conflict as a pattern of the good life is also very much a scriptural thing. Prudentius followed the rhetorical tradition that he had studied, but he also combined it with that of a very similar vein coming directly out of writings specifically Christian in content and thrust. But a love for the well-turned speech, and a carefully balanced play of dialogue were essentially

5. Translation by W. Rhys Roberts in *The Basic Works of Aristotle*, edited with an introduction by Richard McKeon, New York, 1941, p. 1436.

6. C. S. Lewis, *The Allegory of Love: A Study in Medieval Tradition*, London, 1936, p. 69.

rhetorical rather than poetic considerations. To compare this dialogue to that found in the New Testament is to realize immediately the distinction between the literary rhetorical mode and that which can only be termed scriptural.

In this stylistic extravagance so noticeable in Prudentius, but also quite obvious in virtually everything of the period, we find that the rhetorician's usual appeal to the non-rational imagination and emotions has been perverted. For the unsophisticated, a rhetorical appeal strikes with all the energy of an unexpected thunderclap. Because it is not rational, the rhetorical appeal is expected to produce a patterned action which is itself at least partially free of rational control. However, Prudentius, like many others represented in this anthology, was not writing for an audience of unsophisticates. Rather, those who have treasured these poems over the centuries have been men of great learning and ability. This leads us to a formal peculiarity. It begins to seem that rhetoric, as a device or tool, is used not so much to elucidate and enlarge upon a present abstraction, but becomes a means by which the author demonstrates a certain virtuosity in himself and in his audience.

What strikes our ear as rhetorical excess, pretence or preciosity is more properly to be understood as a technique which has become an end rather than a means. Rhetoric here is not so much an exercise in persuasion as it is a demonstration of technical competence and ability, meant to impress rather than move. A pivotal consideration is that of wit. In such an artistic context wit, or simple ability, is used to manifest itself rather than to open up awareness. That we find such writing over-inflated is perhaps a curious demonstration that we, in our own highly rhetorical age, are exceptionally sensitive to excess in a context, here literary, where we do not so often find excesses.

It is in St Augustine (A.D. 354–430) that we find the most significant awareness of poetry and rhetoric with their respective uses. The work of Cicero saw five separate activities proper to the orator: *inventio*, the gathering of material; *dispositio*, the ordering of the material; *elocutio*, the reduction of the material to verbal expression; *memoria*, the memorizing of the speech; and finally *actio*, the method of delivery. In his *De doctrina christiana*, Augustine wrote:

There are two things necessary to the treatment of the Scriptures: a way of discovering those things which are to be understood, and a way of teaching what we have learned. We shall speak first of discovery and second of teaching. . . . But first in these preliminary remarks I must thwart the expectation of those readers who think that I shall give the rules of rhetoric here which I learned and taught in the secular schools. (IV, 1f)[7]

One should consider carefully what is collected in the act of *inventio*. For Cicero rhetoric had a use primarily public and at least ornamental. For Augustine, on the other hand, the primary use of rhetoric, or the art of persuasion, was to convey the good news of salvation found in the Scriptures. For Cicero, because the subject matter was to the uneducated somewhat alien, if not tedious, eloquence was a skill which needed practice in order that perfection might be achieved. Augustine, on the other hand, saw Scripture as lucid, but only to those in whom resided the fullness of goodness, namely the virtues of faith, hope and charity. As Augustine put it, a capable man 'will learn eloquence especially if he gains practice by writing, dictating, or speaking what he has learned according to the rule of piety and faith' (*De doctrina christiana*, IV, 4). In other words, without faith one can preach only with difficulty for one without faith lacks the knowledge requisite to the first act of rhetoric, *inventio*, or the gathering of material.

Augustine's interest in rhetoric and his theory of a Christian rhetoric has a larger interest here. In the earlier three books of the *De doctrina christiana* Augustine developed a critical methodology that has immense significance first to his understanding of the meanings of Scripture and then more widely to a literary aesthetic that continued through the Middle Ages and certainly into the Renaissance. Augustine found that gaining an understanding of a scriptural obscurity or ambiguity was an act both useful and pleasurable. In the second book of the *De doctrina christiana* he saw the obscurities filling several roles. First, they produce humility because even the learned must work to understand, so that a man prizes most highly that which he has worked hardest to achieve. But, more to the point, he understood that by establishing the twin bases of a similitude, he garnered a certain pleasure: 'no one doubts that things are perceived

7. St Augustine, *On Christian Doctrine*, translated with an introduction by D. W. Robertson, Jr, New York, 1958.

more readily through similitudes and that what is sought with difficulty is discovered with more pleasure' (II, 8).

It is from precisely this line of thought that we move when we proceed to an understanding of the figurative and symbolic features of Christian poetry. It was almost a commonplace of classical grammar and rhetoric that a given text had meanings richer in substance than the literal meaning alone might indicate. An allegorical or figurative reading of a poet's text was a time-honoured activity. Augustine realized this direction of thought when he stated in the *De doctrina christiana*:

> Lettered men should know, moreover, that all those modes of expression which the grammarians designate with the Greek word *tropes* were used by our authors, and more abundantly and copiously than those who do not know them and who have learned about such expressions elsewhere are able to suppose or believe. Those who know these *tropes*, however, will recognize them in the sacred letters, and this knowledge will be of considerable assistance in understanding them. . . . And not only examples of all of these *tropes* are found in reading the sacred books, but also the names of some of them, like *allegoria, aenigma, parabola* . . .; an awareness of them is necessary to a solution of the ambiguities of the Scriptures, for when the sense is absurd if it is taken verbally [i.e., literally], it is to be inquired whether or not what is said is expressed in this or that *trope* which we do not know; and in this way many hidden things are discovered. (III, 40)

When applied to the Scriptures, the method of explication learned from the grammarian reveals in seemingly irrelevant passages the highest relevance. That poets, trained like Augustine to read poetry for its figures and aware also of the figurative language of Scripture, should in turn write in figures is hardly surprising.

The poetry of this period, however, shows another, perhaps more tenuous, connection with the rhetoric of the day. Raby asserts that 'there is no clear evidence that the popular verse of the Romans was other than quantitative; rhythmical [i.e. qualitative] verse in the West was entirely a Christian possession and it was never employed by pagan writers' (*Christian-Latin Poetry*, p. 21: see note 4). The qualitative verse which began to be evident in Augustine's day was such that the number of syllables, rather than their lengths, became a determining criterion for the metrical structure. As Raby puts it:

Equality of syllables replaced equality of feet; but the new measures were not, from the first, based on the old by the mere substitution of word accent for the ancient *ictus*. The earlier rhythmical verse was a kind of prose, with no fixed accentual rhythm carried throughout the line, although, as in Augustine's *Psalm*, there might be a regular cadence in the middle and at the end of a line. The nearest parallel to this rhythmical system is to be found in the rhetorical prose of classical times which followed elaborate rules, based on quantity, for the ending (of clauses. (*ibid.*)

Again, the use of rhyme came into poetry through the rhetoricians. A parallel form was very commonly found in rhetorical prose. With this use of parallelism there went also the use of *homoeoteleuton* similar ending: assonance or rhyme). This device was generally used to mark the end of a clause or other structure. As the use of rhyme and assonance passed from the oration to the sermon, it soon became evident that they were also finding their way into poetry. Rhyme, however, was not used throughout an entire poem until about the eleventh century A.D. The devices which Aristotle had seen coming into rhetoric from the poets are here seen returning to the poets from the rhetoricians.

In A.D. 313 the so-called Edict of Milan recognized the juridical status of the Christian Church and its adherents. In A.D. 323 Constantine reunited the Empire under his government. During this age of Constantine there began to develop on a large scale a predominantly Christian literature. Such a literature was no new phenomenon. Indeed, prior to Constantine some of the Empire's most outstanding intellects had given themselves to the practice of Christian letters. But these early writings, however prevalent, had been essentially apologetic and doctrinal in conception. With the expansion of Constantine's authority, however, a new literature began to develop. Instead of a strong feeling of cultural inferiority, the age of Constantine began to manifest a Christianity strongly triumphal in tone. Previously the Church had recognized the classical rhetoric as the only possible mode of expression. With Constantine's revolution, however, the strongly conservative need to be authentically Roman ceased to have relevance. The growth of the Church before A.D. 313 had definitely followed the administrative patterns of the Empire. When Constantine forcibly brought Christianity into the mainstream of Roman culture, he was only achieving a public recognition of the fact that it was already all pervasive.

But it must be noted that all the new things never entirely forsook the traditional. Writing – rhetoric and poetry – was put to new uses in the Christian era but the beginnings remained identifiably classical and pagan. Significantly, Latin culture as we know it began to be less and less a Roman phenomenon. Though Rutilius Namatianus wrote his *De reditu suo* in A.D. 417, an unsuspecting reader might well think him to be leaving an island of cultural splendour and going to a remote and barbarous land quite devoid of all the amenities. Such, however, was not true. Though Gaul had for some years been a parade ground for the various barbarian armies and tribes, it had been and remained a cultural centre which preserved most vigorously its own understanding of Roman grandeur. One is almost compelled to see the urbanity of Rutilius Namatianus as a nascent provincialism. In many ways – and it is entirely possible that he could not comprehend this – he was not so much abandoning the world as he was returning to it.

Each poem and each author included in this anthology is significant as being in some way representative of the age. It was not, by any stretch of the imagination, a golden age of literary achievement; it was an age largely devoid of the stability which produces leisure. It was neither the best of times nor was it the worst of times; it was an age of change and of uncertainty, an age which necessarily looked ahead to the hope of a more possible future. For the most part it was an age of conservation coupled with mad experimentation. While dilettantes revelled in every subtlety of verbalization, ascetics turned their backs on such obvious foolishness to seek another world. But neither extreme persisted and the changing world became a world that neither dilettante nor ascetic could possibly have imagined.

It is by now a necessary commonplace that the translator should piously and gravely affirm the utter impossibility of translating poems from one language to another. Quite properly, translation is a kind of betrayal and Robert Lowell's insistence that he imitates rather than translates hardly advances a possible solution. I most certainly cannot pretend to have solved the problem, except to insist that these poems need to be read again just as they have been read in the past.

But for those who will not read these poems in Latin, I can only suggest that they be read in something of the way they were translated. At no time have I hesitated to use whatever translations were available to me. At times my writing desk was completely covered by first a copy of the Latin, then my pad of paper, and then an assortment of earlier translations all open to the proper page. In the absence of the perfect translation both reader and translator can only hope to build on prior achievements.

My verse form requires some comment. With each poem I have attempted a line which approximates in English the length of the Latin original. This length has, in most cases, been determined on a syllabic basis. That is, my English line achieves its shape by having a given number of syllables, which number is to a certain extent determined by the number of syllables in the particular Latin line. No attempt has been made to link the qualitative characteristics of the English with any feature observed in the Latin. Beyond achieving an approximate equality of syllables, the English makes no attempt to duplicate or translate any quantitative aspect of the Latin line.

My understanding of this period's literature has been formed almost entirely by the writings of the late F. J. E. Raby. His two works, *A History of Secular Latin Poetry in the Middle Ages* (2nd edition, Oxford, 1957) and *A History of Christian-Latin Poetry from the Beginnings to the Close of the Middle Ages* (second edition, Oxford, 1953) have provided not only the impetus to include particular poems, but have also shown me the richly varied secondary materials that surround the various authors and poems. His urbane and polished criticism is constantly supported by the most painstaking and meticulous scholarly apparatus. My tracks must be obvious in his snow, but it is my hope that my reliance on his erudition has in no way detracted from the grandeur of his amazing achievement.

In addition to the work of F. J. E. Raby, I should also mention the work of three other men. Hugo Rahner's *Greek Myths and Christian Mysteries* (London, 1963) is a very significant study which details the absorption of certain elements of paganism by the new Christianity. E. K. Rand's *Founders of the Middle Ages* (reprinted, New York, 1957) is an expansion of his lectures given before the Lowell Institute of Boston in January and February 1928. These essays serve as a very useful introduction to the period which this anthology covers.

Pierre de Labriolle's *Histoire de la littérature latine chrétienne* (2nd edition, Paris, 1924) obviously had a great influence on Raby and his work in the field. Unlike Raby, however, de Labriolle covers only the early period from the end of the first to the close of the sixth century A.D. This book has been translated by Herbert Wilson with the title, *History and Literature of Christianity from Tertullian to Boethius* (London and New York, 1924). This very brief bibliographical note is no more than an introduction to the subject. For the reader who wishes more information, Karl Strecker's *Einführung in das Mittelatein*, which was translated and revised by Robert B. Palmer with the title, *Introduction to Medieval Latin* (Dublin and Zurich, 1966), is an essential introduction to the very extensive body of scholarship surrounding this period of literature.

That this anthology exists is due almost entirely to the encouragement of two ladies: Mrs Betty Radice, its editor, who suggested that it be done; and my wife, Lyn, who recommended that I overcome my early inertia to accept the suggestion.

HAROLD ISBELL

St Mary's College,
Notre Dame, Indiana

31 December 1969

MARCUS AURELIUS OLYMPIUS NEMESIANUS

INTRODUCTION

MARCUS AURELIUS OLYMPIUS NEMESIANUS, a Carthaginian by birth, wrote toward the end of the third century A.D. His poem, *Cynegetica* or *The Hunt*, was in all probability written in A.D. 283 and 284. There are indications that he was a fairly prominent poet during this period. But beyond these very scanty details virtually nothing is known of his life and career.

The text of the *Cynegetica* as we find it is incomplete. After 325 hexameters, the poem ends abruptly in midsentence. Of the extant text the first 102 verses (the first 106 in this translation) are concerned with the usual introductions and dedications. The remaining portion of the poem concerns itself with the preliminaries to the hunt. It is likely that the poem as we know it terminates at about the point where the poet would have turned to a consideration of the chase itself. If this is true, it may perhaps indicate something of the intended length of the completed poem.

Despite the fact that Nemesianus rejected the mythological proprieties as they appeared in so many of the earlier writers, he was still writing very much under the influence of the older poets. When he renounced the stories of antiquity and myth, he took us instead to the less lofty but no less literary consideration of rural and bucolic delights. Still, he reserved to himself the option of treating in a future epic the triumphal deeds of Numerianus and Carinus, the two sons of Carus.

The address to the imperial brothers is only a passage interjected in the mounting praise of rural pastimes. While Nemesianus eschews the formal for the informal, the polite for the rude, even the court for the woods, he attempts the verbal elegance that is so characteristic of Roman pastoral. As the reader is immersed in the rustic, he realizes that the poem is in no way vulgar but is rather a statement emphasizing the balance and order which the refined life requires. As he reminds us in the closing lines of the introduction, the chase is only for those who can

forget about
the courts and their turmoil, the din of the cities,
the noise of war and the greed that makes men sailors.

The pastoral existence is not intended as a substitute, rather it is a diversion. The appeal to be diverted is presented with utmost sophistication; for a man truly urbane, the rustic never ceases to be significant.

The pastoral life which Nemesianus depicts is never presented as real life in opposition to artificial life. Rather, the poem demonstrates that a man's desire to be an artificer can be fulfilled in 'the woods, the green meadows and open fields'. We know that without his arts, man could not survive. For Nemesianus, a satisfactory pastoral existence is entirely dependent on man's ability to adapt to another environment. His audience enjoyed the ultimate in urbanization; his poem is a reminder that sophistication is more than urbanity.

Though clearly not an encyclopedic treatise on all the complexities of hunting, *The Hunt* is a collection of lore on the subject. The advice given is based firmly on commonsense and the reader feels certain that the advice is not only reliable but has also stood the test of time. The recommendations, particularly on the selection and training of dogs, can have been derived only from close and careful observation, whether by Nemesianus or by some predecessor. This imaginatively empirical bias which runs throughout the extant fragment is constantly delightful.

A SELECTED BIBLIOGRAPHY

Baehrens, E. (ed.), *Poetae latini minores*, Leipzig, 1881, vol. III.

Duff, J. Wight and Duff, Arnold M. (eds. and trans.), *Minor Latin Poets with Introductions and English Translations*, London, 1961.

Martin, D. (trans.), *Cynegetica of Nemesianus*, Cornell University, 1917.

Schenkl, H. and Postgate, J. P. (eds.), *Corpus poetarum latinorum*, London, 1905, vol. II.

The Hunt
(*Cynegetica*)

A thousand kinds of hunting I sing; we will tell
its pleasant preparations and its confusion,
all of which are rural concerns. My heart is struck
by the muses' madness; Helicon calls to me
and Apollo makes me drink new inspiration.
After the mind has wandered throughout all the earth
he puts the poet under a yoke and tangles
him in a cluster of ivy so that he can
be guided through deserts where men have never gone.
To heed the god and ride in his golden chariot
is a pleasure indeed. His word takes us across
the fields, and places our feet on the untouched moss.
Calliope would, if she could, distract our steps
and entice us to take the well-travelled highway
but we will break new trails rather than follow old.
 What poet has not sung the fate of Niobe?
Who has not heard of Semele and the fires that
were both her wedding and her death? Who has not told
of Bacchus and how his mother waited nine months?
There are poets who relish the stories of men
that are dead because they saw the rites of Bacchus.
There are the tales of Dirce and Hippodamia
and the daughters of Danaus and their sister
who, as new brides, killed all of their husbands but one.
Everyone has told of the incest of Biblis
and we know of Myrrha and the crime that left her
father defiled and forced her to become a tree.
Some poets describe Cadmus becoming a snake
or the many eyes of Io's jailer. Others
dwell at tiresome length on Hercules and his deeds.
Some tell us of Tereus and Philomela.
There are others who tell of Phaethon's adventure

with the chariot of the sun. And there are those
who sing of flames that were blown out by lightning bolts
and of the stench of the river Padus and of
the swan and the feathers that age brought him and of
trees that always weep because a brother is dead.
The poets tell us over and over the fate
of the house of Tantalus; they tell us about
tables sprinkled with blood and the face of the sun
hidden at the sight of Mycenae polluted
by a father feasting on the flesh of his sons.
We will not bother with Medea and her gifts,
nor with the pretty nereids, nor with Nisus;
we have no time to tell about Circe's cup, nor
Antigone who buried her brother's body.
All of this has been done by too many poets;
the fables of the past are already well known.
We would rather explore the woods, the green meadows
and open fields and hope to find game with our hounds.
We take delight in penetrating nervous flesh:
the hare, the doe who does not escape, and the wolf.
We enjoy snaring the wily fox. All we want
is to wander along the reedy river bank
and spear the rat who challenges the crocodile
or catch a hedgehog and let him fix himself on
his body's needles. We are about to begin
a long voyage into such lofty adventures:
we will set the sails on our little boat and go
across the ocean guided only by our skills
until we have made some poetry that is new.
This tiny boat has never gone beyond the coast
or done much more than cross a harbour with its oars.
But now we will spread its sails before the south wind,
leave our anchorage and try the Adriatic.
I promise, O sons of Carus: after this trip
I will record your great deeds and praise the empire
won by two brothers from the people of the Rhine
and those who live by the river Tigris and those
who live by the Arar and the Nile's headwaters.

Nor will I omit the story of Carinus
and the victory he won in the north nor how
Numerian took the heart of Persia and the
ancient towers of Babylon in revenge for
violations of the eastern frontiers of Rome.
I will also tell of the Parthians' slow flight,
their quivers that never opened, their unstrung bows
and the arrows that were never used in battle.

Songs such as these will be sung as soon as I see
your two radiant, divine faces, gods here on earth.
Already, before I can begin, I feel joy
at the prospect and impatience for the delay;
already, it seems, I see the regal brothers
standing before the people of Rome, the Senate,
the generals and rank on rank of soldiers whose
good souls are moved by bravery and devotion.
The gold standards draped in purple gleam while breezes
set the scales of the awful dragon in motion.

I call on only one of the gods: Diana,
the glory of Latona, who roams the forests,
come quickly to me. Appear to me as you do
with your bow and quiver hanging from your shoulders.
Let your weapons and your arrows be made of gold;
let your feet be fitted with purple hunting boots;
let your cloak be embroidered with golden thread and
let that cloak be held in place with a jewelled belt.
Pull your radiant hair back and tie it with a band.
Let the naiads and dryads follow behind you;
let the water nymphs join the procession and let
Echo repeat the lines of the songs that they sing.
Diana, goddess, come along, lead your poet
through the grass, we will follow you: show us the dens
and the lairs of the savage beasts. Come on with me
whoever loves the chase and can forget about
the courts and their turmoil, the din of the cities,
the noise of war and the greed that makes men sailors.

To begin with, your dogs must be cared for throughout
the whole year. From the moment when Janus opens

the gates and starts the months on their rounds you must choose
a well-trained bitch who will retrieve at your command
and be obedient to all that she must do. She
must be of good blood lines from either Sparta or
Molossus: she should stand high on very straight legs,
her breast should be broad but the body should narrow
to her lean belly, her loins should be strong and her
hips should be broad, her long ears should flap when she runs.
Find her a male with similar features, still young
and in his prime. Do not mate dogs when they are old,
for age brings disease and weakness to the litter.
But it is also important that there be some
difference in the age of the parents: let the male
mate only when he has passed his fortieth month
and let the bitch be at least two years old; this is
the most satisfactory combination. When
Phoebe has taken the moon through two cycles she
will be ready to deliver; the womb that was
enriched by the male will have grown bigger until
she produces her litter. You will have offspring
whining for their mother's warm milk. But disregard
this first litter because it is never the best.
No matter how much you desire dogs, you should wait
for the second and then you must cull out the weak.

If you should decide to keep all that have been whelped,
you will find them lean and weak from competition
for the exhausted bitch's milk. What you must do
is find the strongest as soon as they are born and
protect them from injury. You must test each dog
in the litter before it can walk or see light.
Then, once you have chosen, you must destroy the weak.
You can guess at a young dog's strength by his weight and
you can gauge his running by the size of his bones.
But, besides this, there is another test: set fires
in a circle and place the litter and yourself
inside the fires. The bitch herself will choose without
hesitation which of the litter should survive:
she will select the most valuable dog first.

When she sees her litter threatened she will save them
and thus she will clearly select the nobler dogs.
Since by this time it is spring, you should feed the dogs
whey for it is the season of milk and you should
add bread to their milk so that strong humours strengthen
their bones and guarantee the strength that they must have.

But after the path of Phoebus has reached the heights
and seems to move more slowly, you will soon notice
that the summer's heat is at its greatest. Reduce
the amount of rich food, but keep the whey so that
they do not grow heavy too fast, for at that time
their joints are loose, their stance is still quite unsteady,
and their teeth are not strong enough for heavy food.
Do not keep them in pens or chained to stakes because
you must not harm their future running. Confined dogs,
especially the young, will chew at the posts and gnaw
the door to escape their prison. This will destroy
the straightness of their legs and blunt their teeth. Later,
when they are about eight months old, it would be wise
to mix the gifts of Ceres with their whey so that
they are nourished with the rich produce of the land.
Then you can begin training them with a collar
and chain so that they learn to run while in restraints.
When they have reached the twentieth month, bring the dogs
to a course in a small valley. Release a hare
that cannot escape them: they need an easy prey.
Do this exercise many times until the dogs
can easily catch even the fastest rabbit.
Give them exercise in hunting; force them to learn
and love the praise that merit deserves: they should know
the urgency of a familiar voice whether
it calls them back or urges them to run faster.
The dogs must also learn that when they have their prey
they may only kill without tearing the body.
In this fashion must you select and train your dogs
for each hunting season. Always be concerned for
the dogs as they are prey to serious illness
and the mange can attack a pack of animals

so that, no matter what their worth, the dogs will die:
you must, from year to year, select new dogs so that
the hunting pack renews itself. Protect your dogs
by spreading a lotion of bitter wine and oil
over their skin and then putting them in the sun.
Then, with a knife, pick the worms from their skin and ears.

Dogs are also subject to madness. No matter
where the disease comes from: whether it flows out of
some disease in a heavenly body when the
sun lights the sad world with a dull gleam or whether
when the sun enters the sign of Leo it drives
a feverish heat into the dogs or whether
the earth breathes contagion or whether fetid air
or whether stagnant water – whatever it is,
a burning fire grows in the veins and it excites
the tissues near the heart and with venomous foam
escapes in snarls that compel the poor beast to bite.
Learn the potions and treatment that will restore health:
take a portion of castor and work it until
it becomes soft; mix with it powdered ivory
and blend the two so that they harden together;
mix this with milk and pour it into the dog's throat
to expel the furies who have caused the madness.

Besides the dogs bred in Sparta and Molossus,
you should also raise the breed that comes from Britain
because this dog is fast and good for our hunting.
Nor should you overlook the Pannonian breed
or those dogs that originally came from Spain.
What is more, perfectly good dogs come from Libya
as well as from Tuscany: though they have long hair
and their legs seem clumsy, still they are good hunters
for their nose is so keen that they can track the game
through a field congested with other scents and when
they find their prey they will point to its hiding place.
In a later passage I will describe their strengths,
their ability to track and their habits, but
now I must catalogue the hunter's equipment
and I must give space to the subject of horses.

Let Greece send us her best examples of horseflesh:
let that strong breed remind us of the glorious deeds
of the Cappadocians and let each of them
be well equipped so they surpass their ancestors.
That breed has a very wide and smooth back, their sides
are large and their bellies are trim, their foreheads are
high, they have stiff ears and they carry their heads well.
Their eyes sparkle with energy and restlessness,
the neck is strong and large, the shoulders are heavy,
a moist and steamy breath pours out of their nostrils.
When the beast is standing still he strikes at the ground
with a hoof so that he tires himself while at rest.
These are good horses with a very high spirit.

Beyond the pillars of Hercules, past Calpe,
there is a great land that produces fine horses.
This other breed, the Iberian horse, is fast
and very good for hunting on level terrain.
They are no less beautiful than the Greek horses:
when they pant for air they make a wonderful snort
with a torrent of breath. Their eyes show their spirit:
this breed resists the bridle and fights the harness
and they never relax their ears or rest their legs.
On the other hand, you might prefer the horses
that come from Mauritania in Africa.
It is important with this particular breed
that you take special care in checking the bloodlines.

Or you might select one of those horses raised by
Numidian tribes in the African desert:
this horse has been bred for hard work and also taught
to survive, even in the most hostile country.
Do not be worried by their unattractive heads
or by what seem the grotesque lines of their bellies.
Do not be concerned when you discover that they
have not been broken to the bridle. These horses
are accustomed to being free and their manes fall
across the shoulders. Do not be disappointed
because they are easily driven and you can
turn their heads with the light touch of a leather quirt.

You will find that this horse can recognize commands
that would require a bridle on another horse.
If you race this horse on an open plain you will
discover that he becomes stronger as he runs
so that toward the end he seems refreshed and leaves
the other horses behind choking on his dust.
In like manner Boreas, the north wind, crosses
the waters of Nereus and disrupts the waves
with his shrill howls. All other winds make way for him
while he, glowing with the storm's unearthly light, tops
all the waves and reminds the nereids that he
and only he is master of the stormy sea.

These horses, however, take time to develop
their strength for prolonged running but even when old
you will find that they are more youthful than others.
If the horse remains healthy you will find that its
good qualities, once acquired, will remain intact.
In the early spring feed the colt on soft grain and
then open a vein to let its chronic ailments
escape with the tainted blood. Soon strength will return
to his strong heart and the well built limbs
will quickly be penetrated with a new strength.
Soon a much better and more wholesome blood will warm
every vein in the horse's body. You will find
to your pleasant surprise that they desire nothing
so much as to run without hindrance on the road
or on the smooth ground that passes beneath their hoofs.
When summer has ripened the grain and turned the fields
from green to brown, be sure that you feed them barley
and some kind of light grass. Take care, also, that you
separate the dust from the grain. It is also
good to pat the beast while he eats so that he will
relax and take pleasure from the grain while letting
the nourishment flow through his body with great ease.
For this important job you will need stable boys.

Your grooms should also be taught to weave the netting
for the chase; they must also learn to construct traps;
teach them the way to set a net so that the game

cannot escape; they must learn to make openings
of just the right size between the knots and the cord.
They should also learn to tie feathers in the nets
so that when the net is strung out from tree to tree
the bright feathers and flashing colours will frighten
bears, stags, foxes, boars and wolves and then prevent them
from tearing their way out of the net. You should mix
the feathers so that your nets show varieties
of colour and terror stretched along the cord's length.
Be sure to include feathers from the vulture, from
African birds, from cranes, from old swans, from white geese
and also from the birds that live in the water.
Of these water fowl take birds endowed by nature
with red feathers. There are unlimited numbers
of these and you will find that their colours vary.

Make these preparations during the rainy time
of winter. When spring is about to begin, send
your hounds into the meadows and urge your horses
to run faster and faster through the drying fields.
We will go hunting before the heat of day, while
the soft earth still preserves the tracks made in the night

The Night Watch of Venus

INTRODUCTION

THE *Pervigilium Veneris* or *The Night Watch of Venus* is in many ways one of the larger enigmas of this period. It is thought by various scholars to have been composed between the second and the fifth centuries A.D. Moses Hadas is only a little more precise in placing it between the end of the third and the middle of the fourth centuries A.D. To follow Hadas's argument, it is likely that if one argues from literary affinities, the poem must be placed in the era of Nemesianus (*c.* A.D. 285 – *The Eclogues*) and Tiberianus (*c.* A.D. 350 – his fragments). Hadas notes that it was the emperor Hadrian (reigned A.D. 117–38) who restored the worship of Venus. Inasmuch as the poem combines a sense of *romanitas* with an awareness of the cult of Venus, the historian is tempted to link its composition to the reign of Hadrian.[1]

The poem celebrates the *trinoctium* of Venus which had become an officially sanctioned religious festival. This spring festival celebrated *Venus Genetrix* as the principle of sexual reproduction. The poem's concern with claiming Venus as the foundress of Rome is at best conventional. Its real significance is to be found in the fact of its unusual and strong air of subjectivity. For this, Raby identifies it as 'the last lovely flower of ancient verse and the first romantic poem of the new world'.[2]

It is significant that in the text of the poem the reader catches the ring of an occasional rhyme and even an occasional instance of a qualitative rather than a quantitative metric. Though the poem's subject matter may well suggest Hadrianic composition, it cannot be ignored that the poem's metrical peculiarities are most certainly characteristic of a much later period.

1. Moses Hadas, *A History of Latin Literature*, New York, 1952, pp. 335 f.
2. F. J. E. Raby, *A History of Secular Latin Poetry in the Middle Ages*, 2nd edition, Oxford, 1957, vol. I, p. 46.

A SELECTED BIBLIOGRAPHY

Auslander, Joseph (trans.), *The Vigil of Venus*, New York, 1931.

Clementi, C. (ed. and trans.), *Pervigilium Veneris*, 3rd edition, Oxford, 1937.

Dement, Ruth Sheffield (trans.), *The Lesbiad of Catullus and Pervigilium Veneris*, Chicago, 1915.

Kelly, Walter K. (ed. and trans.), *Erotica, the Poems of Catullus and Tibullus and the Vigil of Venus*, London, 1854.

Mackail, J. W. (ed. and trans.), 'Pervigilium Veneris' in *Catullus, Tibullus and Pervigilium Veneris*, London, 1966, pp. 341–67.

Postgate, R. W. (ed. and trans.), *Pervigilium Veneris, incerti auctoris carmen de vere; The Eve of Venus in Latin and in English*, London, 1924.

Quiller-Couch, Arthur (trans.), *The Vigil of Venus*, London, 1912.

Tate, Allen (ed. and trans.), *Poems: 1922–1947*, reprinted Chicago, 1961, pp. 191–217.

The Night Watch of Venus

(Pervigilium Veneris)

Tomorrow let him love who never loved; he who has loved shall
love tomorrow.

New is the spring, filled with song, the world is reborn.
In springtime the loves come together, the birds mate
and the wood nymph frees her hair in a nuptial rain.

Tomorrow let him love who never loved; he who has loved shall
love tomorrow.

It will be tomorrow that Heaven is married.
Then from the airy humours and the foaming sea,
from the deep-hued flocks and from two-footed horses,
Dione, born of the sea, will appear in the rain.

Tomorrow let him love who never loved; he who has loved shall
love tomorrow.

Tomorrow the goddess of love will make a hut
from myrtle branches in the shade of the forest;
tomorrow she will take her revellers into
the echoing groves while Dione recites her laws.

Tomorrow let him love who never loved; he who has loved shall
love tomorrow.

She paints the purple year with flowers like jewels;
she herself warms the swelling buds with the west wind
and it is she who sprinkles all things with the dew
that is left glittering as the night wind passes.

Tomorrow let him love who never loved; he who has loved shall
love tomorrow.

Shimmering tears tremble as they fall, the falling
bit of dew remains a globe as it drops; as dawn
breaks over the land the wet that comes from the breath
of the stars turns the flowers out of their wet coats.

Tomorrow let him love who never loved; he who has loved shall love tomorrow.

Behold: the purple flowers have revealed their blush
and a blaze of roses has burst from the warm buds;
the goddess herself has made the roses unveil
themselves like new brides naked in the light of day.

Tomorrow let him love who never loved; he who has loved shall love tomorrow.

Made of Cyprian blood and the kiss of Cupid,
blended from gems and flames and the flush of the sun,
tomorrow will that bride without any shame free
from its cluster the crimson hiding in its sheath.

Tomorrow let him love who never loved; he who has loved shall love tomorrow.

The goddess has sent the nymphs into a myrtle
thicket; a boy escorts the girls. But no one thinks
that Love keeps holiday if he wears his arrows.
He has put them down, he has joined the festival.

Tomorrow let him love who never loved; he who has loved shall love tomorrow.

Cupid has been sent unarmed, he has gone naked
so that he injures no one with bow, spear or torch.
But be careful, you nymphs, Cupid is attractive.
Naked, he is himself; unarmed, Love he remains.

Tomorrow let him love who never loved; he who has loved shall love tomorrow.

Venus will send maidens with modesty like yours:
'We request but one thing of you, maid of Delos.
Let the woodlands be unbloodied by the slaughter
of wild beasts, let the shadows fall on the flowers.'

Tomorrow let him love who never loved; he who has loved shall
love tomorrow.

If Venus had thought she could bend your modesty
she herself would have invited you, if proper,
to observe for three nights the dancers passing through
these groves while those assembled kept the festival.

Tomorrow let him love who never loved; he who has loved shall
love tomorrow.

Among the new flowers, among the myrtle groves,
neither Ceres nor Bacchus nor the poet's god
is absent. The endless songs keep the night from sleep.
Dione will be queen and Diana must depart.

Tomorrow let him love who never loved; he who has loved shall
love tomorrow.

The goddess has now established her judgement seat
among the flowers of Hybla; she will announce
her laws with the graces beside her. May Hybla
cover everything with a cascade of flowers.

Tomorrow let him love who never loved; he who has loved shall
love tomorrow.

There will be maidens from the country, from the hills,
and those who roam through the woods, the groves and the
springs.
The mother of the winged god first brought them here and
then forbade them to trust Love, even naked Love.

Tomorrow let him love who never loved; he who has loved shall
love tomorrow.

The rain, which is father to all the year, has flowed
within the lap of earth and commingled himself
with her, so that in passing through the sea and sky
and through the soil he will nourish their progeny.

Tomorrow let him love who never loved; he who has loved shall
love tomorrow.

The mother of all things, from her hiding place, stirs
both the spirit and the flesh with the life she bears.
She implanted Trojan branches on Latin stalks,
she prepared a Roman wedding for the Sabines.

Tomorrow let him love who never loved; he who has loved shall
love tomorrow.

She herself made an unhindered fruitful journey
through the sky, the land and the sea beneath her feet;
she poured the spirit of life into every vein
and taught the universe the ways of giving birth.

Tomorrow let him love who never loved; he who has loved shall
love tomorrow.

She gave the Laurentine maid to be her son's wife
and to Mars she gave a bashful temple virgin.
From them would come the Ramnes and the Quirites
from whom first Romulus then Caesar would be born.

Tomorrow let him love who never loved; he who has loved shall
love tomorrow.

The pleasures of love stir the country; all the land
answers Venus. It has been said that Love himself,
Dione's son, was born in the country: while the fields
begot life, she held him and nursed him with flowers.

Tomorrow let him love who never loved; he who has loved shall
love tomorrow.

Behold, the bulls lay their flanks down on the broom plant
and each herd is enveloped by the marriage bond;
behold, a large flock of ewes bleating with their rams;
behold the birds whose song the goddess has not stopped.

Tomorrow let him love who never loved; he who has loved shall
love tomorrow.

The swans trumpet their rasping cry across the pools;
the maid of Tereus takes up her song beneath
the poplar so that one would think she sang of love
rather than of a sister's plaint against her lord.

Tomorrow let him love who never loved; he who has loved shall
love tomorrow.

While she sings we are silent. When will my spring come?
When will I like the swallow be given a voice?
My muse is silent and Apollo ignores me.
In this way did Amyclae in silence perish.

Tomorrow let him love who never loved; he who has loved shall
love tomorrow.

DECIMUS MAGNUS AUSONIUS

INTRODUCTION

WE would probably never consider Ausonius (*c.* A.D. 310–94) a great poet, yet we cannot help condemning Gibbon for his entirely too harsh, and too frequently quoted, remark that 'The poetical fame of Ausonius condemns the taste of his age.' Perhaps it should be said that his reputation is weakened rather than enhanced by the fact that so much of his work has survived. Almost every student of Latin poetry refers to Ausonius and almost without exception one reads that he is characterized by wit and charm. But it has not been sufficiently noted that Ausonius was writing in a tradition that had lost its focal point, Rome, and was now searching for a new point of cultural reference.

Ausonius, if we are to trust his own testimony, was a proud man who achieved publication by making and sending copies of his poems to his friends. With almost every piece we find some prefatory note addressed to the recipient. Invariably these notes display a mild and self-deprecatory tone though one suspects that had anyone dared suggest corrections the author would most certainly have been offended.

Ausonius tells us that he is a Christian. Yet we find the evidence for his Christianity somewhat less than convincing. He could not be said to have been in any way dissolute or immoral, yet his life style was hardly that recommended by the ascetical writers of the day. For him religion was something done at particular times and in particular places. The time for ending prayers was well established and the business of the day could never be shirked in devotion. Ausonius presents a curious mixture of pagan and Christian. Though baptized, he never hesitated to avail himself of the traditional pagan notions that were common in the declining years of the fourth century A.D.

After many years of teaching rhetoric in the schools of Bordeaux, Ausonius was appointed tutor to the young Gratian and eventually became consul. During this period we find the name of Ausonius associated with that of Paulinus of Nola. Before his retirement from the school at Bordeaux, Ausonius had found in the young Paulinus the brilliance and receptivity that every teacher hopes to find at least once. For Ausonius, dedicated to the life of learning, Paulinus could only have been seen as a successor worthy of the teacher.

But this did not come to be. Shortly before his death Ausonius received distressing news: Paulinus and his wife had decided to retire from the fashionable world to seek perfection in silence and penance. For the worldly and urbane old man this decision could only be extreme foolishness. The series of letters that the two, master and pupil, exchanged is an excellent example of two different temperaments confronting one another in a way neither had before imagined possible.

In Paulinus and men like him the old was destined to be preserved as the forerunner and begetter of a new tradition. In his *De idolatria*, written almost two centuries before the death of Ausonius, Tertullian condemned the decadence and evil that characterized the pagan and his works. Yet Tertullian did not hesitate to remind his readers that this baggage of antiquated paganism could well contain elements valuable to the new order whose advent every Christian eagerly anticipated.

The historian can find much of value in Ausonius. In writing his descriptions of the Seven Cities, in recounting the events of his daily life, in listing and describing the members of his family, Ausonius provides an interesting and colourful account of aristocratic life and customs in the provinces of Rome. In the lifetime of Ausonius the barbarians were still being held in check at the frontiers. Although many towns in Gaul had erected heavy fortifications, the order and consequent tranquillity of peace were much in evidence.

There is much good to be said for Ausonius and his work. Like many writers, he has had the misfortune of having his better works indiscriminately ranked with his inferior. When judging the *corpus* of Ausonius's poetry, the critic weighs the good against the bad and finds a disappointing preponderance of the latter. Still, certain of his works have been almost universally liked by anyone taking the time to locate often inaccessible texts.

A SELECTED BIBLIOGRAPHY

Blakeney, E. H. (trans.), *The Mosella*, with a foreword by J. W. Mackail, London, 1933.

Flint, F. S. (trans.), *The Mosella*, London, 1916.

Lindsay, Jack (trans.), *Ausonius: Poems*, London, 1930.

Pieper, Rudolph (ed.). *Bibliotheca scriptorum graecorum et latinorum teubneriana*, Leipzig, 1886.

Schenkl, Karl (ed.), *Monumenta Germaniae historica: auctores antiquissimi*, Berlin, 1883, vol. V:2.

Stanley, Thomas (trans.), '*Cupid Crucified*' in *Poems and Translations by Thomas Stanley*, London, 1647, pp. 25–34.

White, Hugh G. Evelyn (ed. and trans.), *Ausonius with an English Translation*, 2 vols., London, 1961.

Bissula

Ausonius to his friend, Paulus, greeting:

Well, Paul, I am at last giving you what you wish. Though you have been introduced to the secret rituals, you are still forcing your way into the chambers of my muses, a place once shrouded in the darkness proper to sacred mysteries. Though I have never thought of you as one of the vulgar mob which Horace would ban from the muses' precincts, yet I must state my conviction that every deity has its own rites so that Ceres is not approached as one approaches Bacchus, even by the same worshippers. These fragments which I had written so capriciously for my little serving girl are still in the rough, half-finished form that they have always known. They were intended as nothing more than little verses to be read by the fire. I put them aside with no misgivings and they enjoyed their obscurity. But you have compelled me to bring them into the light of day. Surely you must desire to crush me in my shyness by demonstrating the extent of your influence. Your persistence surpasses that of Alexander who cut the knot he could not untie so that he entered the oracle's cavern on a day when it was to have remained closed. Use these lines, then, with the freedom, though not the assurance, with which you use your own, because your works can stand in the public eye while mine make me blush, even in private.

Farewell.

I

Paul, as you've requested, I send the lines
done for that Swabian lass, Bissula.
I must confess that they were written down
more to kill my time than seek my glory.
You've worn me out with your tiresome demands;
you must read the dreary songs as they stand.
What you've begun to eat, you shall finish.

As that saying of the slave would have it:
let the blacksmith wear the shackles he makes.

II

Now don't raise your eyebrow because you hold
a little book of rough and unkempt verse.
Weigh these hefty songs with your brow wrinkled.
These off-hand lines will chant Bissula's praise,
but I warn you now, drink before you read.
I've never written for a fasting man;
a taste of wine is good before my verse.
But sleep is better than a little wine,
for when sleeping one thinks my songs are dreams.

III

Bissula, born beyond the banks of the Rhine,
saw the Danube start its drop to the sea.
She was captured in war but later freed
by order of him to whom she belonged.
Lacking a mother and needing a nurse,
she never felt the hand of a mistress.
Her birth and fortunes never caused her shame
because she barely knew her slavery.
She was Latin but remained a German
in her pretty face, blue eyes, and blonde hair.
Although she was a child of German birth,
her youthful tongue found our language easy.

IV

Pleasant, charming and loving; though foreign,
my daughter has conquered all the Latins.
Bissula, gentle girl with rustic name,
you need never fear your master's anger.

V

Neither wax nor paint will ever capture
in its art Bissula's form or colour.
The reds and whites of other girls are caught
by painting the shades of powder and rouge,
but hands won't catch her beauty as it is.
Let a painter mix the lily and rose,
still that colour comes to her from the air.

VI

Artist, if you plan to paint our daughter,
be diligent in your art like the bee
who finds a sweetness and colour among
the flowers high on the rocks of Athens.

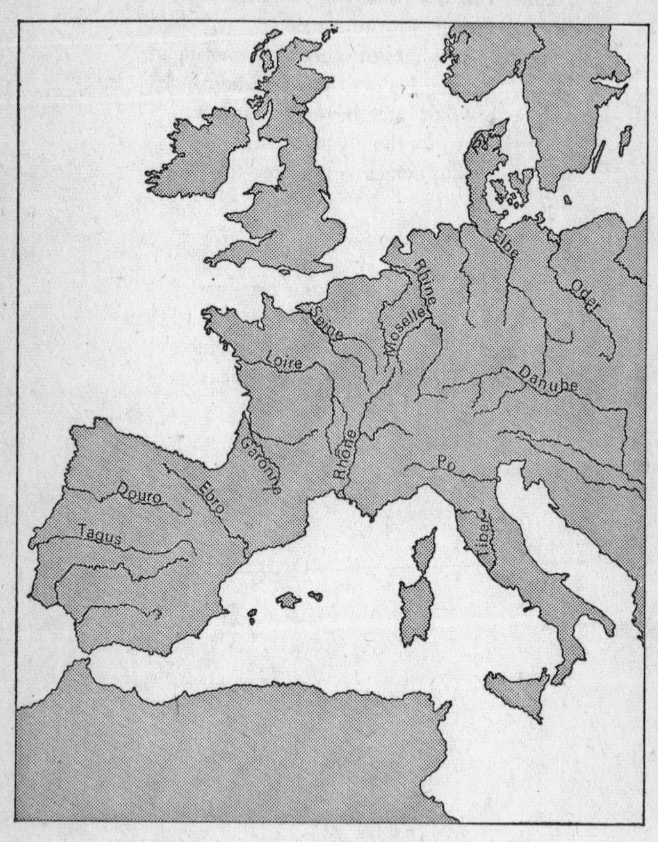

Western Europe showing major rivers

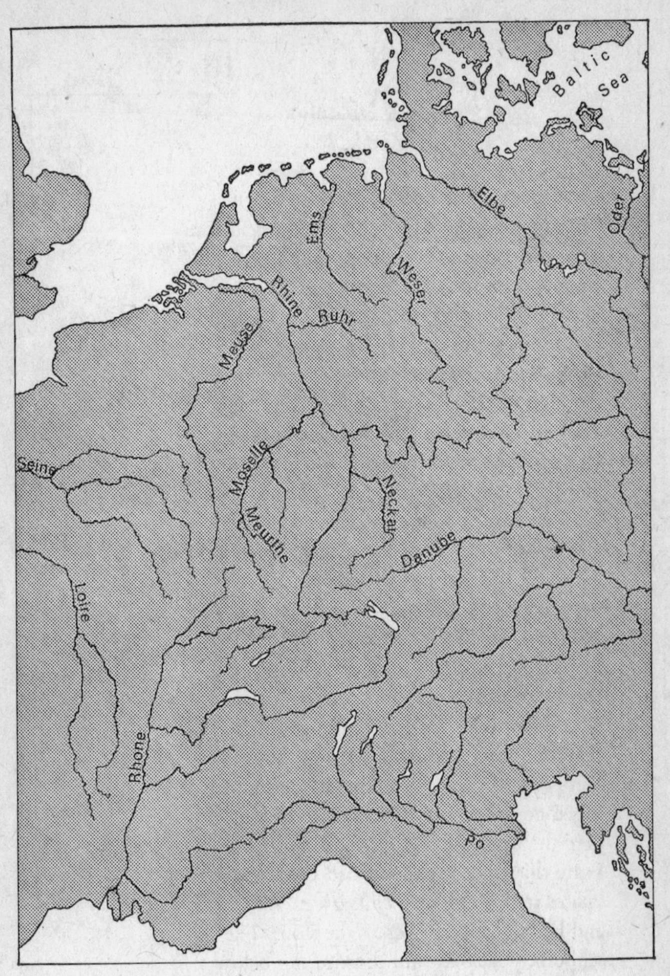

Detail map showing the Moselle and surrounding area

The Moselle

(Mosella)

I had crossed the murky Nava and seen
with wonder the new walls around Vincum.
This is the place where the soldiers of Gaul
fought bravely as the Romans at Cannae
and left their men, strength of the land, alone
and unburied in a misty forest.
From that place my journey continued on
through nameless forests which never saw men.
I passed Dumnissus and its fields drying
in a drought that cracks the soil and ruins crops;
and I saw the cool spring at Taberna
pour an endless stream of water and life;
and my journey took me past those tired fields
allotted to barbarians whose luck
deserted them in frontier skirmishes.
Then on the edge of Belgian soil I saw
Neumagen where – or so the old men say –
the victorious Constantine made camp.
The air on that plain was pure and more sweet
than the misty breaths I drew in the woods.
Here one sees the sky without branches twined
together, green and dark, buried in fog;
here the brightness of daylight never hides.
I saw this land of well-tended fields and
estates set on hills and cliffs green with vines
and hedges running across the slopes like
schoolboys at play and murmuring below
in the valley, the Moselle, my new found
river hurried along. The pleasant scene
recalled to me my distant home, Bordeaux.
  May I pay my respects to the river
praised by every man working in his field?

You bring the honour of empire to Trier.
The channel can float a sea-going ship,
yet your stream slopes and glides like a river.
Pools bright as water in crystal goblets
mimic the mountain lakes I've seen at dawn.
Your current rushes like a narrow brook
and gourds of water lifted from your pools
are better than water from wells or springs.
You glide along hardly rippled by wind
or hidden rocks which might hurry your course
and detract from the glory of your name.
A man can travel this stream in two ways –
he can let his raft drift with the current
and with an oar beat the water to foam
or men can drag his craft along the shores
never slacking the rope stretched from their necks
to the oak mast of a ponderous barge.
Have you ever thought of your twisting stream
and supposed its given speed rather slow?
Your shore is not matted with muddy grass,
the long shallows are not heavy with silt,
your banks are dry down to the water's edge.

Go now, foolish men, and lay out acres
of marble; build floors good enough to rest
under the fine mosaics of your walls
while I scorn the fruits of wealth and marvel
at the work of nature rather than join
that waste which only leads to poverty.
Firm sand covers the moist shore and the beach
cannot remember the shape of a foot.

As the gentle air is clear to our eye
and the resting winds do not hamper sight,
my vision, when it pierces this deep stream,
finds the open secrets of the bottom.
I see the sand is wrinkled with furrows,
the grasses sway green in the river's bed,
pebbles gleam and gravel adorns the moss.
Under the rolling waves of my Moselle,

weeds of many colours reveal scattered
pebbles quiet in the dancing current.
This is like the remote coves of Scotland
where one can find green seaweed, red coral
and pearls – the rich fruit of any oyster's shell.
The toys of men are there beneath the tide
and under a wave this river mimics
the fashions men decree for jewelry.
After watching the stream's bottom my eye
wants to follow the schools of darting fish.
But all the different kinds weave in and out
and the changing numbers leave me confused.
Neptune would never tolerate my voice,
I'll call the nymph to name the fish I see.
The scales of the chub gleam among the weeds,
his meat is crowded with bones yet tender;
he cannot be kept for more than six hours.
The back of the trout is starred in purple,
the bones of the roach are not too pointed
and the grayling swiftly darts out of sight.
I see the bearded barbel who has fought
through the narrowing chasms of the Saar
where the channel is turned by six stout piers.
But when that stream becomes the Moselle he
finds in old age hard-earned dignity and rest.
And could I forget the rosy salmon?
The casual beat of his tail is seen
in a splash rising from the deepest pool.
Salmon, your gleaming corselets of armour
will someday grace an epicure's dinner,
yet you endure the years and rocks and wait
with the fat of your belly fresh as dawn.
And you, tasty lamprey, a migrant fish,
were carried overland from the Danube
to the pleasant stream men call the Moselle –
a famed river welcomed a famous guest.
Lamprey, how nicely nature dresses you:
your sleek back is marked with brown and black spots

set in rings of the rainbow's precious hues.
Blue, deep as the sky, stretches to your tail;
the flesh as far as the middle is rich
but from there on back it is dry and rough.
  And now the perch, delight of our tables.
Only you can be ranked with the mullet.
Your body is plump and your flesh is rich
and divided in segments like an orange.
Lucius, the pike who haunts the frogs, is graced
with a Latin nickname, yet lives in sedge.
He is never invited to dinner,
his meat is cheap and sold in shops that stink
with the rank odour of his frying flesh.
  All of us know the green tench that comforts
plebeian appetites; the bleak provides
sport for boys and their hooks; the shad hisses
on the hearth and is food for common men.
A fish whose species is a mystery
(neither salmon nor trout, something between)
is also in this river, the Moselle.
I cannot forget the bearded gudgeon:
no longer than my palms laid side by side,
the belly is flat till heavy with spawn.
  Now I think we've had enough of the deeps.
Nature must always have something to boast:
the sheat-fish is the pride of our Moselle.
Your back glistens like olive oil from Greece,
your movement is graceful as the dolphin
while the length of your body is hampered
by sand bars and weeds growing by the shore.
But when you swim down our majestic stream
the green banks are dutiful and the fish
are like plebeians at a noon parade.
Your progress raises a swell of water
and the green sedge bows unwilling respect.
Even the whale, pride of the ocean,
can be tossed up on the shore like a chip;
he displaces a tidal wave and men

are afraid. But the sheat-fish does no harm.
Enough of the stream and its mysteries.
The processions of vines which ride the hills
bring the gifts of Bacchus like spectacles
drawn through cheering crowds in the city streets.
These vines spread their grip over the long peaks
of the naked rocks which wind in and out
to form new theatres on the hillsides.
Other rivers have their shores decked the same:
the Garonne reflects the rows of my vines.
Gaurus, Rhodope, the Pangean hills –
all these mountains and ridges are softened
by green plants both wild and cultivated.
The hills of the Moselle stretch themselves down
the slopes of Bacchus like a yeoman's bow.
The landsmen are gay as children playing
while the hard-working farmer happily
labours in song on the brow of the hill.
A traveller feels he must sing with these men;
the banks hear their songs roll through the valley.
But the valley has more than scenery.
Here the satyrs and grey-eyed nymphs must meet
while old Pan and his goat-foot troop riot
with their clumsy strokes in the green shallows
and frighten the nymphs under the water.
Panope, the river's lady, often
steals a bunch of grapes, joins the mountain nymphs,
and is chased through the countryside by fauns.
They say that when the sun reaches high noon
and men hide themselves away from the heat,
the satyrs and river nymphs meet beside
the stream and dance outside the human gaze.
The river nymphs love to splash the satyrs
whose stroke is weak and too clumsy to catch
these charming tormentors, who slip away
in the long waves rolling over their home.
Now there is nothing wrong in my speaking
of things which men have never before seen.

I only wish to reveal them in part
while I leave the greater secrets hidden.
  There is a sight I can easily draw:
the blue river reflects the shadowed hill,
the stream seems to bear leaves and twisting vines,
all the ridges swim on darkened ripples,
the leaves and even the clusters of grapes
are captured here on the clear crystal waves.
The confused boatman counts out the green vines,
the helmsman steers his bark in the channel
of the river where the hill's image blends
with water and the edges of shadow.
  And how nice it is to watch the oarsmen
row their boats together in the middle
weaving makeshift pageants on the water.
They circle in and out and build a dance
which touches the sedge growing by the shore.
The bargemen run from bow to stern like boys
playing their summer games, and the farmer
rests his back and gaily watches these feats
of skill played on the river's flat surface.
While he watches, the farmer can forget
the setting sun and the cares of his land.
All things – river, painted boats – give these lads
that appearance which only youth can wear.
Liber (some would say 'Bacchus') must have seen
the same when he strolled the slopes of Gaurus
and measured the rising Cumean tide,
or watched the vineyards on Vesuvius
raise their wine-rich clusters under a cloud,
or when Venus (happy for Augustus)
commanded Cupid and his troop to act
the battle fought by the navies of Rome
and Egypt below Apollo's temple,
or when the Avernus bears the acting-
out of the naval battle at Mylae.
  When Hyperion unleashes the heat
of the sun the crystal surface reflects

the crews as crooked and up-ended men.
While the oarsmen force their hands back and forth,
the rippling water parodies their strength.
The boys take delight in these illusive
images the river gives back to them.
When they see this mockery the sailors
are each innocent as a growing child
who has never seen a mirror and thinks
the image he sees is another boy.
This inexperienced infant would like
to smooth reflected hair, straighten the shirt
and would even kiss the polished mirror.
The boys on the boats while their time away
with shapes that are sometimes true, often false.
But where the shores can be easily reached
no fish is safe from the fisherman's skill.
The deep pools and devious currents seem
defence enough, almost sanctuary,
yet this false security is shattered
with each foot splashing across the surface.
One man out on a sandbar balances
himself and his nets against a current
which sweeps up innocent fish like a broom
and at the same time makes the hook wiggle
like a drowning insect teasing a fish.
Nets buoyed up by corks, hooks dragged down by lead,
the river's water betrays the dumb fish.
No fish has ever told another of danger
lurking in those knit fabrics or drawn wire –
the bite of iron in the soft gullet
or the pinch of linen cords at the gills –
the green wand bows to the fish it has caught,
the dutiful corks bob in pert respect.
Unthinking, excited, the hungry boy
whips his catch from the stream onto the grass
and I think of a scourge falling on flesh.
Under the water a fish is alive,
but in the sun he will strangle in air.

The dying body quivers helplessly,
the tail is feeble, the mouth is open:
the gills cannot breathe out life in that gasp
every animal tries to make at death.
Those shining gill covers once were beating
like a bellows in a blacksmith's workshop.
Now these gills cannot use the air they suck.
Then again I have seen fish almost dead
leap up high in the air like tumblers
and throw themselves back into the water,
swimming off, to the fisherman's surprise.
When this happens, the boy will make a dive
and try to catch them as they swim away.
Glaucus was stunned to see his catch of fish
flip themselves back into the waiting sea.
He tasted the herbs the fish had lain on
and found he could not avoid the ocean
but would be happy to live as a fish.
All these strange things I think of when I see
those young boys try to catch a fleeing fish.
These scenes are acted along shores and banks
within sight of old country estates perched
high on the crumbling cliffs which overlook
a quiet valley and a rolling stream.
How many have seen the waters divide
Asia and Europe but forget the bridge
that Xerxes tried to build across that strait?
Yet our Moselle is much better than this,
for never in the memory of man
has it had the mad fury of that strait,
and we have never seen a nor'wester
boil the restless waters with snow and ice.
On these shores one need never raise his voice,
the opposite bank echoes every word
so that talking is almost touching hands.
Who is so good with words that he can tell
in every detail the accomplishments
of all the great architects time has known?

Daedalus would not allow one of these
to capture Icarus in golden forms
because the forms were too much like his son.
Philo of Athens is known as well as
Archimedes and his weapons of siege,
and seven ancient architects are known
because their work was good and still endures.
The works of Menocrates, Ephesus,
all these are monuments to skilful men.
Ictinus did well with the Parthenon.
And have you heard of the owl whose cold eyes
were so made that birds were charmed to their death?
Among these count Dinochares who drew
the plans that became Ptolemy's palace.
And don't forget the pyramid that fools
the sun because it stands on its shadow.
The Cretan who honoured the sister-wife
of Ptolemy is always remembered.

Maybe these men or others with like skills
built such wonderful homes on Belgian soil,
buildings which are this river's ornament.
One, over there, is high upon a cliff,
that one on the edge of a jutting bank,
another folds the river in a bay.
This house is high in clouds and has a view
of the fields and wastelands around its base
as though all other lands belonged to it.
Another lifts a tower in the clouds
like Ptolemy's lighthouse built on Pharos;
yet this grand structure above our river
rests its foot on the fertile river plain.
Another is built so the river flows
through its walls and fish are caught in stone nets.
Another glowers down on a river
made much more distant by the tumbling fog.
Must I mention courts beside green meadows
with their roofs balanced on marble pillars,
or the baths built close to the sloping shore?

Here the boiler smoke is drawn by Vulcan
through red-hot flues that heat the cold water
hot enough for an old gentleman's bath.
I have seen some weak from too much bathing
plunge in running water rather than still
because the river is more refreshing
and its current provides them with more sport.
And if a stranger should come from Cumae
he would think our river were a copy
of the streams he had known all of his life:
its charm is refinement without excess.
River, how can I begin the listing
of tributary streams when you are like
the sea with his countless flowing sources?
These streams hurry to lose their names in you.
Although its own swift current is enriched
by the Prüm and the Nims, the Sauer hastens
to bury itself beneath your waters
and by this its name is lost in glory
matched only by flowing into the sea.
The Kyll and the Ruwar (known for marble)
both rush on to swell your brimming river.
The Kyll is well known for delicious fish,
and the Ruwar hears the screams of his mills
as they furiously saw the marble
and make the distant shore-line, hills and trees,
ring with the din of a marble quarry.
I pass the Lieser, the Thron and the Salm
and turn to the ship-bearing Saar which rolls
its weary and overstretched stream beneath
the dignity of imperial walls
that share minor majesty with the Saar.
Ranked next to the Saar is the happy Elz
whose banks are burdened with fruit trees and grain.
A thousand other streams rush to join you
as though nothing else could satisfy them.
But if you had been given the poets
of Smyrna or Mantua, Simois

renowned on the Trojan coast would give up
its famous name and even the Tiber
would be forced to offer homage to you.
Please pardon my extravagance, Tiber;
I meant no insult to your august name.
To you belongs a higher praise because
you guard the seat of sovereign government.
But all hail to you, Moselle, the mother
of a rich farmland and healthy children.
Nature has given virtue to your sons:
their spirits are blithe, their bodies are strong
and perhaps in time their wisdom will match
the ancients, Cato and Aristides.
But I am running away with myself.
Come my muse: end the song; put up your lyre.
I hope to have many years yet to live.
If I exhaust the river's praises now
my old age will be barren and boring.
When I become old and tired of writing
I shall smooth my brow with your name's glory
and I shall sing songs about your heroes.
The muses then shall weave me songs with yarn
woven at fast looms strung with a soft woof.
Spindles filled with imperial purple,
of whom shall I not be able to write?
The peaceful farmers, the skilful lawyers
will be subjects of my pen as well as
those brilliant attorneys who plead the case
of justice and virtue for men accused.
These great men are a senate of their own
and stand in traditions of eloquence
equal to the fame of Quintilian.
Men like these rule their cities with wisdom
and without the shedding of warlike blood.
This stock has supplied vicars and prefects
as governors of Britain and the north.
One of these became consul with Gratian
and found himself, though not highest, still peer

of the highest. May fortune return him.
But enough of famous men and their deeds;
let me tell you about the happy Rhine
which rushes madly through the countryside.
The Rhine must measure a dignified space
to receive the waters of my Moselle;
let them share honour like brothers ruling.
The Moselle brings a most precious gift for
he has seen father and son defeat foes
far beyond the Neckar at Ladenburg,
a feat not found in Latin chronicles.
The Moselle's tale of this victory comes
to the Rhine and others will follow it;
they will be joined and press back the blue sea.
This union can cost the Rhine no esteem
because a host can never be jealous.
Endless fame is only swelled by union.
Rich in waters and rich in water nymphs,
the Rhine's channel can afford to give birth
to twin streams branching out from either bank.
When they see the Rhine's flowing majesty
the barbarian tribes are filled with fear.
The doubled horns of a river's person
are not found at the high source of the Rhine,
but further down where swollen by Moselle.
I, Ausonius, a Roman by name
but a Gaul by birth, find myself daring,
though gifted with only a little lute.
I have tried to sing of Belgian honour,
feeling myself not qualified by birth
or name but many weeks spent as a guest.
I hope it has not been a sin to touch
this holy stream with what my muse affords.
I do not covet praise, only pardon.
This river has caused many to trouble
the Aonian maids and Aganippe.
But so far as poetry will allow,
when I finish my service as tutor

to the growing sons of the emperor
and I return as consul to Bordeaux,
my native lands where I will spend my years,
I will write more in praise of the Moselle.
I will write long poems about cities graced
by the silent channel of this Moselle;
I will tell of fortresses built for war
but by now converted to granaries;
I will tell of rich men on either shore
and how the river parts the fertile fields.
The Loire, the Aisne, the Marne, the Charante
shall never prefer their greatness to yours
even though they measure the boundaries
of peoples known for strength and bravery.
The waters of the Dordogne rush madly
yet they yield to the Moselle. Gold-bearing
though it is, the Tarn is ranked much lower,
and though the Adour rushes swiftly on
it never outstrips Moselle in glory.
Moselle, you are known through foreign lands
and not only at your source or along
the gifted shores of your beautiful stream.
If any man choose to read this poem,
if anyone spends leisure on my verse,
your name must become common property
and the lips of men will recite your praise.
Lakes and living springs will learn your greatness,
rivers and groves will hear our cities praised.
The Drome and the Durance will honour you
as they wander along their shifting banks.
The cold alpine streams and even the Rhône
will admit your glory higher than theirs,
and I will sing your praise to the Garonne.

[1–13]

The Crucifixion of Cupid

(Cupido Cruciator)

Ausonius to his son, Gregorius, greeting:

Have you ever seen a picture painted on a wall? Of course you have, and you remember it. At Trier, in the dining room of Zoilus, there's this picture: certain women who have obviously suffered the pangs of love are nailing Cupid to a tree! Don't misunderstand me. These are not the lovers of our day who casually fall into love with their eyes wide open. Not at all. These are the great lovers of the heroic age who absolved themselves of guilt by blaming the gods. Naturally you remember that Virgil presented something of the sort in his *Aeneid* when he described 'the Mournful Fields'. I was quite impressed by both the subject and the technique of that picture. Subsequently I turned my astonishment into what I must now confess are silly verses. Only the title of the poem pleases me. Nonetheless, I commend the blunder to you. We love our scars and warts. It is not enough that we muddle along in our foolishness, we always seem to insist that others love our effusions as we have loved them. But why should I bother to plead the case of this ecologue? I know very well that whatever comes from me will be welcomed by you. It is this good reception I desire, more than your praise. Good-bye. Think well of your father.

In that 'blest Elysian ground' which Virgil describes
(where the saddened lovers are shaded by myrtle),
the heroines are conducting their rites, each one with
some sign of the death she died. They wander about
in a dank forest with an ominous light. Reeds
and poppies grow in the stagnant ponds and silent
streams. Flowers of evil thrive in the flickering gloom.
Here are the names of the ancient heroes and kings:
Narcissus, Hyacinthus, Crocus, Adonis
and Aeas, whose name for many meant tragic woe.
These are the names that extend the memory of sorrow

after death. The heroines are summoned to live again
the anguish that brought them down to this dreadful place.
Semele is here, both pregnant and in despair:
shrieking at her lonely labour in the lightning,
she fears the empty cradle her body became;
the fire that seared her now burns only in her mind.
Caenis became a man but now she weeps because
she lost the precious gift that brought her happiness;
without hope, still she hopes to be a man again.
Procris still bleeds from the one wound Cephalus made:
she died at his feet, loving the hand that killed her.
Hero carries a sooty terracotta lamp
and throws herself again and again from the tower.
Sappho was much like a man but fell in love and
was slain by love for Phaon: she stands, threatening
to leap from the high foggy cliffs of Leucas.
Eriphyle was saddened by both her husband
and her son, again she rejects Harmonia's gems.
The tale of Minos and mountainous Crete flickers
like a picture sketched in faint lines: Pasiphaë seeks
the tracks of her white bull and Ariadne holds
that ball of string in her hand; her sister, Phaedra,
studies the letter she sent to her husband's son.

One carries a noose, another a hollow crown,
one is ashamed to enter the heifer's belly.
Laodamia cries for the joy of those two nights
spent with her lords, one dead and the other alive.
There are others with drawn swords: Thisbe, Canace
and Elissa. The first carries her husband's sword,
the next her father's, the third the sword of her guest.
Luna, with her torch and a crown of stars set on
her two horns, wanders here as she did when she
tried to seduce the sleeping Endymion. More,
at least a hundred, are there remembering their grief.

But suddenly Love scatters the gloomy darkness
of that place by breaking in on his beating wings.
Each one, you can be sure, recognizes him and
each one remembers that he is her enemy.

The steamy air hides his splendour but they know him.
They catch him; that is a place that cannot be his.
The wings that have been his glory are useless there:
the unending dusk is heavy and saps his strength.
A crowd of angry women soon surrounds him and
he cannot escape from them. Fear makes him tremble.
They drag him into the open and there they choose
a myrtle tree. They know that species well because
Proserpine had tortured Adonis with it
when he loved Venus: it is the tree of vengeance.
They bind him hand and foot and hang him high
on the tree. He cries for mercy but there is none.
They pronounce him guilty without accusation.
Condemned without a judge, Love must pay for his crimes.
Each one acquits herself and blames him for her sin.
Accusing him, each one holds the sign of her death.
Those are fine weapons indeed; that is sweet revenge.
One comes with her noose, another her ghostly sword,
another shows him bottomless rivers, pointed
rocks, a white surf and the quiet depths of the sea.
Some in their anger threaten his skin with torches
that burn without flame. Myrrha stands in front of him,
neither living nor dead, but locked in the form of
a tree. She tears her ripe womb and gathers the drops
of yellow amber that flow down her wounded stem.
She hurls the grisly wealth at his trembling body.
Some of them mock him by pretending to pardon
while they pierce his beautiful skin with sharp needles.
Roses grow from the drops of his blood while the flames
of their lamps move across his delicate body.
His mother, Venus, is among that screaming crowd.
Without fear she approaches her suffering son.
She does not beg for mercy but her bitterness
doubles his fear and intensifies their fury.
She blames him for her disgrace, for all her troubles,
for her shame when she and Mars were snared together
in her husband's bed. She accuses him because
the grotesque Priapus, her son, is mocked by all.

She blames him for the cruelty of Eryx and
for the fact that Hermaphroditus is neither
man nor woman. Speech alone is not enough:
after lashing him with words, golden Venus beats
him with her wreath until he cries, fearing harsher
torture. His broken body colours the roses
with a redness that becomes brighter and brighter.
The menacing voices soon fade away when the
punishment seems to exceed the crime. The ladies
themselves, shocked by a mother's display of hatred,
try to soften her anger by blaming the fates
for the cruelty of their deaths. Then Venus turns
away and becomes again a loving mother.
She thanks those ladies of the past for their mercy
which overlooks their grief while they pardon her son.

These visions and idle fears come from the darkness
even now to disturb his sleep. When he suffers
through the night with terror he escapes from his gloom
by fleeing through the gate of ivory to the gods above.

On the Freshly Blooming Roses

INTRODUCTION

THE poem, *De rosis nascentibus* or *On the Freshly Blooming Roses*, has frequently been edited with the works of Ausonius yet it is in fact a poem of unknown authorship. The poem's immediate importance lies in the fact that it was once attributed to Virgil. It is, however, not likely to have been written much earlier than the fourth century A.D. The poem, which has in it so much of medieval imagery, can be traced through the centuries by either direct translation or allusion in the work of Despérier of Lyons, Ronsard and Edmund Spenser until it appears again more strongly in the English lyric as the source of Herrick's

> Gather ye rosebuds while ye may;
> Old time is still a-flying.
> And this same flower, that smiles today,
> Tomorrow will be dying.

A SELECTED BIBLIOGRAPHY

Pieper, Rudolph (ed.), *Bibliotheca scriptorum graecorum et latinorum teubneriana*, Leipzig, 1886, vol. XXII.

Schenckl, Karl (ed.), *Monumenta Germaniae historica: auctores antiquissimi*, Berlin, 1883, vol. V:2.

Waddell, Helen (ed. and trans.), *Medieval Latin Lyrics*, reprinted Harmondsworth, 1968, pp. 36–9.

White, Hugh G. Evelyn (ed. and trans.), '*Appendix to Ausonius*', *Ausonius with an English Translation*, London, 1961, vol. II, pp. 277–81.

On the Freshly Blooming Roses
(De rosis nascentibus)

It was the spring of the year and the daylight
returned on the breath of golden dawn.
The biting cold of winter was ended but
a fair breeze blowing just before dawn
gave me clear warning of the day's coming heat.
I strolled through the paths of my garden
to seek the freshness of a day newly born.
I saw the grass bent down by hoar frost
which touched the sweet leaves of the kitchen garden;
the cabbage heads sparkled with bright drops.
I saw rose bushes like those grown at Paestum
smiling in the dew of the fresh day.
On the frosty green leaves pearls of dew glistened
until the sun's light made them vanish.
I could not say whether Aurora's colour
came from the roses or whether they
were dyed by tones borrowed from her countenance.
The dew and the redness are one and
together they are the morning, for Venus
is queen of both rose and morning star.
Perhaps the fragrance of both is also one;
but hers is mingled in the bright skies
while this rose in my garden breathes a sweetness
that I can detect quite easily.
The Queen of Paphos, goddess of both the star
and the rose, colours them both the same.
Then it was the moment for the bursting buds
to divide and open their sections.
One was capped close with a cover of green leaves,
another's sheath was flecked with purple
while a third was parting the tip of her spire
to free the tight-folded scarlet and

another was unfolding her packed grandeur
  ready to count the newborn petals.
The glory of that smiling cup was opened
  and one could see all the saffron seeds.
Another whose bloom is past, fades, abandoned
  by her falling petals. I noticed
how swiftly the passing season works ruin
  so that roses wither while they bloom.
While I said these words another flower lost
  the blazing petals from its head and
the earth gleamed with a fresh carpet of crimson.
  All these appearances, all of these new things,
all this birth and change is the work of a day
  which ends the blossoms it has begun.
Nature, we lament because such beauty ends
  so quickly. Once we have seen your gifts
they are immediately taken away.
  For only one day does the rose live;
the shortness of youth and length of age are one.
  The bloom whose birth the morning star saw
is the withered bloom found in the evening.
  But even sudden death can be good.
Though the rose must die she survives her death and
  lengthens life by springing up again.
Young ladies, gather rosebuds while both the rose
  and you are young, for life too soon ends.

CLAUDIUS CLAUDIANUS

INTRODUCTION

CLAUDIUS CLAUDIANUS was probably born in Alexandria about A.D. 370. With his death probably occurring sometime during the first decade of the fifth century, it quickly becomes obvious that his life spanned one of the most significant periods of Roman history. During these thirty to forty years, the frontiers experienced constant pressure from various barbarian tribes. In A.D. 378 the Roman legions were defeated by the Visigoths who had been forced into battle by the incursion of Huns from the north and east. Finally, in A.D. 382, after the Roman armies under Theodosius had been victorious, the Visigoths, like the Goths, became allies – at least temporarily – of Rome. For a few years this uneasy alliance sufficed to hold back the Huns.

In the western half of the Empire these latter years of the fourth century were characterized by repeated wars and political assassinations. In A.D. 395 Theodosius, whose military skill had saved the Empire on several occasions, died, leaving the Empire to his sons, Arcadius and Honorius. Stilicho, who had been one of Theodosius's generals, was a Vandal. However, in spite of his non-Roman ancestry, Stilicho served the young Honorius well by defeating Alaric's rebel Visigoths in Thrace, Macedonia and Thessaly.

Stilicho had taken as his wife Maria, the adopted daughter of Theodosius. In A.D. 398 their daughter, also named Maria, became the bride of Honorius. It was this wedding and the persons involved in it which prompted Claudian's 'Epithalamium for Honorius Augustus and Maria, Daughter of Stilicho'. At Easter in 402 Stilicho defeated Alaric who had again turned rebel and devastated Italy. This battle must have been the last important event to fall within Claudian's lifetime. He probably died about the year A.D. 404.

The poems by which we know Claudian seem to have appeared at Rome from about A.D. 395 to 404. A substantial collection of his poetry has survived and the critic can only conclude that much of it was written to win the favour and patronage, even the affection, of powerful men. Claudian is thought to be representative of the finest Latin poetry. Yet his faults are many and his admirers are always cautious. As Raby says, it is easy enough 'to convey the sense of tedium that falls upon the reader of these remorselessly competent, hard and glittering verses' (*A History of Secular Latin Poetry in the Middle Ages*, 2nd edition, Oxford, 1957, vol. I, p. 92). If Claudian's poetry were nothing else, it would represent most adequately the verbal skills of antiquity. Whatever his accomplishments might have been, it should be noted that Claudian's greatest gift was his power of description. In his long poem, *The Rape of Proserpine*, there are many passages which contain descriptions as fine as any to be found in the literature of Rome.

Claudian opens the poem by detailing the burden of poetic inspiration. He affects to be not merely anxious, but so obsessed by the divine inflatus that all human considerations have been expelled from his breast. But beyond the descriptions, he has little enough to say. It is interesting to note that in two places Claudian engages in cosmological description. Yet each passage reports the events not as fact but as pictorial representations worked into a piece of embroidery. Claudian clearly evades the intellectual issue by merely telling us what images satisfied the characters of his poem. The cosmologies here presented were already, in Claudian's time, quite outmoded. However, it should be noted that such an antiquated description functioned as an artistic device to heighten the verisimilitude of an account clearly meant to be 'prehistoric'.

It is likely that *The Rape of Proserpine* was written early in his tenure at the Milanese court. In all probability the poem's period of composition extends from early in A.D. 395 to near the end of A.D. 397 when Florentinus, to whom the poem is dedicated, lost the favour of Stilicho. Apparently out of loyalty to Stilicho, Claudian left the work unfinished.

A SELECTED BIBLIOGRAPHY

Digges, Leonard (trans.), *The Rape of Proserpine*, 1617, edited by H. H. Huxley and reprinted Liverpool, 1959.

Hawkins, A. (trans.), *The Works of Claudian, translated into English Verse*, London, 1817.

Claudius Claudianus

Howard, Henry E. J. (trans.), *The Rape of Proserpine, a Poem in Three Books*, n.p., 1854.

Hughes, Jabez (trans.), *The Rape of Proserpine from Claudian*, London, 1714.

Koch, J. (ed.), *Bibliotheca scriptorum graecorum et latinorum teubneriana*, Leipzig, 1893.

Platnauer, Maurice (ed. and trans.), *Claudian with an English Translation*, 2 vols., London, 1963.

Pope, R. Martin (trans.), *The Rape of Proserpine in English Verse*, London, 1934.

Strutt, Jacob George (trans.), *The Rape of Proserpine, with Other Poems from Claudian, Translated into English Verse with a Prefatory Discourse and Occasional Notes*, London, 1814.

The Rape of Proserpine

(De raptu Proserpinae)

BOOK I

The man who was first to build and float a ship stirred
the waters with crudely carved oars. Putting
hope and his craft in the wind, he conquered nature.
In the beginning he sailed only when
the seas were calm and he could stay close to the shore.
Soon he began to sail across the bays
and then he spread his sails to Notos, the south wind.
As he lost his fear, he sailed where he wished
until, one day, he could sail on the open sea.
He followed the heavenly markers and
passed triumphantly through the Aegean tempests
into the turbulent Ionian Sea.

*

My impatience asks that I sing of many things:
the black horses of that thief from the underworld,
the stars blotted out by his chariot's shadow
and the dark, dismal palace of Proserpine.
Leave me alone, unless you understand these things.
The divine madness has expelled all human thoughts
from my breast: I am filled with the breath of Phoebus
who has become my spirit and now I can see
the holy place swaying. Its deep footings quiver
and that light glowing in the doorway is the sign
that the god himself is present now in his shrine.
Even the earth roars like a bull. Cecrops' temple
catches the noise and hurls it back while the ancient
city, Eleusis, waves its holy torches.
The snakes of Triptolemus raise their necks and stretch
their red, hooded heads and smoothly they glide along.

Three-headed Hecate rises in the distance
and with her the beardless Bacchus, crowned with ivy,
who wears the pelt of a Parthian tiger, its
claws dipped in gold and tied together, while the staff
which he and his followers carry guides his feet.
I call on the gods who are served in Avernus
by the unnumbered hordes of the dead; I call on
the gods into whose hungry treasure house there fall
all who have died on earth. Your fields are surrounded
by the colourless Styx while Phlegethon runs through
the steaming rapids. I summon all of these gods.
Open for me the secrets of your world, unfold
the deepest mysteries of your sacred stories,
tell me how the god of love brought light to your world.
Tell me how Proserpine received her dowry,
how Ceres looked for her daughter, tell me why men
learned to eat grain and soon lost their taste for acorns.
The lord of Erebus became swollen with rage
and, since he himself had no wife, threatened the gods
with war because he wanted the joys of marriage
and the happiness of paternity. Quickly
the monsters of Hell formed ranks and the furies swore
an oath against the Thunderer. Tisiphone,
with the bloody snakes clustered on her brow, brandished
her torch and called the armed yellow ghosts to battle.
The powers of nature might even have broken
their chains, the horde of Titans might have seen again
the light of day and bloody Aegeon, escaped
from his bondage, might have challenged the strength of Jove.
But the goddesses of fate who saw the danger
knelt together before the lord of Hell and touched
his knees while they wept. It is their hands which govern
all things, their calloused thumbs spin out the thread of fate
and the endless ages are wound on their spindles.
Lachesis, her hair tangled, was the first to speak:
'Lord of the night, great King of the dead, it is you
who commands us to spin out the fate of all things.
You announce the beginning and the end, your word

prescribes birth and destruction, yours is the power
of living and dying. Anything that exists
acknowledges you as the giver of its life;
after a cycle of years you, and only you,
return these souls to bodies. Do not violate
the peace which we have spun for you; do not disrupt
the treaty which binds both you and your two brothers.
Why must you make war? Why must you free the Titans?
Ask Jove. He will answer your request for a wife.'

Pluto stopped at once. Her reason calmed his spirit,
though he was still not willing to forget his wrath.
In such a way Boreas, the north wind, while armed
with the gales and heavy with snow, his wings frozen
with hail, attempts to threaten the sea, the forests
and the fields with a storm. But if Aeolus bars
the door, his fury fades and the storm soon retires.

Then Pluto commanded that the son of Maia,
Mercury, come to him. At once the messenger
was there carrying his wand and wearing his cap.
Pluto's awful majesty ascended his throne,
his sceptre was heavy with the dust of ages,
his presence was foul, his huge head was wreathed in clouds.
He sat there stiff, unbending, a pitiless god
made more terrible by the force of his anger.
Then he raised his head and these words came like thunder:
'Grandson of Atlas, born in Arcadia, god that
goes between Heaven and Hell, god for whom the gates
of both must always open: part the winds, go fast
and take my demands to Jove who sits in Heaven.

'Cruel brother, have you been given dominion
over me? Has harsh fortune taken both power
and light? Because I have lost the vision of day
have I also lost my own strength and my weapons?
Am I weak because I cannot tease the heavens
with thunder? Am I cowed because I do not have
spears hammered out in the forges of the Cyclops?
Surely you must be satisfied with me here
in darkness compelled by that third choice and this place

while your majesty adorns the heavens' brightness.
All of this is yours, must you forbid my marriage?
The daughter of Nereus embraces Neptune;
Juno, sister and wife, holds you close to herself
when you are tired of your weapons; and in secret
you loved Leto, Ceres and Themis. But enough.
You wanted children and now you are surrounded
by a crowd of offspring. I am in this empty
palace with no joy, no fame and without the love
of a child to quiet the torment of my pain.
I will not tolerate such boredom, I swear by
the unending night and by the stagnant waters
of Hell, if you refuse to hear this, my request,
I will open Hell itself and free its monsters.
I will break the chains of Saturn and plunge the sun
once again into darkness, I will blend the light
of Heaven with the shadows of Hell, I will tear
the world from its place, nothing will be as it was.'
While he spoke the silent halls trembled at his voice;
the dog who watches at the gate put his three heads
on his paws; Cocytus stopped his tears; Acheron
waited while the river, Phlegethon, ceased to flow.
All of Hell became silent at the tyrant's words.

Almost before he finished, the messenger left
the gates of Hell. The Father heard the demands and,
taking counsel with himself, tried to think of one
who might prefer the caverns of the river Styx
to the brightness of the sun, he must soon decide.

Ceres, who is worshipped at Henna, had only
one daughter, a much-loved child, because the gods had
granted no second child to her exhausted womb.
Mothers of one are prouder than mothers of two;
Proserpine was a daughter finer than most.
She was her mother's only concern, Ceres cared
for her with a fierce devotion no less than that
of an old cow tending her helpless calf until
curved horns can grow on the forehead of the beast.
As the years passed, Proserpine was a woman

ready for marriage. Though she dreamed of a husband,
her innocence and modesty made her afraid.
There were suitors everywhere, their voices echoed
throughout the palace. Mars and Phoebus presented
gifts: Mars would have given Rhodope while Phoebus
offered Amyclae and Delos and his temple
which stands at Claros. Juno and Latona each
wanted Proserpine as the bride of her son.
But Ceres with the golden hair rejected both
and sent Proserpine to Sicily so that
the child would be safe. She did not know the future.

Sicily, with its three headlands, was once a part
of Italy but storms and tides cut it away.
Nereus broke loose to fill the narrow valleys
and leave the mountains standing over a channel.
This three-cornered island stands alone in the sea:
at one end of the island Pachynum spits back
the wrath of the Ionian Sea; another point,
Lilybaeum, stands where the African currents
rise and beat against the shore; at the Pelorus
the unrestrained Tyrrhenian Sea shakes the land.

The burned cliffs of Aetna rise out of the island.
This mountain is a standing monument to Jove's
conquest of the giants; this mountain is the tomb
of Enceladus whose body, tied and beaten,
breathes endless brimstone clouds from its smouldering wounds.
Whenever his restless shoulders shift this burden,
the very foundations of the island quiver
and the crumbling city walls sway from side to side.

The summit of the mountain can only be seen
because no man has climbed its peak. The lower slopes
are green but the higher slopes have never been tilled.
The mountain vomits dense smoke and darkens the day,
then it begins to quake and threaten the heavens
with destruction; it feeds the flames with its body.
Though it boils and sends out such heat, still it observes
a contract with the snow: the ice and ashes cool
together, protected from heat so that the fires

lick the frost with a breath that does not melt the ice.
What monstrous machine hurls those boulders? What power
can pile rocks one on the other in such fashion?
From what awful spring does that blazing river flow?
I do not know. Perhaps the wind, forced underground
and into some confining cave tries to escape
and sweeps the hidden caverns with its mighty blast.
Perhaps the sea, flowing into the blazing bowels
of the sulfurous mountain, bursts into flame as
its waters are driven together by the heat.

When Ceres, the mother of Proserpine, gave
her daughter to Henna, she went to Cybele,
in Phrygia, driving a chariot drawn by
two serpents who leave venomous spots on their bits
and as they pass open wide the clouds of heaven.
At first they swam in circles through the air and then
they skimmed across the waiting fields and sowed the land
with golden kernels until their path was yellow.
Sprouting stalks covered their tracks and rich crops of grain
stood where the sister of Pluto had crossed the land.

Soon the speedy chariot left Aetna behind
and the island disappeared. She knew what must come;
her cheeks were marked with tears, she looked back to her home
with words like these: 'Be joyful, dear island, because
I have left my daughter to be safe on your soil.
I entrust her to you, she is my only joy,
she is the fruit of my desire and my labour.
You will be well rewarded. Keep her from danger
and I promise that your rich land will never know
the pain of the hoe or the cruel steel of the plough.
Your fields will bear fruit and without working the soil
your people will have a harvest sown by itself.'
Before long her serpents brought her to Mount Ida.

Here stands the shrine of Cybele and in this place
the statue of the goddess is shaded by pines
so that though there is no wind the creaking branches
remind the visitor that the place is sacred.
In the temple the followers of the goddess

raise their wild chants: Ida resounds with their howling
and the woods of Gargara bend over in fear.
When Ceres arrived, the drums became quiet
and the shouting choirs grew still; the corybantes
halted their mad dance and laid their knives on the floor;
the pipes and cymbals were still; even the lions
bent their necks in welcome. Cybele ran out of
her shrine, bowed her towering head, and kissed her guest.
Jupiter, on his high throne, saw everything.
He confided in Venus: 'This is my concern.
Long ago I decreed that Proserpine must
be the bride of the prince of Hell. Old Atropos
desired this, Themis prophesied that it would be.
Her mother has left her alone, now is the time.
Make a visit to Sicily; urge the maiden
to play in the meadows when dawn lights tomorrow
with its rosy glow; use those tricks which can inflame
all things, even you. Why should Hell be free of love?
Every land must know love, even the dead must burn
with the fires that Venus kindles; now is the time
when even the dismal furies must feel passion;
the heart of Dis will be softened by love's arrows.'
Venus hurried away. Pallas and Diana,
the huntress, obeyed Jupiter's word. Like a star
falling from Heaven, Venus plunged toward the earth.
A glowing ball of bloody light is an omen
of evil: the sailor who watches it will die,
the nation which sees its passage will be destroyed;
for the ship it means a tempest, for the city
it means that an enemy will attack with fire.
The goddesses soon reached the palace of Ceres;
they saw its walls, built by the Cyclops, the polished
iron, the burnished gates, the doors bolted with steel bars.
Neither of Vulcan's apprentices, Pyracmon
nor Steropes, ever built anything so well,
nor did the bellows ever breathe such a wind, nor
did the streams of molten iron ever run so deep.
Even the furnaces were wearied by this task.

The great hall was panelled with ivory, and the roof
was spanned by long beams of bronze on amber columns.
 Proserpine was busy stitching a present.
On the cloth she traced in embroidery the course
of primordial things, the house of the Father
of the gods, and she depicted Nature bringing
order out of Chaos so that the elements
parted and went, each of them, to its proper place:
those that were light went up, the heavier went down;
the newborn air became bright and fire found its place;
the sea began to flow and the earth hung in space.
The girl adorned this marvellous scene with many
threads. The stars were edged with gold, the sea was purple.
The shores sparkled with precious stones and her needle
imitated a pattern of waves on the sea.
One could think he saw seaweed thrown against the rocks
while hearing the waves hiss across the thirsty sand.
She measured out the five zones of the world: red yarn
showed the hot centre, the desert was dry and its
threads were baked by the sun's heat. The temperate zones,
where mankind lives, showed a climate mild and pleasant.
At the top and bottom she traced the frozen zones,
showing the horror and gloom of eternal cold.
She went on and showed the throne of her uncle, Dis,
and his attendants with whom she must one day live.
All at once her maidenly cheeks were wet with tears;
she knew the prophecy, she could see this omen.
 Then she began to stitch in Ocean's crystal depths
on the edge of her cloth but at just that moment
the doors opened to the goddesses and she left
her work unfinished. A bright flush came to her cheeks
and lit the lamps of her modesty: ivory
stained with scarlet dye was never so beautiful.
 Then the sun lowered himself into the sea and
the mists of night came scattering sleep to all men.
As darkness fell, Pluto prepared to leave his realm
and make his way to the upper air. Allecto
yoked to his chariot four horses: Orphnaeus,

cruel and fast; Aethon, faster than an arrow;
Nycteus, pride of Hell; and Alastor, branded
by Dis himself. These horses drink from the stagnant
pools of Lethe and let oblivion drip from
their thick, pendulous lips; these four animals graze
by the banks of Cocytus and roam the meadows
of Erebus. They stood in harness, impatient
to enjoy the plunder they were destined to have.

BOOK II

When Orpheus rested and put his songs to sleep,
  the nymphs complained because their joy was gone
and the rivers missed the sweet and soothing music;
  once again, all of nature was savage.
The heifer listened for the silent lyre to calm
  the hungry lion; the rugged mountains
grieved in his absence and the woods that had often
  swayed to his songs were standing in silence.
But then Hercules, going from Argos, came to
  the plains of Thrace and destroyed the stables
of Diomede and put the horses out to graze.
  Then the poet took up his lyre again
and touching the strings with a quill made sweet music
  while his fingers danced on the ivory board.
As before, the wind and waves were stilled and Hebrus
  flowed more slowly in his reluctant stream.
Rhodope, eager for the song, stretched out her rocks;
  Ossa bent down and shed his coat of snow.
The poplar, pine and oak left the slopes of Haemus;
  even the laurel was drawn to the song,
though at one time it had despised Apollo's art.
  The dogs of Molossus played with the hares
and the lamb was still while the wolf lay by its side.
  Does played friendly games with the tiger and
the Massylian stag did not fear the lion.
  All of nature was again in repose.

Orpheus sang a song of a stepmother's wrath;
he sang about the deeds of Hercules
and the monsters defeated by that strong right arm;
he told how the infant in his cradle
had strangled the snakes and given their torn bodies
to his terrified mother and then laughed
because dangers such as that meant nothing to him.
Orpheus made a list of those labours:
'Neither the bull that shook the cities of Crete nor
the wrath of the hound of Hell frightened you.
Neither the Nemean lion nor the wild boar
from Mount Erymanthus terrified you.
You stripped the Amazons of their weapons and shot
the birds of Stymphalus. You drove the herds
home from the west and snatched from the jaws of Geryon
a triple victory. Antaeus sank
to the earth for nothing and the Hydra sprouted
new heads in vain. Diana's deer could not
escape; the fires of Cacus were put out; the Nile's
flood was red when you wounded Busiris.
Pholoë stank from the slaughter of the centaurs
and beasts were born from the clouds of the air.
Even the shores of Libya respected your name;
Tethys, wife of Ocean, admired your strength
when you lifted the heavy earth to your shoulders.
On your strong neck the heavens were secure,
the sun and the stars were tethered to your shoulders.'
That was the song of the Thracian poet.
You, Florentinus, are a Hercules to me:
it is you who moves my quill; it is you
who wakes the muses from their long sleep; it is you
who leads them from their caverns to the dance.

*

Not yet had day brightened the Ionian waves.
The light of dawn burned the surf and flickered across
the blue sea. Proserpine forgot her mother's
jealous worry and went to the green, wet meadows.

Such had the fates decreed; she was led by Venus.
Three times the hinges of the doors gave their warning,
three times did Aetna thunder prophecies at her,
but she could not be stopped. Blinded and deafened by
this divine deception, she hurried to her fate.

The goddesses attended her; Venus went first,
pleased with what she was doing. She could see the theft
of Proserpine, she knew that soon she would rule
the depths of Chaos; love must conquer even Dis
and Venus would govern the spirits of the dead.
The hair of the goddess, combed out and then braided,
was wrapped around her head in great folds that were held
in place by a pin made on Cyprus while a brooch
that Vulcan forged held a garment studded with gems.

Diana, queen of Parrhasia, and Pallas,
who guards the fortress of Athens, are both virgins:
one the huntress, the other the goddess of war.
On her polished helmet Pallas Athena had
the image of Typhon, his upper body dead,
the lower body writhing; her spear, like a tree,
pierced the clouds as she brandished it; she hid the neck
of the gorgon within the folds of her jewelled cloak.
Diana's expression was mild, she is much like
her brother: her cheeks and eyes might well belong to
Phoebus; only a woman's form makes the difference.
Her arms were bare, her long hair was blown by the breeze,
her bow was slack, her arrows were tied to her back;
the tunic which came from Gortyn, on Crete, was held
by two belts that let it hang down to her knees; her
undergarment was embroidered with her birthplace,
Delos, in a golden sea that moved as she walked.

Proserpine, the pride of Ceres and her grief,
walked as an equal with them. She looked like Pallas
without her shield, like Diana without her darts:
her dress was held with a brooch of polished jasper;
her young body dignified the loom and shuttle,
never before had cloth so beautiful been made
nor had there been embroidery so true to life.

In the pattern she had stitched the birth of the sun
from Hyperion's seed and the birth of the moon,
she showed the two nurtured by Tethys and she showed
the dark plains of Ocean lit by their youthful light.
On her right shoulder Tethys carried the infant
Titan, pictured as gentle, with a slight flame that
came and went as he cried. Titan's sister, the moon,
was on her left shoulder and suckled at the breast.

That was the marvellous design of the girl's dress.
She was attended by the naiads, goddesses
from the Crimisus, the Pantagias, and from
the Gela, whose name has been given to a town.
In addition to these who came from Sicily,
there were naiads from the Camerina, and some
from the Arethusa who came under the sea
to Sicily with the river god, Alpheus.
Cyane was also there, tallest of that group.
They moved together like that band of Amazons
led by Hippolyte as they march after war
with the Getes or after harassing the country
beside the Don with axes forged in their homeland,
they moved together like a procession of nymphs
keeping the feast of Bacchus. These Lydian nymphs
were fathered by Hermus in whose river they play,
wet with his golden waters. The god of that river
is glad and spills a generous flood from his springs.

Henna saw the crowd of goddesses from her hill
and called down to Zephyr in his windy valley:
'Dearest Father of springtime, who rules my meadows
with your breezes and brings rain to the summer's fields
with your unending breath, observe this gathering
of nymphs and see the noble daughters of Jove who
are happy to play in my meadows. Favour them:
let my trees be heavy with new fruit; let Hybla
be jealous of this new garden; spread the fabled
sweetness of Panchaia's resin, spread the odours
of India and all the spices of Phoenix
which bring life out of death. Scatter this wealth throughout

my veins and freshen the countryside with your breath;
let my leaves be worthy to grace their sacred brows.'

Those were her words. Zephyr shook nectar from his wings
and soaked the ground with dew. The brightness of springtime
followed his flight. The fields grew a thick green carpet
and the dome of heaven shone without any cloud.
He made the roses red, the hyacinths blue and
the fragrant violets purple. What belts, even those
made in Parthia for the body of a king,
are adorned with such a treasure of gems? Is there
cloth, even that dyed with Tyrian purple, more
handsome? The wings of Juno's own bird are shabby
beside such beauty; not even the rainbow has
such colours when it bridges the winter sky with
an arch of rain that glows among the open clouds.

The countryside surpassed even the bright flowers:
the plain, with its easy slopes, rose into a hill
and streams poured up out of the fractured rocks to flow
through the grassy meadows; a tree softened the sun's
intensity and with the shade of its branches
preserved the coolness of winter around its trunk.

The pine, whose trunk becomes a ship's mast; the cornel
tree, whose wood is tough and good for spears; the useful
oak, sacred to Jove; the cypress which grows on graves;
the red oak which has honeycombs, the laurel which
knows the future; the box tree which has a thick crown
of leaves; the creeping ivy and the vine that grows
on the elm were all growing in that place. Not far
away is a lake, Pergus, surrounded by trees.
Anyone who looks down into that lake can see
the deepest secrets that lie there on the bottom.

Venus stopped the procession. 'Come here, my sisters.
Let us waste no time; the newborn sun is shining
through the moist air and Lucifer drives his damp team
and waters the fields of flowers.' As she said this,
she plucked the flower that grows in the memory
of her grief. Her companions explored the valleys
like a cloud of bees led out of their wax fortress

by their king and swarming in search of some sweetness.
The humming army finds the rich blossoms of thyme
and then, one by one, returns to the hive. The fields
were stripped of their beauty: one goddess wove a crown
of white lilies and purple violets, another
draped herself with marjoram, a third crowned her brow
with roses, another was decked with white privet.
Hyacinth and Narcissus, once beautiful boys,
but now the pride of spring, were gathered by their hands.
Hyacinth, born at Amyclae, and Narcissus,
Helicon's son: one died when struck with a discus,
the other died dazzled by his own reflection.
The god of Delos, his brow turned down in sorrow,
wept for one; Cephisus mourned for the other's death.

Proserpine wanted to gather wild flowers.
Her happy baskets made of river weeds were filled,
she made a flower crown and put it on her brow,
but she did not see this grim prophecy of marriage.
Even Pallas Athene, goddess of bugles
and the weapons of war, picked flowers with the hands
that know hand to hand combat and how to pull down
the gates and walls of an enemy encampment.
She put down her spear and wore a crown of flowers
on her helmet. The blossoms bent her plumes, the buds
hid the martial austerity of the spearhead.
Diana, like the rest, no longer roved the slopes
of Parthenius with her hounds, but made a rope
of flowers to hold her long flowing hair in place.

While the ladies sunned themselves, suddenly a noise
was heard: towers fell to the ground and whole cities
swayed and collapsed on their foundations. No one knew
what had happened; all except Venus were confused.
The goddess of Paphos knew that sound; joy and fear
filled her breast. The king of the underworld had left
his throne and was making his way through the dimness
surrounding his dark domain. The ghostly horses
crushed the body of Enceladus as they rose
to the upper air; the giant, writhing in pain,

had his limbs torn from his body as he struggled
to tangle the wheels of the smoking chariot.
The third son of Saturn came like some enemy
tunnelling under the walls hoping to surprise
the foe by piercing every defence with their picks.
Pluto struggled up through the earth hoping to come
out beneath his brother's sky. No door was open;
boulders lay in his path; the earth was a prison.
He could not tolerate delay; he struck the rocks
with his staff. The caverns of Sicily thundered;
the Aeolian islands shook; Vulcan left his forge
and the Cyclops dropped their burning bolts of lightning.
The guardian of the frozen Alps heard the noises
as well as he who swam in your water, Tiber,
even before your stream flowed under the glory
of Italy; and even he who rows his boat
down the Po heard of Pluto's coming to our world.

In like manner, when the lake with its rocky shores
covered all of Thessaly, Neptune struck the cliff
with his trident and Ossa fell back away from
Olympus and made a channel so that the sea
could have her streams and the farmer could have his fields.

When the island of Sicily felt Pluto's blow
and opened herself, a sudden fear seized the sky.
The stars fell out of their orbits, the great Bear fell
into the ocean, the lazy Boötes set
and even Orion trembled. Atlas turned pale
when he heard those horses neighing. Their smoky breath
darkened the heavens and the bright sun frightened them,
who were so accustomed to darkness. Stunned by a
world they had never seen, those horses stopped in their
tracks and for just an instant they threatened to turn
the chariot back the way they had come. But they felt
their master's lash and learned to bear the sun's brightness.
They were faster than a stream in spring, quicker than
an arrow, faster than a Parthian's dart, the
south wind's rushing, faster than a thought in the mind.
Their bits were warmed by blood, the air was infected

by their breath and the dust was poisoned by their foam.
The nymphs escaped; Proserpine was caught and dragged
off, begging for help from the goddesses, her friends.
Pallas Athena unveiled the gorgon's head and
Diana strung her long bow and hurried to help.
Neither would yield to her uncle's violence. They fought
for the virginity that each possessed; they fought
because anger was aroused in them by that deed.
Like a lion bloodied by a fresh kill, Pluto
scorned the feeble anger that raged around his head;
like a lion who has slaughtered a prize heifer
and has torn the helpless flesh and spent his fury
on all the limbs, Pluto rested in his conquest.
'Master of the listless, vilest of three brothers,'
Pallas screamed, 'what furies roused you, what furies
have prodded you with pikes and burned you with torches?
Why have you left your throne? How dare you come to foul
the upper air with your team? You have the furies,
that hideous curse of Hell, and all the other
gods who roam that world. Any of them are worthy
to be your spouse. Get out of our brother's kingdom,
leave the realm that is now another's; go away.
Be content with the darkness you already have;
do not try to mingle the dead with the living.
Leave. Do not be a guest in this unfriendly world.'
She finished. Blocking their progress with her shield, she
struck the horses and drove them back by raising high
the head of Medusa with the hissing curling
snakes that are its hair. She then threatened the horses
of Hell with her weapons; even darkness was stopped
in its tracks by the gorgon's head that is mounted
on the shield of Athena. She picked up her spear;
its radiance drove the shadows out of that chariot.
She had almost thrown it when Jupiter leaned down
from Heaven and hurled a burning bolt of lightning.
The clouds were torn apart and the thunder became
a marriage hymn that was heard throughout the world and
the flaming heavens confirmed the marriage contract.

The goddesses had no choice. Diana, in tears,
put her weapons down and said, 'Do not forget us,
farewell. We cannot disobey our own Father,
we cannot help you now, we cannot protect you;
we have been defeated by a greater power.
Our father plotted this: he has abandoned you
to the silent kingdom where you will never see
the sisters and friends who want just a glimpse of you.
What fate has taken you from the upper air? Why
have the heavens been condemned to such deep mourning?
Never again will we take pleasure in setting
our nets on the slopes of Parthenius; never
again will we wear a quiver. Let the wild boar
roam where he wants; let the lion roar as he will.
Even the mountains will weep for you; the ridges
of Maenalus and the summit of Taygetus
will forget the hunter. Cynthus will mourn for you;
my brother's shrine at Delphi will become silent.'

While these sad words were said, Proserpine, weeping,
was carried off in that chariot. Her hair streamed
out in the wind, she beat her hands together and
shouted her words at the sky: 'Father, why is it
that you have not struck me with your bolts? Did you wish
to give your own daughter to the spirits and drive
her out of the world? Can you not be moved by love?
Do you not have a father's feeling? In what way
have I offended you? When the land of Phlegra
was torn apart by the insanity of war,
I was not one to raise my hand against the gods.
For what crime, for whose guilt have you banished me now
to the bottomless lower world? Happy the girls
who have been carried away by other brigands.
At least they can live in the light of day, but I
and my virginity lose the sight of Heaven.
Both daylight and virtue have been taken from me;
now I must leave my world and be the bride of Hell.
Why did I ignore the wisdom of my mother?
Why did I not detect the trap that Venus set?

Ceres, my mother, wherever you are, hear me:
if in Ida listening to the Lydian mode,
if you are on Dindymus where the galli howl
and the swords of the curetes flash, hear my plea.
Escape from that noise, then stop Pluto's lust and catch
the reins of the horses who draw this funeral coach.'

Her words and tears overcame even Pluto's heart
as he felt the stirring of love. He wiped her tears
with his dismal cloak and soothed her grief with these words:
'Proserpine, do not trouble yourself with care
and groundless fears. You shall have a sceptre and you
shall have a husband worthy of all of your gifts.
I am the child of Saturn, whose wishes command
the world and whose power extends throughout the void.
You have not lost the brightness of day forever:
my world is another world; I have other stars.
You will see a purer light and you will be stunned
by Elysium's sun and by those who live there.
A richer age, a golden race, dwells in that place;
we possess forever what men win only once.
Meadows and flowers like Henna has never seen
breathe sweetly in a breeze softer than the west wind.
There is a tree in the groves whose curving branches
are bright with golden fruit. That tree belongs to you.
You shall be the autumn queen and enjoy its fruit;
you shall be mistress of all things wrapped in the air,
all things that grow in the earth, all things by the sea,
where the rivers roll along and the marsh lands are,
all living things beneath the moon will become yours.
Kings in purple robes will kneel at your feet as will
poor and common men, for death makes all men equals.
You will send the wicked to suffer and give rest
to those who die in goodness; as they come to you
and stand before your throne the wicked will confess
the evil of their lives. You will control the stream
of Lethe and the fates will obey your command.'

While he spoke he reined in his horses and entered
Tartarus. The ghosts of the dead were gathered there

thick as a storm of leaves driven by the south wind,
heavy as rainclouds coming in summer, countless
as the ocean's waves or sand flying in a gale.
The dead from every era hurried on to see
the bride. Soon the lord of that place entered with joy
and smiled at their bantering laughter; he was changed.
Phlegethon rose up as the couple passed by him;
the monster's beard glistened with fires that lit his face.

Slaves hurried to meet the master and his new prize:
some pulled the chariot off, others led the horses –
tired and hot – to graze in their familiar pastures;
some opened curtains, others made decorations
for the chamber. The ladies of Elysium
attended their new queen and calmed her awful fears:
they gathered her hair into braids, they veiled her face
to hide the chaste colour that had come to her cheeks.

Joy filled that colourless place; the crowd of buried
men and women kept the festival as they should:
the manes wore crowns of flowers while joyful songs
broke the dreary silences. There was no wailing;
the squalor of Erebus was broken and the
darkness of the eternal night became softer.
No lots were drawn from the urn of Minos, the sound
of beatings ended and Tartarus was silent.
Ixion's pain stopped as the wheel stopped its turning;
the pond no longer fled the lips of Tantalus:
Ixion was free and Tantalus could drink deeply.
Tityus was allowed to straighten his body
and the unwilling vulture was dragged away from
the dark flesh that now no longer would be renewed.

The furies lost their wrath and made a bowl of wine
from which they drank. The snakes that live on their foreheads
lifted their mouths to the wine and became happy
like all the monsters and fiends of Hell. Then the birds
flew safely over the poisonous Avernus
and the lake, Amsanctus, gave off no more vapours.
The river stopped its flow and the whirlpool was still.
It is said that at that same time the springs that feed

Acheron began to flow with sweet new milk while
Cocytus, wreathed in ivy, drifted in sweet wine.
Lachesis took no more lives and nowhere was heard,
while the marriage songs were sung, the funeral dirge.
Death did not walk on the earth and no parents wept.
No sailors died on the sea; no soldiers were killed.
Death, the destroyer, was forgotten by the towns.
Charon wove sedge into his tangled hair, he sang
while he worked the weightless oars on an empty boat.

Then an evening star shone in the underworld and
the maiden was led to the chamber, night was clothed
with stars and stood beside her like a sponsor; she
touched the couch and blessed a union they could not break.
The happy ghosts of the dead raised their voices and
beneath the roofs of Dis began their sleepless song:

'Daughter of Ceres and son of Juno, Pluto,
the brother and son-in-law of the Thunderer,
may you both know the union of sleep together;
pledge fidelity as you hold one another
in your arms. Your children will be happy; nature
is waiting for gods who are not yet born. Give us
and the world a new divinity; give Ceres
the grandchildren she has always wanted to have.'

BOOK III

Then Jupiter ordered Thaumantis to summon
all the gods. Like a rainbow spanning the sky she
passed through the heavens and called the gods of the sea.
She scolded the nymphs for their delay; she summoned
the river gods from their damp caverns. All hurried
in doubt and confusion because this disturbance
of their peace filled them with fear. The starry heavens
opened and all were seated according to rank.
This was no contest in which chance named a leader:
the heavenly orders were first, after them came
the gods of the ocean, Nereus and Phorcus,
and in the last place were Glaucus and Proteus.

The ancient river gods had seats while a thousand
other streams stood like young men among their elders.
Water nymphs, still dripping, leaned against their fathers
and fauns silently admired the starry heavens.
The majestic Father spoke from his mountain throne:
'Again, the affairs of mankind have troubled me.
Since that day when I observed the reign of Saturn,
I have neglected that unhappy race. I saw
them, then, buried in the torpor my father
permitted in that stagnant age. I urged mankind
by goading them with necessity so that crops
would no longer grow without their cultivation;
I forbade the forest trees to drip with honey
and I stopped up those springs that poured a flood of wine
into every cup that was dipped into their pools.
I was not jealous of their blessings – gods cannot
be envious – but luxury is the enemy
of a life centred on the gods. Wealth blunts the minds
of men. I arranged that necessity, mother
of invention, would spur their lazy minds so that,
little by little, they might discover the cause
of things that are both hidden and open to view.
An age of industry replaced a golden age.
'But now Nature is endlessly complaining that
I have failed to help the human race. She calls me
cruel and says that I am a tyrant; she recalls
my father's reign and she says that I have hoarded
her riches because the world is a wilderness:
fields are overgrown with weeds and there is no fruit.
She complains because she, who was called a mother,
has now become more like a hateful stepmother.
She accuses me: "Is it any good if man
has wisdom from on high? What good is it if man
can raise his head above the earth while he wanders
like a beast in the desert? Like the animals
with whom he lives, he crushes acorns for his food.
Can a life that is hidden in a forest bring
happiness to one who is more than animal?"

Over and over I heard these complaints. At last
I took pity on man and decided to free
him from his dependence on the fruit of the oak.
I have decreed that Ceres will wander across
the earth mourning the loss of her daughter until,
finding a trace of the child, she will rejoice and
in her joy give to mankind the gift of grain; then,
as her chariot speeds through the sky, she will scatter
such fruits as men have never known. But if any
god dares to tell Ceres who has stolen the girl,
I swear by the might of my kingdom, by the peace
that is in the world, that whoever he may be –
son, sister, spouse, or even one of those daughters
proud to be born from my brow – that divine person
shall feel the lightning bolt, the anger of my arms;
he shall curse his birth and pray for a speedy death.
Mangled and torn, he will be received by the king
of the lower world, my son-in-law, to suffer
in the place he thought he might betray. He shall learn
that Tartarus has but one lord. So let it be,
let the fates fulfil my decree.' He finished and
set the stars shaking in terror at his power.

Far away from Sicily, Ceres was anxious
because she felt that she had suffered some great loss.
For a very long time she had lived securely
in that cave which always echoes and re-echoes
with the noise of worship. But dreams troubled her sleep
and during the night she saw Proserpine gone:
she dreamed that a spear pierced the body of her child;
she saw the garments of her daughter changed to black;
she saw an ash budding and growing in her house;
she saw the laurel that shaded her daughter's grove
cut off at the roots and dragged through the dust. She asked
the meaning of this and – in her dream – the dryads
told her that it was the furies from Tartarus.

Next the image of Proserpine herself came
to Ceres and announced what had happened: she saw
her daughter locked up in a dark prison and bound

with chains. The child had not looked like that when she left:
this was no child running in the fields; this was not
Proserpine playing on the slopes of Aetna.
The hair which had been more beautiful than drawn gold
was fouled; the darkness of night had dimmed both her eyes
and the frost had driven the roses from her cheeks.
The beautiful hue of her skin and those arms, white
as morning frost, had become the colour of Hell.
She saw the vision, but could not see her daughter.
She looked more closely; she examined the features
and then, though still she doubted what she saw, she said:
'What awful crime could have deserved such punishment?
What does this mean? Who has such power over me?
Why are your soft arms fettered like a beast? Are you
my child or am I deceived by some illusion?'
Then the vision answered: 'Detestable Mother,
you have ignored your daughter's fate, you are worse than
a yellow lioness. How could you forget me?
Was I nothing because I am your own daughter?
Perhaps my loss will make me precious in your eyes.
Can you enjoy dancing while I am confined and
tortured in this cave? Can you relax in Phrygia?
If you, Ceres, are really my mother, save me.
Unless you have forced a mother's love from your breast,
unless I was whelped by a tiger from the shores
of the Caspian sea, I know you will return me
to the upper world and save me from this prison.
But if the fates prevent this, visit me, at least.'
She reached out her trembling hands but the iron fetters
held her close. The noise of the chains woke her mother.
Remembering the dream, Ceres was rigid with fear.
She rejoiced because she could not believe her eyes,
though she was sad because she could not touch the child.
But the fear returned and she rushed to Cybele:
'I cannot stay here in Phrygia. I must leave.
My daughter is surrounded by many dangers.
Surely, my Mother, you understand. She is young.
I do not trust her safety, even in the walls

that were forged at the Cyclops' hearth. I am afraid
that rumour will reveal her hiding place; I fear
that Sicily will not properly guard my trust.
It is a place that is now too famous. I must
find a home that is much more obscure. Men will know
what we have done; the groans of Enceladus will
tell anyone who cares to listen. I have dreamed
of disasters: you know this is a bad omen.
Not a day passes without something to scare me:
my crown has dropped from my head, blood flows from my breasts;
tears come to my eyes and my hands beat at my ribs;
if I play the flute, all that I hear is a dirge;
the cymbals have a muffled sound. There is trouble
behind all these things; this journey has injured me.'

Cybele answered: 'May the wind disperse your words;
the Thunderer has weapons to save his daughter.
But go so that you may return free of worry.'

After this Ceres left. But she could not hurry
fast enough. Her dragons seemed sluggish; she lashed them
across their wings though they could not have moved faster.
She was afraid of all things and hoped for nothing.
Like a bird who has left her fledglings behind while
she goes to gather their food and then finds herself
fearful that the wind has destroyed the nest and left
her young to the mercies of men and snakes, Ceres
hurried along, seeing nothing but her terror.

She found the gatekeepers gone, the hinges rusty,
the doorposts tipped and the passages desolate.
She needed to see no more: she tore her garments
into rags and pulled the golden grains from her hair;
she could not speak or breathe or even weep. Trembling
started in her heart and shook even her marrow;
she could not walk, she could hardly stand. She wandered,
then, through the deserted palace and recognized
the loom with its tangled threads. What her daughter had
left unfinished there the spider would soon complete.

Ceres did not weep or cry, but she kissed the loom
and held it to her breast as though it were her child.

Proserpine had used those spindles, she had tied
those threads and left it all when she went out to play.
She saw the child's innocent bed and her chair. Like
a herd returning to find all its steers murdered
by a lion's fury or wandering wolves, she
gazed in silence at the place where life once had been.
Ceres found Electra, Proserpine's nurse, who
loved her daughter like a mother. It was the nymph,
Electra, who carried the child to her father,
Jove, and let her play on the divine knee. She was
the girl's companion, guardian, and almost, mother.
With her hair torn and smeared with dirt, she was weeping
because her foster child was stolen from her care.
Ceres approached the woman and said: 'What is this
ruin? Who is my enemy? Is my husband
still lord of the gods or have the Titans triumphed?
Who would try something like this if the Thunderer
were still alive? Has Typhon destroyed Ischia?
Has Alcyoneus escaped Vesuvius?
Has Enceladus escaped the jaws of Aetna?
Briareus, the giant with a hundred arms,
must have attacked my household. Daughter, where are you?
Where are my thousand servants, where is Cyane?
What strength could have driven away the winged sirens?
Is this the way a trust is kept? Is this honour?'
The old nurse trembled, shame overtook her sorrow;
she would have died to escape the face of Ceres.
For many minutes she did not move; she delayed
because the villain's name meant certain death for her.
She spoke weakly: 'I wish the giants had done this.
It was the goddesses, her own divine sisters,
who conspired to ruin us; jealousy did this.
The house was quiet. Obedient to your last words,
the child would not leave even to run in the grass;
she busied herself with the loom, the sirens sang
for her pleasure, she chatted with me and with me
she slept. Within these walls all her delight was safe.
Suddenly Venus came attended on each side

by Diana and Minerva – I do not know
who showed them the way to this hidden place; at once
the three visitors put on happy faces and
kissed Proserpine and called her "sister" until
they had her trust. The three complained that mothers who
hide such beauty must be unnatural mothers;
they said that a goddess should be close to Heaven.
The gullible child enjoyed their speeches and she
ordered that a feast be prepared for her three guests.
She put on Diana's armour and took her bow;
she put the helmet with horse-hair plumes on her head
and tried with her young arms to lift the heavy shield.

'Venus, the most conniving of the three, mentioned
the beauty of Sicily's mountains and valleys.
Feigning ignorance, she asked the child to describe
the beauties of this island. She pretended doubt
when told that the roses bloom even in winter;
she could scarcely believe that the cold months are bright
with flowers; she persuaded the child to show her
the place. How easily youth in its weakness falls.
My tears meant nothing, even my words meant nothing.
Away she went, trusting her sister's protection,
followed by nymphs nearly lost in the confusion.

'They went to the hills and gathered flowers at dawn
when dew whitens the land and violets are freshened.
But when the sun at noon had reached the higher air,
suddenly the sky was wrapped in the cloud of night
and this place shook as horses drew a chariot
across the land. No one knew the driver's name,
he might have been a messenger or Death himself.
The meadows took on the colour of a deep bruise,
the rivers were stopped, the fields seemed to be poisoned.
Anything touched by the horses' breath soon withered:
the cypress lost its colour, the roses wilted
and the lilies died on their stalks. When the driver
turned his horses back the way he had come, daylight
returned as night disappeared. Your daughter was gone.

'The goddesses, their work finished, had left in haste.

We found Cyane out in the fields nearly dead.
She wore a garland and a crown of blackened leaves.
We asked about the child. She had been a witness.
Then we asked about the horses and their driver.
She said nothing but turned to water as we watched;
her body, as though it were eaten by poison,
melted until our feet were standing in a stream,
The others have fled: the sirens are living now
on the coast of Pelorus and in their anger
will no longer sing unless their songs can destroy.
Their pleasant voices will stop any ship and once
the song is heard the oars can never move again.
Only I remain to spend my years in mourning.'
  Ceres was still anxious. Although nothing happened,
she still dreaded what the future might bring. She raised
her eyes and voice to heaven and cursed all the gods,
even the least significant. Just as the rocks
of Niphates shake when the tigress roars because
her cubs have been taken to become royal playthings,
so did the island tremble at this mother's rage.
Faster than the west wind which is her living breath,
the tigress rushes the hunter who shrewdly shows
the beast her image in a mirror and stops her charge.
Ceres climbed Olympus and cried, 'Give me my child.
I am no water nymph, nor am I a dryad.
I am not of common birth; Cybele bore me
as Saturn's child. Where are the commands of the gods?
What has happened to the law of heaven? What use
is it to live a good life if this is my prize?
Even after she had been caught by Hephaestus
Venus managed to overcome the shame of sin
and become chaste again; now she cannot be shamed.
After such brazen behaviour she knows no guilt.
I call on all of the unmarried goddesses:
is this the way virginity should be treated?
Are you so changed that now it means nothing to you?
Have you become partners with Venus and her crowd?
Your cults cannot be gentle. What caused your anger?

In what way might Proserpine have injured you?
Did she drive you away from your favourite pastimes?
Did she bore you with a child's idle chattering?
Did she perhaps interrupt your elegant dance?
That was not it. She was hidden in Sicily
far away from the places you like to frequent.
What good was this? Nothing appeases jealousy.'

In that manner she addressed the heavens. But they,
because of the Father's commandment, held their tongues.
Either they said nothing or wept when Ceres spoke.
What could she do next? She changed the tone of her voice
and lowered herself to humble pleading. 'If I
have let my love get out of hand, if I acted
with too much boldness, forgive me now, I beg you.
Like the lowest beggar I kneel at your feet and
beg that you tell me what has happened. Let me know
what I am now: tell me, and I will call it fate;
I will not even accuse you of injustice.
If nothing else, let me only see my daughter.
You have won your victim; possess it now in peace.
But if the villain has already succeeded
and has sealed your lips with oaths, at least Latona
will tell his name. Perhaps Diana, your daughter,
has confessed the crime. You have borne children, you have
worried for their health and you have also loved them.
You bore twins, Diana and Apollo, but this
one child was my only child. I pray that you live
a happier mother than I. Enjoy your twins.'

She began to weep. 'Why am I shedding these tears?
Why are my prayers answered with nothing but silence?
All living things have abandoned me to my grief.
I cannot stay here; I am at war with Heaven.
I shall seek my daughter on land and sea;
I will peer into every crevice of this earth:
I will not rest until I have found what is lost,
even though she be buried off the coast of Spain
or lost in the depths of the Red Sea. I will go
even to the frozen north where the Rhine flows and

to the frosts which are on the Alps; I will not fear
the raging tides of the African coast; I will
go south and seek her in the snows of Boreas;
I will climb to the summit of Atlas and peer
into every cavern with my smoking torches.
May Jupiter observe my travels; may Juno
feed her jealousy with the sight of my ruin.
Enjoy yourselves, you gods of Heaven; be happy
in the proud victory you have at my expense.'

She went to the slopes of Aetna to make torches.
On the slope of that mountain there is a forest
watered by the Acis, in which Galatea
swims when she finds the ocean too violent. Those woods
are dense and wrap the mountain in twining branches.
It is said that the father of the gods left his
arms and spoils there after the war with the giants.
There are trophies taken on the plains of Phlegra
and they are hung on every tree. Here are the jaws
and skins of the giants; their faces still hang there
threatening all who pass. The huge bones of serpents
are ranked everywhere still smoking from the lightning
which struck them down. Every tree has a famous name:
one tree is bent double by the swords taken from
the hundred hands of Aegaeon; another boasts
of Coeus; another has the arms of Mimas
and another tree has the weight of Ophion.
But higher than all is one with spreading branches:
it has the stinking weapons of Enceladus,
the king of the giants who were spawned by the earth.
It would have fallen without an oak that grows near.
Because of all these things, this is a hallowed place;
no one will touch these ancient trees or their burden.
None of the cyclops lets his flock graze in that place
nor would one of them dare to hew even one tree;
Polyphemus himself avoids the sacred place.

But Ceres was not afraid. The grove angered her
because it was sacred to all her enemies.
She carried an axe and would have struck Jove himself.

With care, she surveyed the timber. Hesitating
between the pines and the cedars, she looked for trees
that would best serve her purpose. She was like a man
building a ship who chooses different kinds of wood
for the different parts: the trees that grow tall and straight
become yardarms to stretch the sails, the helm is strong,
the oars are pliant and the keel is waterproof.
There are two cypresses, twins, growing in that place.
Neither the Simois nor the Orontes have
watered trees like these. You would know they were sisters
for they were the same height. She wanted those two trees
for torches. She tied her skirts up and swung her axe.
First one and then the other trembled at her strokes;
together they fell and lay in the dust. The gods
of the forest wept over the dirty branches.
Ceres took both trunks and, panting for air, began
to climb the mountain. She passed the flames and then crossed
the lava that no human can touch. In this way
Megaera takes the trunks of yew trees to light up
her crimes, whether in Mycenae or in the town
of Cadmus. That one lights her torches on the shores
of Phlegethon where even water turns to flame.

When Ceres had climbed up to the edge of the pit,
she hurled the two trunks into the mountain and closed
the cavern on all sides. The mountain quaked and then
it began to tremble from the flames within it.
Vulcan was imprisoned; the smoke could not escape.
The flames burned away the cones and then the branches.
But before the trunks were consumed, Ceres sprinkled
them with a drug that keeps a thing from being burned.
The potion was that one which Phaethon throws over
his horses and the moon sprinkles on her bulls. She
addressed the flames and ordered that they neither die
nor sleep. She had finished her work, now she must go.

The silence of night had fallen, all the world slept.
Ceres, with her burning heart, began her journey.
'I never thought, my daughter, that I would carry
torches like these. All my dreams were a mother's dreams:

marriage and marriage torches and a wedding song
to be sung in Heaven. I dreamed of nothing else.
Are we, even though we are gods, subject to fate?
Must we suffer the enmity of Lachesis
just as mankind suffers? How fortunate I was.
I was beset with suitors seeking my child's hand.
Though I had only one daughter there were more men
about the house than many mothers ever see.
You were my first joy; now you are my final joy.
For that one child they said I was prolific.
You were my pride, my sustenance, the dear object
of a mother's eye. While you lived I was divine;
your safety made me equal even to Juno.
But now I am forced to wander like a pauper.
It is the Father's will. But why should I blame him?
It was I who deserted you; I left you there
at the mercy of your foes: I was too concerned
with the noise of Cybele's shrine. I was playing
with the Phrygian lions when you were carried off.
But look and see how I have been punished. My face
is scarred with gashes and long deep cuts mark my breasts;
my womb beats within me trying to forget that
once it carried you inside my body. Where now
shall I look for you? Who will even show me the way?
Whose chariot was it? Who held the horses' reins?
Did he come from the earth or was he from the sea?
Can I find the tracks left by his wheels? Wherever
I go, following one step after the other,
I will go happy that I am searching for you.
The mother of Venus herself should suffer this.
Will I succeed? Will we ever again embrace?
Are you still beautiful? Are your cheeks radiant?
Or will I find you as you were in that vision?'

She cursed the flowers on the slopes of Aetna and
began to drag herself away from the guilty
place where Proserpine had been stolen. She found
the tracks of the chariot and, raising her torch,
she lighted the fields so that she could see the path.

Every rut was moistened with her tears and she wept
at each mark she found in the fields. Like a shadow,
she flew over the sea and her torch lit even
the coasts of Italy and Africa. The light
reached the cavern of Scylla, whose dogs frighten men
with silence while other dogs continue to bark.

Epithalamium for Honorius Augustus and Maria, Daughter of Stilicho

(Epithalamium de nuptiis Honorii Augusti)

When Pelion's slopes became a bridal chamber
  and readied a welcome for all the gods;
when Nereus, the bride's father, with his daughters
  tried to tie up all the days in one feast;
when Chiron, resting his horse's legs and body
  offered a cup of the finest to Jove;
when Peneus made nectar from water, and wine
  poured down the cliffs and valleys of Oeta:
Terpsichore slapped the waiting lyre with her hand
  and led a crowd of young girls to the caves.
Not even the Thunderer scorned these songs because
  all knew that lovers' vows fit the music.
The centaurs and fauns, however, ignored the feast
  because they are not moved by any lyre.
Hesperus trimmed his lamp for the seventh time and
  a seventh day was breaking; Phoebus touched
his lyre and sang the promise of Achilles' birth
  and the Trojans he would kill in battle.
This is the god whose songs have power enough to
  move the rocks and gravel of the mountains.
The wedding chants echoed on Olympus and back
  and forth from Othrys even to Ossa.

*

Honorius had not known before such a fire
as he felt for Maria: the heat of passion
burned in his heart but he did not know what it was.
The warmth in his face, the sighs, were all confusing
because he was only a beginner. Horses,
hunting and spears no longer intrigued him; the wound

of love was always on his mind. But his secret
was known to others because he could not control
the colour of his young face or his groaning heart.
Many times he found his hand writing out her name;
he prepared many fine gifts for his beloved
and selected from the imperial treasures
jewels that had been worn by the royal women,
though she was more beautiful even than Livia.
A lover is impatient and hates to delay:
like a stallion he chafes at the bit; the long days
seem to stand still and the moon does not seem to change.
Deidamia, a girl from Scyros, inflamed
the young Achilles and taught his strong hands to spin
thread like a woman. She stroked the head of the man
who would bring terror and destruction to Ida.

Honorius talked to himself: 'Does Stilicho
still reject my suit? Why does he postpone our vows
when he has already approved our love? Why should
he still refuse my chaste desires? I am not like
those rich princes who live in luxury and want
only handsome flesh; I have not dealt with panders
who hawk their pretty merchandise from door to door,
nor have I tried to select my beloved by
carefully considering the economic
and political advantages of marriage
into this or that particular family.
I have not chosen for myself another's wife.
My beloved was pledged to me by her father,
and by her mother's noble birth we are cousins.
Without the purple, I have gone as a beggar;
ministers of state have carried my petitions.
Stilicho, I do not seek some trivial thing, but
just as my imperial father gave you your wife,
surely you must give Maria to be my wife:
give to me, the son, what you owe to my father;
return to this household one who belongs to us.
Perhaps her mother, Serena, will hear my prayer.
Daughter of my uncle Honorius, whose name

is mine, you are the pride of the river Ebro.
Though my cousin, you cared for me like a mother.
In your arms I grew strong; your love made me a man.
Though you did not bear me, still you are my mother.
How is it that you keep your two children apart?
Let your own daughter marry your adopted son.
What is the day? When will our wedding night be blessed?'

With such words the young man eased the pain of his love.
Cupid laughed to hear such a sad speech. He hurried
away to share the news with Venus, his mother.

A mountain casts its shadow over the western
end of Cyprus: it faces Pharos and the mouths
of the Nile; nothing can violate it. No man
has climbed its slopes; it never has frost; the winds and
the clouds do not attack its cliffs. It was made for
pleasure and is a shrine to Venus. The climate
never changes; the seasons are always the same;
it enjoys the grandeur of an eternal spring.
The slopes become a level plain surrounded by
a golden hedge which guards the meadows from the world.
It is said that this estate was Mulciber's gift
to his wife. The enclosed land is bright with flowers,
though the only gardener is Zephyr; no bird
may enter its peaceful groves until the goddess
herself approves the quality of its singing.
Those which please her are admitted, the others leave.
The very leaves on the trees live only for love
and every tree comes to know the power of love.
Palm bends to mate with palm; poplar sighs for poplar;
plane whispers to plane; alder whispers to alder.

There are two fountains: one sweet, the other bitter.
One has honey mixed with its water, the other
is poisoned. It is in these two streams that Cupid
dips his arrows. Cupid's thousand brothers with their
quivers play on the banks of those streams. Together
they are like Cupid both in age and appearance.
They are the sons of nymphs while Cupid is the one
son of Venus. All things are subject to his bow.

From the stars of Heaven to the lowest of men,
there is no one who cannot know the sting of love.
Other gods also live within this enclosure.
Unfettered Licence and mercurial Anger,
wine soaked Sleeplessness, innocent Fears, the Pallor
that is the lover's badge, trembling Audacity,
pleasant Fear, fickle Pleasure and the lovers' Vows
who play in every passing breeze. And among them
there is always Youth closing Age out of the grove.
  From a great distance the palace of Venus can
be seen in the green light of the grove: Vulcan built
it of precious stones and fine gold which he mingled
by the jeweller's art. Columns carved of amethyst
support beams hewn from emeralds; the walls are covered
with beryl, the doorsills are of polished jasper
and the floor is paved with agates which are walked on
as though they were only dirt; the inner courtyard
is covered with a sod that releases perfume;
there are plants that produce balsam and cinnamon
to sweeten the air and give pleasure to Venus.
  Cupid flew down to this place after his journey;
with a joyful heart and a proud step, he entered
his mother's house. Venus was on her throne having
her hair combed; by her stood the three sister graces.
One poured an ointment of nectar on her head, one
parted her hair with ivory combs and a third
braided the hair and then arranged it in its place
with one lock escaping to enhance her beauty.
Her face eagerly sought the mirror's opinion:
that image was reflected by the palace walls
and wherever she looked she was pleased by the sight.
She saw her son's shadow and quickly embraced him.
  'Why are you so pleased?' she said. 'Have you been fighting?
Who is your latest victim? Have you again forced
the Thunderer to bellow among the heifers?
Is Apollo vanquished or Diana summoned
to some shepherd's hideaway? You look as though you
have overcome some god who was quite powerful.'

Lingering over his mother's kisses, he said:
'Rejoice. We have won a battle. Honorius
has felt the sting of our arrows. Surely you know
the girl, Maria, and her father, the general
whose armies guard Gaul and Italy. And you know
her mother, Serena, a nobly born lady.
Hurry. Hear their regal prayers and bless the union.'
Cytherea opened her son's arms, bound her hair,
gathered her dress over her arm and wrapped herself
in the garments whose charms can stop a flooding stream
and calm the sea, the winds and the angry lightning.
She spoke to her thousand adopted sons: 'Which one
of you will plunge in this surf and summon Triton
who can carry me quickly across the ocean?
Never before have we needed him more than now.
The marriage I am asked to witness is sacred.
Hurry. Perhaps he is blowing his conch in the
Libyan Sea, maybe he swims in the Aegean.
The one to find him will get a golden quiver.'
They formed bands and each one went a different way.
Triton was swimming in the Carpathian Sea
in pursuit of Cymothoe, the nereid.
She was afraid of that suitor and she escaped
by slipping her wet body through his embraces.
One of his pursuers saw the act and shouted:
'For shame! The ocean itself cannot hide your games.
Be prepared to take our mistress where she commands.
In payment for your services you will receive
the maiden who has just eluded you. Venus
will make her eager for your affection although
she despises you now. Come and win your reward.'
The savage god rose out of the sea. His unkempt
hair fell over his shoulders and cloven hoofs grew
where a fish tail was attached to his human form.
With four strokes he was thrown on the beach of Cyprus.
To protect the fair goddess from the wind and sun,
he arched his tail over his head and let her sit
on the scarlet scales that cover his back; Venus

reclined on that couch with her feet in the water.
A band of attendants flew beside the goddess
and the beating of their wings created a wind.
Flowers were thrown everywhere in Neptune's palace.
Leucothoe, the daughter of Cadmus, played
in the water and Palaemon drove his dolphin
with a harness of roses. Nereus scattered
violets in the seaweed and Glaucus adorned
his grey head with immortal plants. The nereids
heard the news and joined the procession. They mounted
the various beasts of the ocean: one, who was
both girl and fish, rode the tiger of Tartessus;
another rode the Aegean ram who shatters
ships with his forehead; a third was riding the neck
of a sea lion; a fourth clung to a sea calf.
They competed with one another in bringing
presents for the bridal pair. Cymothoe brought
a jewelled belt, Galatea a precious necklace,
Psamathe a crown heavy with pearls she gathered
in the Red Sea. Doto gathered coral which is
a plant in the water but a jewel in the air.

The nereids surrounded Venus and they sang
her praises: 'Venus our queen, we beg you, take these
gifts to Maria, the queen of queens. Not even
Thetis nor even our sister Amphitrite
received anything so grand when she was married
to Neptune, the Jupiter of our ocean world.
May Stilicho's daughter see the sea's affection
and may she know that Ocean himself is her slave:
it was we who guarded her father's fleet when he
embarked to avenge the destruction of the Greeks.'

Then the breast of Triton touched the sandy shoreline
of Liguria and his coiled body rested.
At once Venus flew over the land to Milan,
a city built by the Gauls, which has on its seal
the pelt of a sow covered with fleece. As she passed,
the stunned clouds retreated and the Alps shone brightly
in the pure north wind; the foot soldiers were happy,

though they felt no reason for joy; the staffs of war
suddenly burst into bloom and the spears sprouted
a most unusual growth of leaves. Then Venus
spoke to her attendants: 'Listen, my followers:
keep this palace safe from the god of war; let it
be mine, if only for a time. Banish the fears
inspired by bright armour; put the sword in its sheath.
Let the emblems and flags of war stay where they are.
This camp will be surrendered to me. Let the flutes
replace the bugle; let lyres drown out the trumpet.
Let the soldiers, even those standing watch, rejoice;
let the beakers spill foam on the shining weapons.
May the imperial majesty put away
its mighty pride and join the crowd of wedding guests.
Such a deed will ennoble men of common birth.
Place no restraints on joy, even the law should laugh.

'Hymen, it is time now to prepare your torches.
Let the three sisters gather flowers. Come, Concord,
and weave these blossoms into crowns. And you, my sons,
be useful wherever your help is requested.
Let none be lazy: some of you hang out lanterns
because the banquet cannot end when darkness falls;
the doorposts must be hung with myrtle; light incense
so that the house has an Arabian sweetness;
open out the yellow silks that come from the east;
cover the floors with Sidonian tapestries.
Use every skill to decorate the marriage bed:
let its canopy be embroidered with jewels
and raised high on carved columns more beautiful than
those made in Lydia for Pelops or those raised
over the sleeping Bacchus. Make piles of their wealth;
bring out everything that the first Honorius
won from the Moors and the Saxons; let all men see
what his son with Stilicho beside him brought home
from his many wars. From the Ukraine in the east
to Armenia and the headwaters of the Nile,
a backward place where men wear arrows in their hair,
came tribute and booty to make these men more rich.

Even the Medes bought peace with gifts from the Tigris.
Let the couch be adorned with these treasures; gather
in that wedding chamber the riches of conquest.'
Then, suddenly, she entered the house of the bride.
Maria, however, had no idea that
at that very time her wedding was being planned.
Unaware of the preparations, the maiden
was listening to the wise words of her mother.
The child was being taught the ways of nature and
the practice of old fashioned virtue. With the help
of her mother, the child studied the old authors.
She read Homer and Orpheus and Sappho's songs.
In the same way Latona taught Diana and
Mnemosyne gave instruction to Thalia.
The two women noticed that the sky had brightened
and that a sweet breeze was blowing through the palace.
They noticed the pleasant perfume of scented hair.
Then the goddess appeared and stood there admiring
first the girl's beauty and then that of her mother.
Like a new moon and a full moon, they were alike.
Like a laurel sprouting beneath the parent tree,
the child showed the promise of her mother's beauty.
They were like two roses blooming on the same bush:
one in full bloom, the other only beginning.
Venus spoke to Maria: 'All hail, Serena's
daughter, child of kings and – some day – mother of kings.
I have left Paphos for you. I came here because
I do not wish you to hide yourself and permit
Honorius to suffer the passion of love.
Your birth demands the position he offers you:
take the crown your children will wear; enter into
the palace and the household that was your mother's.
Even if your blood were not royal your beauty
would still make you more than worthy of a kingdom.
What face deserves a sceptre more than yours? What face
could ever adorn a palace better than yours?
Your lips are redder than roses; your neck whiter
than frost; your hair is more yellow than fresh pansies;

no flame can equal the brightness of your two eyes.
How delicately placed are your eyebrows; your blush
is the perfect blend of red and white; your fingers
are more pink than the fingers of dawn; your shoulders
have bones prettier than Diana's. Your mother
should be proud that her beauty is surpassed by yours.
If Bacchus turned Ariadne's flowers to stars,
why is it that you do not have a crown of stars?
At this moment Boötes is gathering stars
to weave into a crown for you. Heaven gave birth
to new stars so that your forehead could be adorned.
Go. Be the wife of one who is worthy of you;
let him share an empire that covers all the world.
Let the Danube pay homage to you; let all men
praise your name. The Rhine and the Elbe will be your slaves;
you will be queen of the Sigambri. That is all.
I will not list an empire's wealth. All of the world
will rejoice when you become the wife of its lord.'

While the goddess spoke she clothed the child with the gifts
the nereids had prepared: she parted her hair
with the point of a spear, she belted up her dress,
and then with her own hands arranged the bridal veil.
A procession stopped at the outer doors. The prince
wanted to run to meet his bride. He longed for night.
Like a stallion, he was ready to take his love:
the horse's nostrils flare as he greets his partner.
The master smiles for the future while the mare finds
pleasure in the mate who has come in search of her.

Meanwhile the armies put down their arms. The soldiers
put on white and congratulated Stilicho.
Even the men of lowest rank scattered flowers
like rain upon their general. Crowned with laurel,
they sang: 'Holy father, Theodosius, whether
Heaven or Elysium is your home, behold:
Stilicho has kept his promise. He has repaid
you for what you gave him. You arranged this marriage
and now he has given his daughter to your son
just as you once gave Serena to Stilicho.

You need never regret what you have done. The love
of a dying father did not deceive your mind.
The young man is worthy to be your heir; he is
worthy to marry this man's child. The state is safe
in his hands: we could tell you about his courage
in battle, the fame of his arms and the terror
that he strikes in the enemy's heart; but the gods
of marriage say that such tales are not proper now.
Our song must be in harmony with the singing.
Whose counsel is wiser than Stilicho's? Who knows
the laws and customs better than he? Stilicho,
you join strength with wisdom, fortitude with prudence.
Was there ever a man with so noble a face?
You are worthy of the highest places; your heart
alone has the strength to endure many worries.
In a crowd, men would know that you are Stilicho.
You are the finest example of majesty:
your words are not arrogant; you are not pompous;
you are not given to making haughty gestures.
Nature gave you the manners that others must learn.
Your modest nobility is quite evident
and grey hairs enhance the appearance of your face.
Although dignity is the mark of age and strength
is the mark of youth, you enjoy the best of both.
You are the best example of fortune's kindness.
Never once have you lifted a sword unjustly;
never once have you incurred the hatred of men.
Your justice, tempered with mercy, is always pure.
That we fear your power confirms our love. You are
the law's interpreter; you are the guardian
of an honorable peace; you are the greatest
leader; you are first among our country's elders.
Since you are the father of our emperor's bride,
we owe him an allegiance stronger than before.
Put on these flowers, forget your rank and join us.
Do this so that your son can surpass even you
and your other daughter can be married like this.
Do this and Maria's womb will soon grow bigger

until another Honorius draws his breath
and a son of kings sleeps on his grandfather's knee.'

AURELIUS PRUDENTIUS CLEMENS

INTRODUCTION

PRUDENTIUS was born in Spain in A.D. 348. Toward the end of his life, he composed a brief *Prologue* for his works which gives a few scanty biographical details. Like Augustine before him, he tells of his early schooling and confesses a proper shame at having learned and then practised the deceits of rhetoric. After a period of licentiousness, he found himself a lawyer suffering the frustration of defeat in his intense desire to win at the law. He proceeded then to be a magistrate or prefect on two occasions. It is quite possible that he went to Rome and took a position at the court of Theodosius. But after a life of such public productivity, he realized that

> It must be said to me:
> 'Whoever you are, the world you desired
> is lost. What you sought means nothing to God.'

Late in life, he resolved to turn away from the trivialities of the world; after a successful public career he resolved to turn his energies to writing and singing the praises of God.

It is no easy matter to separate in his *Prologue* those sentiments which are genuine from those which are uttered as a matter of propriety. Every man always has the privilege of redirecting his energies to new or more elevated ends. But the reader becomes almost painfully aware that Prudentius's 'confession' is strongly set in a tradition already well established and recognized. Still, the reader cannot help being touched by this man's statement of what seems to be only a trite awareness. Awareness of the reality of the passing years and a desire to escape the ravages of death come eventually to every man.

Since the 'Prologue' makes reference to the passage of fifty-seven years since the author's birth, its composition may be placed with some accuracy in A.D. 405. As such, the *Prologue* constitutes the last certain evidence of his life. It is quite probable that his various writings were the product of his adult life, while the *Prologue* was

written toward the end as a preface to a collection of his poems. The *Epilogue*, which is included in this anthology, is of questionable authenticity. It makes no reference to time and its composition cannot be dated by internal evidence. We are certainly free to presume that these verses were composed and added to the authentic text by a nameless scribe for much the same reason that impelled Prudentius to compose at the end of his life a *Prologue* to his work. The uncertainties, the fears, in short the problems posed in the *Prologue* demand an answer. But a man schooled in the writings of Seneca would not expect an answer this side of the grave. The poet of the *Epilogue*, on the other hand, seems assured that his impoverished state is wealth indeed and that his inadequate service will be rewarded with a largesse proper only to a kindly and paternal God. Fear and mercy are conjoined realities. In the *Prologue* Prudentius suffers from a most salutary fear of the Lord. In the *Epilogue* we find him mellowed and even secure in his awareness of divine mercy.

This transition from one psychological state to another is interesting. The *Epilogue* reflects an ease of optimism which I find nowhere else characteristic of this poet. Prudentius, like Chaucer and Milton after him, was a man of the world whose experience in worldly matters must have been not only profound but also such as to colour every experience with the brightness of practicality and a strong awareness that Faith always remains no more than 'the substance of things hoped for'. To rest securely in an awareness of divine beneficence is really to deny the psychological impetus which dictated the 'Prologue'.

I have argued against the authenticity of this *Epilogue*. The argument rested on the premise that there exists within the duration of a man's life a certain consistency against which all reported actions may be tested to determine whether they are substantive or diversionary. The patent falseness of that premise need not be outlined. Prudentius was a man who might well have come to the end of his life and been willing to see it also as the end of only his first career. The appeal to Faith as an explanation for specific patterns of behaviour is necessarily an appeal to chaos and confusion for in establishing the substantiality of Hope one necessarily flies in the face of a lifetime of accumulated wisdom. The *Epilogue* is included here on the possibility, however remote, that it is the work of Prudentius. If it can be shown for a certainty that it is not authentic, then we must see it as an example of that passion for symmetrical expression that so characterized the centuries after Prudentius.

In the *Psychomachia* or *The Battle for the Soul of Man* we find first a continuation and then a beginning of the tendency to allegorize. Prudentius must have known the personifications of Statius in the *Thebaid* as well as those of Apuleius in his *Metamorphoses*. Prudentius is significant to us because it is in this work that we find the old pagan modes and fashions turned to a Christian purpose. Using the language and the exalted sentiments of his tradition, Prudentius strove to achieve a similar grandeur for the ideas motivated by Christian doctrine. In his *De spectaculis* (chapter XXIX) Tertullian recognized, almost in passing, that the taste for gladiatorial combat could be purified, if not with extermination, at least by being redirected to serve the ends of Christianity rather than the ends of pagan religion. Prudentius, for whom the conflict between the old and the new religion was very real, addressed himself to the problem of establishing a cultural birthright that was first of all plainly Christian but at the same time clearly and unmistakably Roman in character and structure.

We cannot avoid the recognition that in Prudentius the twilight of the gods received a new impetus so that we can definitely identify in his *Psychomachia* a new cultural awareness. When Prudentius makes the virtues stand in the battlefield exchanging blows with their enemies, the vices, the reader finds himself immersed in the weary and creaking machinery of the classical epic. But toward the end of the *Psychomachia* all the virtues and strengths, all the resources of man are summoned before their enthroned leaders. In that summons we find a departure from the antique and outmoded norms of the literary battlefield. Here the leaders invite rather than compel; here the masses are free rather than subject. Whether or not such a change is a true description of the results of applied Christianity, it still represents clearly and unmistakably the ideals which Christian teaching presented to the Empire. In Prudentius we find another attempt to deal with the relation between the city of God and the city of the world.

It has been suggested that Plato's *Republic* is a psychological as well as a political treatise. Such a theory sees a polity – in this case the republic – as a thing whose structure and internal action is closely analogous to that complexity contained in one man.[1] In the *Psychomachia* the allegory rests firmly on the presumption that a polity – in this case a theocentric polity – is a proper analogue to explain that polity which is a man.

Prudentius's audience was already well aware of the facts of political life. Drawing on his wide background in Roman law and civil service, Prudentius was able to suggest not only more satisfactory modes of government, but also, and more properly, the way in which a man can, through a lifetime of vigilance and discipline, bring under control and subjection the unruly members of his own person. The vision which sees this psychological act as a political act is the vision of a man whose poems are a pivot around which both future and past necessarily turn.

The history of medieval moral theology is closely related to the history of the personification of moral good and evil. These personifications, because they function in the work – whether treatise, sermon or *Psychomachia* – as figures, are necessarily one-sided. Experience tells us that no man is entirely good or entirely evil. Yet moral allegory demands this essential and basic unreality for the ends which it tries to achieve. Personification as a rhetorical device functions in many ways. First, and most importantly, the personification is an aid to memory. If the abstraction is given flesh and then made to act like a man, the audience is more disposed to remember. The personification also functions as an almost irrefutable argument for the author's conclusion. Because the personification appeals to reason through the medium of the sensory imagination, and because a personified argument is essentially a non-verbal argument, the impact of the allegory is greater and much less subject to the exercise of the critical judgement. The homiletic impact of such a presentation is of prime importance: the individual given to the sins of the flesh easily resists every

1. See especially Werner Jaeger, 'The State within Us' in his *Paideia: the Ideals of Greek Culture*, translated from the 2nd German edition by Gilbert Highet, 2nd edition, New York, 1945, vol. II, pp. 347–58. A. E. Taylor makes the same point when he writes: 'It has sometimes been asked whether the *Republic* is to be regarded as a contribution to ethics or to politics. Is its subject "righteousness," or is it the "ideal state"? The answer is that from the point of view of Socrates and Plato there is no distinction, except one of convenience, between morals and politics' (*Plato: The Man and His Work*, New York, 1956, p. 265).

argument which logic frames, while an appeal to the sensory imagination by personification is more compelling precisely because it is an appeal to the modes of thinking which permit the vice to continue.

Though C. S. Lewis was convinced that the *Psychomachia* was a bad poem, it must be understood that its impact on medieval and even renaissance literature was profound.[2] The medieval appetite for allegory which Lewis found so notably satisfied by the *Roman de la rose* was something whose richness pervaded much of the culture of western Europe.[3] If indeed there is beauty to be found in the horror of medieval life, it must be a beauty derived from allegory and the devices of personification. In a time when even the rich and powerful were necessarily subject to all the vagaries of life's transience, the allegorist's art often provided through imagination the only escape. I have mentioned that the history of medieval moral theology is essentially a history of the personification and pictorial representation of moral qualities. As the abstractions of moral and ethical teaching became persons rather than qualities, there developed a rhetoric and iconography of the moral condition. The morality plays were only a small and relatively late part of this larger imaginative effort. One hardly turns a page of the medieval or renaissance writers without the realization that Prudentius is not far removed.

By way of comparison, the *Cathemerinon* or *Hymns for the Various Hours and Days* is a work quite different from the *Psychomachia*. Instead of using the epic appearances, the *Cathemerinon* deals with the small, the close and the personal situation. The work is presented as a collection of hymns for the various hours of the day with certain adaptations to the seasons and certain special events. But the reader should not conclude that these poems were actually written to be sung. Though various passages have been set to music, it is not likely that the entirety could have been sung with anything approaching ease.

The poems in the *Cathemerinon* display a variety of classical metres. Ambrose before Prudentius had written hymns, but his were quite different in form and texture. The poems in the *Cathemerinon* remind the reader more of the odes of Roman antiquity, though their subject

2. C. S. Lewis, *The Allegory of Love: A Study in Medieval Tradition*, London, 1936, p. 68.

3. ibid., pp. 112–56.

matter is clearly Christian and represents quite a new force in Latin culture. Ambrose had written with the limited intention of producing a liturgical poem, the hymn. Prudentius, on the other hand, freed himself of the real limitations of worship and produced poems which have the largeness of literature. In this departure Prudentius clearly set himself apart from his fellow Christian poets.

If there is any quality which runs through the poems, it is that transcendent hope which sees victory in death itself. It is important to remember that the poems were written in an era which witnessed the destruction of the old certainties. Pagan and Christian alike must have been stunned to recognize that immortal Rome was again not secure against the barbarians. As Augustine had demonstrated so clearly, a military defeat can never be an event of trivial importance.

Because Prudentius represents a touch point for both the pagan and the Christian traditions, it is interesting to note the way in which he reflects attitudes which are both pagan and Christian. Both pagan and Christian alike saw the dead as beings of power who might be invoked as intercessors. The difference, however, was in the Christian belief that life after death could well be desirable while for the pagan life after death was not only a matter of the greatest uncertainty but more than likely to prove distinctly unpleasant.

Prudentius, like other poets, was learning to use a new mythology derived from Scripture. The Hebrew heroes and villains became the figures for Christ and the various aspects of the Christian's life. Prudentius had studied the writers of antiquity. Still, these writers were forbidden him and he found instead the type and symbol of the New Testament in the Old Testament. The poems present a richly developed symbolism which sees in the literary as well as the natural event an analogue for the supernatural event.

A SELECTED BIBLIOGRAPHY

Bergman, J. (ed.), *Corpus scriptorum ecclesiasticorum latinorum*, Vienna, 1926, vol. LXI.

Eagen, Sister M. Clement, C.C.V.I. (trans.), *The Poems of Prudentius*, 2 vols., Washington, 1962 and 1965. These two volumes are Nos. 43 and 52 in the series, *The Fathers of the Church: A New Translation*, edited by Roy Joseph Deferrari and others.

Lavarenne, M. (ed. and trans.), *Psychomachie, texte, traduction, commentaire, avec une introduction historique*, Paris, 1933.

Pope, R. Martin and Davis, R. F. (eds. and trans.), [*Cathemerinon*], London, 1905.

Smith, Ernest Gilliat (trans.), *Songs from Prudentius*, London, 1898.

Prologue

(Praefatio)

I lived for fifty years
and now the sun has gone through another
seven years, unless I am mistaken.

My time comes and each day
God gives me is in the zone of old age.
What worthwhile thing have I done in this time?

In my early years I
wept at the snap of the rod; the toga
taught my tongue the art of telling a lie.

Lewdness and indulgence
to my great shame and sorrow soiled my youth
with the squalor and dirt of wantonness.

Argument strengthened me
and an evil desire to win at law
made me suffer many cruel defeats.

With law as my bridle,
twice I governed cities and gave justice
to the good and terror to evil men.

Next I was advanced close
to the side of power where I then stood
with those who are nearest and most favoured.

While I was occupied
with such trivialities, old age caught
me forgetful of how it all began.

Salia's consulship
saw my birth. Too many winters have passed;
my grey head tells how many springs are gone.

What will all of this mean,
whether good or bad, when my flesh is dead
and death will have destroyed all I have been?

It must be said to me:
'Whoever you are, the world you desired
is lost. What you sought means nothing to God.'

As my last day draws near,
may my soul abandon its foolishness;
let it praise God with words if not with deeds.

Let my hymns link the days;
may no night pass without singing his praise.
May I fight falsehood by preaching the faith.

May I trample the rites
of heathen men: tear down your idols, Rome;
sing of martyrs and praise the apostles.

While writing or speaking
of these things may it be my good fortune
to be free to have what my tongue has told.

[1–33]

The Battle for the Soul of Man

(Psychomachia)

The faithful old man who first showed the way
of faith became a father late in life:
his sons became a race blessed by God and
his name, Abram, which his father gave him,
became Abraham when God spoke with him.
He made a sacrifice of his first born
and showed us that the only sacrifice
pleasing to God is one which offers what
is dearest to our hearts. He warned us that
we must fight unholy men; he himself
showed us that no child is pleasing to God
or virtuous until the spirit kills
the monsters lurking within the child's heart.
Vicious kings captured Lot and made him stay
in Sodom and Gomorrah where he was
known as a great man, though an alien.
A messenger brought to Abram the news
that his kinsman had been placed in bondage
by barbarians. He armed his own servants,
slaves who had always lived in his household,
to pursue the enemy and catch them
while they marched burdened by the victory
and the great weight of booty they had seized.
Abraham himself, filled with God's Spirit,
took a sword and drove those insolent kings
into a lumbering flight. He killed them
and trampled their bleeding bodies; he broke
the chains and released the plundered riches –
gold, young women, children, jewels, mares, cups,
clothing and cattle. Lot himself was freed,
and straightened his neck and massaged himself
where the chains had rubbed and blistered his skin.

Abram, after destroying that triumph,
returned covered with glory because he
had saved his brother's son from slavery
so that their race would not be subjected
to the rule of wicked, barbarian kings.
While Abram and his men were on the road
from this slaughter, a priest stopped their journey
and gave them heavenly food. This great priest,
a mighty king, had no known mother and
no known father: without parents, without
children except those known only to God,
he fed the father of undying sons.
Then a trinity of angels under
the form of three men came to the old man's
cottage for food and rest. Sara conceived
and was astounded to find her old womb
alive with the strength and promise of youth;
she was becoming a mother after
the time for bearing children had gone by.
She rejoiced for the heir and regretted
her laughter when she had heard the promise.
This picture of the ways of God and man
has been drawn as a model for our lives
to show again that our hearts must have faith
and that every part of our captive flesh
must be freed from the foulness of desire.
We must see that we have servants enough
from within our own house to overcome
the evil that always rages in us.
Christ himself, who is the only true Priest,
the Son of one whose name cannot be said,
will feed the victor and enter his heart
to let it entertain the Trinity.
The Spirit will embrace the childless soul
and make it fertile with eternal seed;
late in her life, this richly endowed soul
will be a mother and produce an heir.

*

O Christ, you have always been revered because you
have always had compassion on the misery
of man; you are always revered for the powers
you share with the Father – it is one power for
it is only one God yet it is not merely one
God that we worship since you too are also God
born of the Father. Tell us, great King, how the soul
is endowed with strength to fight and expel our sins
from our hearts; when our thoughts are scattered and when strife
rises within us, when evil desires rebel,
tell us how to guard the liberty of the soul;
tell us about our defences against the fiend.
For you, good leader, have not left us here helpless
before the onslaught of vice without the virtues
to help us in battle and renew our courage;
you yourself are in command of legions that fight
this battle where the attack is worst. You yourself
can arm the spirit with precious skills which permit
it to resist and fight for you, conquer for you.
The path to victory is there before your eyes.
We must study the features of the virtues and
the dark monsters waiting there to challenge their strength.

Faith is the first to appear on the field to face
the uncertainty of this conflict. Her rough dress
is dishevelled, her shoulders are bare, her long hair
is untrimmed and her arms are uncovered. The glow
on her skin is caused by the prospect of sudden
and unexpected battle. She burns to enter
new contests, she ignores the demands of armour.
Faith puts her confidence in her strong heart and arms.
She scorns the dangers of hand-to-hand combat and
intends to destroy her foe by exhausting him.

The first adversary approaches Faith; it is
Worship-of-the-Old-Gods (we have no better name)
who proposes to accept the challenge of Faith.
But Faith strikes the enemy's head and it tumbles
in the dirt where it lies, with its be-ribboned brows
and the wide mouth that ate the warm red flesh of beasts.

Faith tramples the head and takes particular pains
to squeeze the dead grey eyes out of the bloody skull;
the monster's throat is closed and its breath is throttled
in its passages until it gasps a hard death.
The spectators, who have been assembled by Faith
from among the ranks of the martyrs, become brave
enough to face the foe: she crowns her followers
with blossoms and gives them robes of flaming purple.

The next person to step out on the grassy field
is Chastity, the virgin, shining in armour.
Lust, who has come from Sodom, is armed with torches.
The vice thrusts a burning pine knot dipped in sulphur
and tar into the maiden's eyes. But without fear
she strikes the hand with a stone and the blazing torch
is knocked away. With only one thrust of her sword,
she pierces the throat of the whore and stinking fumes
with clots of blood are spat out; the foul breath poisons
the near-by air. The virtuous queen then cries out:

'It is done, this will be your end – you will always
lie prostrate, never again will you dare to spit
your flames against the men and women who are God's;
their hearts are kindled by the torch of Christ's pure love.
Do you think, molester of men, that you can get
your strength and be warmed again by the breath of life?
Remember the head of Holofernes: it soaked
the cushions of his couch with the blood of passion;
Judith, an honest woman, refused his jewelled bed
and stopped his fervour with one thrust of her dagger.
Weak woman though she was, her hand never trembled
as she fought for my cause with heavenly boldness.
But perhaps you think that because such a woman
acted under the old law, a physical law,
she and others like her would be powerless now
that the battle has been moved to spiritual realms.
But I tell you that feeble hands can still sever
the heads of the mighty: a virgin has now borne
a child. On that day when the flesh lost its nature
and the power of God made for us a new flesh,

a bride who was never a wife conceived the Christ
who is both man because of his mother and God
because he was conceived by the Spirit of God.
Ever since that day, all flesh is godlike since it
conceives the Son of God and assumes his nature
by a compact of partnership. The Word of God
has not become another thing by taking flesh.
The majesty of God is in no way reduced
by the limits of bodily experience.
But mankind is raised to understand nobler things:
God remains as he always is though he begins
to be something that he was not; we are no more
as we had been because we have been born again
to a better condition. He gave of himself
to men, without detracting from what he is; he
has not been diminished by taking what is ours,
but by adding what is his to what is ours he
has elevated us to the height of his gifts.
'That you, foul Lust, lie here defeated in the dirt
and cannot challenge me because of Mary is
the gift of God to men. You are the way of death;
you are the gateway to ruin. You stain our flesh
and you plunge our spirits into the pit of Hell.
Bury your head in the abyss of grief; you are
a pestilence without power, you are frozen.
Die, whore; go down to the damned. May you be enclosed
in Hell and be thrown in the dark crevasse of night;
may the blazing rivers toss you on their currents;
may the flood of darkness and the pools of sulphur
fling you among the rapids of their roaring streams.
Never again, Prince of fiends, will you tempt Christians;
their bodies will be kept clean and pure for their King.'
That was the speech of Chastity. She washed her sword
in the Jordan because the hammered steel was stained
red by the blood that had gushed from the monster's wound.
The victorious queen cleansed her blade in the stream,
dipping it again and again until the clots
had washed away. Then, because she was afraid that

it might rust in its tight sheath, she consecrated
it in a Catholic temple from which the river
of God flows. In that place the sword cannot be dimmed.
When Chastity has retired, Longanimity
or Patience comes on to the field. She is standing
by the side watching the uproar of that combat:
her quiet expression never changes as spears
inflict their mortal wounds. Wrath, from a great distance,
spies the easy-tempered virtue and all at once
becomes enraged. Baring her teeth in anger and
letting flecks of foam fall from her gaping black mouth,
the vice darts her bloodshot eyes this way and that and
challenges Patience to fight both by brandishing
the weapons of combat and by making a speech:
she mocks Patience for keeping a place on the side.
Infuriated by such reticence, Wrath throws
a spear and abuses the meek, long-suffering
virtue: 'This is for fools like you who stand aside
and watch the combat without expressing favour.
Take this wound in your gentle breast without crying;
you would be dishonoured to admit any pain.'
With these words a shaft of pine is hurled through the air.
Thrown with a good aim, the long sharp shaft strikes against
the belly of Patience but falls into the dust.
The virtue has wrapped her body in a jacket
of steel links: this garment is three layers in thickness
and its fabric is stitched together with leather.
Longanimity stands there quite unruffled while
a storm of weapons falls at her brave feet; she keeps
such a line of defence that nothing injures her.
While she stands unmoving, Patience watches her foe
rage in an uncontrolled frenzy. But Patience waits
because Wrath will perish by her own violence.
When that opponent has finally exhausted
her strength and used all of her weapons her right hand
is useless and the ground is littered with weapons.
Then she reaches for a sword: raising the steel blade
high over her head, she brings it down on the head

of Patience, but a helmet of forged bronze only
rings under that great blow. The sword, its edge blunted,
rebounds; the unbending helmet shatters it and
Patience still stands there, unmoved, as she was before.
The fury of Wrath is multiplied: with her sword
scattered about her feet, she throws the hilt aside
and finds herself without weapons. Only one thing
remains: she had spent all her energies and won
nothing for herself; her unreasoning anger
turns on herself and she prepares for suicide.
She picks up one of her useless weapons; she puts
the shaft in the dirt and falls on the upturned point.
Patience stands over Wrath and speaks: 'We have conquered.
With no danger to life our accustomed virtue
has won the day again. This is the way we live,
wiping out the devils of passion and all their
attendant evils by standing as they attack.
Wrath is its own enemy, Fury kills herself.'

As she turns away and walks among the martyrs,
a noble man appears there as her escort. Job
had stayed by her, enduring the battle with her.
Before his expression was grave and he panted
as he watched the conflict. But now he is smiling
as he thinks of his healed sores and the scars he shows
as his glory after thousands of hard-won fights.
Heaven's King invited him to rest and he gave
Job those spoils of battle that he will never lose.
Patience herself walks through the raging battlefield
without injury. Patience allies herself with
the other virtues and freely gives assistance
wherever it is needed. No virtue enters
the battle without the help of Patience. Only
Patience has the strength needed by all the others.

It happens that Pride is riding about the field
on a high, spirited horse. As usual, she
is all inflated by her own great importance:
she has laid a lion's pelt across the horse's
strong shoulders so that she can look more important

as she keeps her disdainful poise above the field.
She has braided her hair high on her head so that
there might be a lofty and more imposing peak
above her haughty brows. A mantle made of fine
Spanish linen is thrown across her shoulders and
gathered high at the bosom so that her breasts are
made more prominent. A long veil hangs from her neck
like a transparent scarf; when the wind blows around
her, it flows and billows like a vessel's pennant.
Her horse, a charger who cannot stand still, carries
himself in haughty fashion unwilling to have
his jaw curbed by the bit. Since the horse is restrained,
he cannot enjoy the freedom he seeks: he stamps
with rage because the reins press hard against his neck.
In such fashion does this virago show herself.
Head and shoulders above the opposing troops, she
parades up and down on her horse and glares at those
confronting her. Her enemy is poor in arms
and numbers, a force conscripted by Lowliness.
Though noble, Lowliness has need of another
since she cannot rely on her own resources.
Hope is her friend, a virtue whose estate is rich
and raised above the earth to be a place of wealth.

Mad Pride looks over Lowliness and her motley
crew. She makes this speech: 'What kind of nonsense is this?
Surely you must be ashamed, poor men, to challenge
someone so famous as me with troops so tattered.
How can you raise your swords against a tribe of such
distinction whose skill at fighting has won it wealth
and given it power to rule the richest lands?
Can it be that some penniless upstart presumes
to overturn a most ancient race of princes?
Are we to see you as the new nobility
bearing in your hands the sceptres that have been ours?
Is it you who will plough a furrow over plains
whose sod was first broken by us? Will you poison
our soil with alien steel and drive off the land
those who have cultivated for our benefit?

You are a pretentious crowd. When one of your own
draws his first breath, we embrace the man that he is
and pour our power into the newborn body;
we and only we are masters of those new bones.
Where in that person are you allotted a place?
There is nothing for you; we possess everything.
Both the house and its masters were born the same day.
As the years pass, we all grow together so that
from the time when Adam, dressed in skins, left Eden,
all that has happened to him and his race happened
because we commanded and men rushed to obey.
'What army is this that has come from God knows where
to annoy us? You lack spirit, luck, elegance,
and good sense. The rights you claim now have been assigned
to those who claimed them first. I suppose that you trust
those vain whispers which encourage wretches to dream
about some future good and console their hunger
and unmanly laziness with expectations.
What a silly hope that must be: it flatters them
but still they ignore the bugle's call to battle
and their courage does not strengthen their feeble souls.
Chastity's frozen liver is of little use
and the sweetness of Brother Love is soon undone.
O Mars, O my heart, such an enemy shames us:
must we take up weapons against frivolity?
Must we enter combat with a chorus of girls
with whom are the beggars, Justice and Honesty,
parched Sobriety, Fasting with her pasty face,
Purity and her bloodless cheeks, Simplicity
exposed to every injury and Lowliness
always bent double to the ground without freedom
and so distressed that one must see her cheap spirit?
This avenging horde will be trampled like stubble:
we will not show the courtesy of using swords;
we will not dip our blades into your sluggish blood;
we will never win an unmanly victory.'
Pride spurs her horse into a fierce gallop; she flies
along with the reins slack hoping to stun her foe

with her shield's weight and then trample Lowliness.
But her horse stumbles and Pride is thrown in a pit
that Deceit has already dug across the field.
She is one of the vices – that damned pestilence –
who is always busy with her tricks. She had seen
the war about to break out and had touched the earth
so that the enemy would be caught in the rush
of their attack against the lines of the vices.
She camouflaged the pit with branches overlayed
with sod so that it all seemed to be quite solid.
But Lowliness, not even presuming to know
the ways of those more crafty than she, has not yet
ordered her troops to advance and engage their foe.
It was impetuous Pride, in all her grandeur,
who galloped into a trap made for Lowliness.
As the horse falls she clings to his mane and is thrown
among his thrashing legs. The self-contained virtue,
on finding her opponent crushed and nearly dead,
walks calmly to her side, raises her face a bit,
and combines a look of kindliness with her joy.
She refuses to do anything more, but Hope,
her true companion, gives her the sword of vengeance
and fills her meek spirit with a love of glory.
She grasps the bloody foe by the hair, drags her out,
and turns the face toward her own. Pride implores her
to have mercy, but Lowliness bends the head back,
cuts it from the body and raises the grey face
for everyone to see. Hope speaks to those around:
'This is the end; this is what your grand words produced.
God shatters arrogance; even the great must fall.
All bubbles burst; inflated Pride must be flattened.
Do away with supercilious airs, watch out
for the pit that may open up under your feet.
Let all men who are proud take a warning from this.
How well we know the word of Christ that the lowly
will rise to high places while the proud are put down:
we have seen how the mighty Goliath was felled
by an infant's hand; a little stone from a sling

struck a hole deep in the forehead of the giant.
He was a terrible threat, boastful, menacing,
and given to bitter speeches. At his pride's peak,
raging and preening himself, threatening the sky
with his shield, one instant taught him what a child's toy
can do. A bellicose man died by a boy's hand.
I led that boy into that battle: from that day
his courage ripened in my service; his mature
spirit was part of me. Because I take my rest
at the feet of our omnipotent Lord, all men
who live as I command are taken there at last
while their sins reach after us beseeching mercy.'

Lowliness strikes the resounding air with the wings
that are touched with gold, at once she is in Heaven.
The virtues see her go and are impressed by this.
If the unending warfare did not constrain them,
all the virtues would accompany Lowliness;
instead they resume battle and prepare themselves
to win the promised victory and just reward.

From the far edges of the world, where the sun sets,
comes their enemy, Indulgence. Reputation
means nothing to her, for it is already lost.
Her curls are perfumed, her restless eyes are not still,
her voice is languid and bored. She lives for pleasure,
she wants all feelings to be calm and gentle, she
finds delight in her unlawful games and she tries
to destroy her mind by making it more feeble.
As she arrives on the scene she is lazily
belching because of a long feast she has just left.
She comes with dawn because she has heard the trumpets
calling her to fight. She leaves the cups of warm wine
and her dizzy feet slip as she walks through puddles
of wine and perfume; her bare feet crush the flowers
on the pavement: drunkenly she goes off to war.
In her chariot her beauty inspires the army
of her compatriots. It is a strange battle:
she does not shoot arrows from her bow, no lances
are hurled at the enemy's lines, she holds no sword.

Rather she throws baskets of violets and roses
and scatters blossoms over her fierce enemy.
The virtues are won by her charms. Her sweetened breath
dilutes their manly courage, her strong odours strike
their lips and hearts so that their iron-clad strength is crushed.
 Their courage fails; surely they have been defeated.
They put down their spears and their feeble hands are still
while they gaze at the chariot in which she came.
They stare at the gold-encrusted tinkling harness
and they are awed by the axle of solid gold.
The costly spokes, made of purest silver, support
the wheel's bright rim which is made of precious amber.
As this happens, the entire army suddenly
finds itself pervaded with an intense desire
to surrender. More than anything else they hope
to abandon their standards and become the slaves
of luxurious Indulgence. They welcome the yoke
of a dissolute mistress and the tavern's law.
Sobriety, a virtue with a strong will, weeps
at the sight of such a reverse. She weeps because
an invincible army has been defeated
without a battle, but she is a good general.
 She plants her flags where each one can see and restores
their courage with a speech: 'What blind madness troubles
your confused minds? What is the fate you are seeking?
To whom have you pledged allegiance? Are these fetters?
You are men of iron, how can flowers restrain you?
These yellow bouquets with white lilies, these circlets
of red flowers, is it by these that your strong hands,
trained in the iron arts of warfare, will be bound?
Must you now have your hair wrapped in a gold turban
with a band to soak the perfume? Are these the heads
that once were anointed with oil in the King's sign,
a sign that guaranteed his eternal favour?
Is it your purpose to walk sedately and sweep
your paths with expensive hems? Where is the tunic
woven by Faith and given as a protection
to the young hearts which she had already renewed?

You will be busy: you will attend great banquets
that last through the night; huge foaming tankards will spill
wine and costly dishes will drip on the board; your
couches will be soaked with drink and their silk emblems
will still be wet with yesterday's dew. Remember
the thirst in the desert; remember the water
that gushed from the side of the rock when the prophet's
staff struck the stone and made a spring where there was none.
Were your fathers' tents not filled with heavenly food?
Was this food not like that which Christ gives us today?
After such a feast, can you let Drunkenness and
Wantonness take you to the den of Indulgence?
You are an army that has survived every threat.
Neither the fury of Wrath nor Idolatry
could halt you, but a drunken dancer has you now.
'Do not go, I beg you. Remember who you are:
remember Christ, who is our all powerful King;
consider your people and your reputation;
do not forget our Lord and our God. You are sons
of Judah, your line reaches back to God's mother
who gave flesh to the Son of God. Be awakened
by the memory of David who never sought
relief from the burden of war. Consider, too,
Samuel who forbade his men to touch the booty
they had seized in battle and who executed
uncircumcised kings as soon as they were taken.
He was afraid that if the captive survived he
might again bring to them the ravages of war.
He thought it wrong even to make them prisoners.
You, on the other hand, desire to be conquered.
Repent of your wish to pursue this pleasant sin;
I beg of you, by the fear of God's justice, repent.
If you beg his kind forgiveness your betrayal
will not destroy you. Jonathan repented when
he broke his long fast with a piece of honeycomb:
intrigued by a wish to be king, he was careless,
but he repented of that deed and we rejoice
because his cruel fate did not occur. Come with me;

do battle under the flag of Sobriety
and all of the virtues will join me in forcing
that vice, Indulgence, to pay the great penalty
which she earned by tempting you to abandon Christ.'

With these last words, she raises the cross of Christ high
before the horses who draw the chariot of
Indulgence. She pushes the holy wood against
the bridles. The beasts are frightened and run away
down a steep path; the chariot and its driver
are dragged helplessly along. Dust blows in her face,
she is thrown out and her body catches in the wheels
so that she is the brake that stops the runaway.
Then Sobriety strikes the death blow by hurling
a great stone that she finds nearby. Chance found the stone
and then Chance directs its short flight so that the nose
and teeth of Luxury are smashed and her red lips
are driven into the arch of her ruined mouth.
The teeth are loose in their sockets, her throat is torn,
and the chopped tongue spits out bits of its bloody flesh.
This meal of her own body sickens her: she swallows
the crushed bones and vomits the lumps she has eaten.

Sobriety speaks: 'Drink up. You drained many cups
before, surely you can stomach your own body.
You have revelled in your excesses of sweetness;
you should enjoy morsels like these. The taste of death
must be bitter in your mouth; this last draught of wine
must turn your previous pleasures to gall.' Then she dies.
Those who enjoyed her company scatter in fear.
Jest and Impudence throw their cymbals away for
they in their foolishness imagined that battles
are won by instruments of noise. Lust also flees:
pale with fear for his life, he abandons his darts
tipped with poison; his bow slips from his shoulders and
he leaves his quiver where it fell. Then Vanity,
who parades in hollow grandeur, is stripped naked
and her long flowing robes are swiftly dragged away.
The garlands that adorn Allurement are shredded
and left behind. The gold ornaments are broken

and the confusion of Strife shatters her jewels.
Pleasure is more than happy to flee through the thorns
with injured feet. She endures her painful exile
because fear of dangers toughens her tender soles.
Wherever the routed army turns as it runs
seeking an escape, things are lost and left behind:
hairpins, headbands, ribbons, buckles and little veils,
body stays, diadems, and precious necklaces.
Sobriety and all of her comrades refuse,
because they remember Samuel and his command,
to even touch these spoils. Their unpolluted feet
trample the causes of sin into the dirt so
that nothing can make a good man trip, nor compel
him to turn his disciplined eyes to sinful joys.

It is said that Greed then folds her robes in a huge
pocket and gathers up everything of value
left behind. With her wide mouth open and gaping,
Greed admires the trinkets as she sifts through the sand
for broken bits of gold. When her pockets are filled,
she stuffs money bags and purses with her treasure.
As she works, the bag is held in her left hand while
with her right she combs the field with fingers like rakes.
This last monster is followed by her allied fiends,
Care, Hunger, Fear, Anxiety, Perjury, Dread,
Fraud, Fabrication, Sleeplessness and Sordidness.
Among them are the crimes born and nurtured by Greed
so that the brood grows strong on its mother's black milk.
Like ravenous wolves, her young prowl across the field.
If a soldier sees his brother wearing a jewelled
helmet, he will not stop at murder to get it.
If a son finds his father dead after battle,
he stifles his grief and strips the corpse of its wealth.
Civil war permits brother to steal from brother.
Pride of Possession, who is never sated, spares
no one; Gluttony robs even his own children.

These follow the advent of Greed. Such a slaughter
is set loose in the world that droves of living things
are destroyed. One man blind and with his eyes pried from

the pits of his skull is left to wander by night
over every hurdle without a staff to help.
She catches another with his eyes wide open
by showing a grand thing. When he reaches for it,
her sword catches him; he sighs as it finds his heart.
Many men, like pigs, are driven to furnaces
where gold is being burned out of its rock. Each man,
though it dooms him to death by fire, stretches his hand
into the glowing chamber hoping to find gold.
The entire human race is seized by Greed; all men
are destroyed before mortality can be saved.
Of all the vices there is none more frightening:
Greed wraps the lives of men in calamities that
they only escape when they are thrown to Hell's fire.
She even tries – it is too much, even I can
scarcely believe such a horror – to tempt the priests
whose pure lives are spent in the service of the Lord.
They are the leaders who stand in the battle lines
doing battle for the virtues and blowing horns
to encourage and guide those who follow their steps.
Greed will have attacked them and destroyed their bodies
if Reason, the guardian of the tribe of Levi,
has not covered her foster sons with her great shield
and saved all of them from the deadly rush of Greed.
With the assistance of Reason, the priests are saved
and remain strong and uninjured in the battle.
Only a few of them feel the lance of Greed and
they are only scratched. Most infamous pestilence
that Greed is, she is astounded to see her spears
turned away so neatly from her enemies' throats.

With a scream of rage, her passion begins to speak:
'We are losing. Because we lack stamina we
cannot maintain our attack. Our power to hurt
is feeble, though before no one could resist us.
No man, not even a man with a will of iron,
was so hard that he could ignore money or gold.
Every kind of man has been sent to Hell by us:
hearts that are tender and hearts that are rough and hard;

minds that are learned as well as those that are not;
the stupid and the wise; the pure and the impure
have, like all the others, been easy prey for us.
I and I alone, avaricious Greed, have brought
to the Styx all who have ever crossed that torrent.
The greedy river has enjoyed the gifts of Greed.
Hell was enriched by us and it is in our debt.
How can it be that now our strength is turned aside
while fortune turns her twisted smile on our weapons?
Christians have no concern for faces stamped on coins;
they have no concern for hammered silver; no treasure
has value for they think its glory is tarnish.
What does this newly found fastidious pose mean?
We won the Iscariot, one of Christ's chosen
followers who even broke bread with his Master.
With the most compelling reasons for loyalty,
Avarice destroyed him with only a few coins.
He sold the blood of God and bought an infamous
field. He atoned for this deed with a strangled neck.
The people of Jericho were destroyed by us
when they found that their safety had turned to defeat.
Though Achan enjoyed the victory of the Jews,
he was destroyed because he touched the golden spoils.
He picked a bright bauble from the city's ashes
and covetously hid what he thought was his own.
Nothing could save him from the curse of the prophet.
His tribe's great prestige, his own descent from Judah,
a patriarch from whom Christ would come so that all
the sons of Judah would be favoured by God, all
this meant nothing. Achan died for his avarice.
Men who live for Greed are men who will die for Greed.
I cannot win any battle if men know me.
I will wear disguise and trick the sons of Judah
and Aaron, their chief priest. I will recoup my loss.
Who cares if the battle is won by arms or tricks?'
  She finishes her soliloquy and changes
her bearing to one of nobility. She lays
her weapons aside and changes her expression.

In the form and dress of simple austerity,
she becomes the virtue that men have known as Thrift,
a virtue who likes a moderate, saving life.
In this new guise she looks like one who never takes
anything with grasping hands. With her careful airs,
she earns the reputation she has constructed.
Bellona also wears the appearance of Thrift
so that men will not see the liar that she is.
With a delicate veil of maternal concern
she hides her wanton hair so that the inner rage
will be disguised. She hides her plundering thievery
and miserly hoarding of stolen goods under
the commendable name of care for her children.
With deeds like these she tricks and fools gullible men.
People follow this awful monster because they
think her work is virtue. The wicked fiend finds them
cheerful victims happy to live in her shackles.

Meanwhile the strong battle line begins to falter.
The virtues waver because their priestly leaders
are confused while the rank and file is confounded.
The monster's appearance easily misleads them
since they cannot distinguish their friend from their foe:
Greed's appearance is a fluid and changing thing
that makes them doubt their unsteady eyes. Suddenly
Good Works comes to the aid of her confused comrades.
She enters the fight last but by putting her hand
in the battle, she can guarantee their success.
Every impediment is thrown aside, she moves
through the ranks without armour or even a shield.
She has lightened herself of many burdens. Once
she had been heavy with riches and money but
she is able to be freed by helping the poor.
Generously she scatters her inheritance.
Now, rich with Faith, she examines her empty purse
and then estimates the value of her estate
in Heaven with the interest that accrues to it.
The sight of Good Works strikes Greed like a lightning bolt.
Shivering with fear, her senses suddenly numbed,

she cannot move because she knows her end has come.
What more can she do? What tricks remain to her so
that she can regain the wealth that she now has lost?
The brave virtue leaps on her and before the vice
can escape, her neck is seized by hands strong as iron.
The virtue strangles her, squeezing blood from her throat
until it is dry. Like steel bands beneath the chin,
her hands press tight until life is finally gone.
There is no wound, the breath is stopped and the body
suffers inside itself the agonies of death.
As the vice struggles, her victor presses a knee
to her breast and stabs her through the ribs. After death,
the virtue strips the body of its precious spoils.
Nuggets of gold, decaying money bags, green coins,
all these hoarded things are given to the needy.
Then, with exultation, she speaks to her army:
'Take off your armour, honest men, drop your weapons.
The cause of our troubles is dead. The pure can rest
now that the desire for gain is gone. It is good
to wish for nothing that is not needed. Simple
food and only one coat are enough to refresh
and ease our weak bodies. With nature satisfied,
there is no need for anything more. When you set
out on a journey do not take a wallet nor
should you worry about another change of clothes.
Do not worry about tomorrow, for your food,
our daily bread, comes to us as the sunlight comes.
The birds live only for today; they do not care
because they know that God will provide food for them.
The fowls of the air trust in God; even sparrows
have a certain belief that the Lord cares for them.
They will not perish. But you are God's beloved
and have a strong resemblance to his Son. Can he,
your Creator, ever desert you? Do not fear:
the giver of life will be the giver of food.
Look for nourishment in the teachings of Heaven;
find your strength in the food that also enlightens,
a food that strengthens the hope of unending life.

The maker of all things also cares for their needs.'
At these words their troubles ended. Suffering,
Fear, Violence, Crime and Fraud, which deny the faith,
are driven from that land. Then the kind lady, Peace,
with her enemies gone, expels the storms of war.
All of the awful equipment is thrown aside.
They unfasten their buckles and take off their belts.
Their flowing robes fall to their feet and their quick step
slows to the pace of men who are their own masters.
The curved bugles are silent, the swords are returned
to their sheaths, the dust of battle settles and light
from Heaven begins to beautify all the place.
The army is happy to see war end: they see
the face of God, the Thunderer, smiling on them
and Christ on his throne rejoices in their conquest
and opens his Father's home for his followers.
Concord gives the command to take the victorious
pennants and flags back to camp. There is no army
that ever looked so fine, or so glorious, as
she leads her troops marching back in double columns.
The foot soldiers sing psalms on one side of the line
while the mounted soldiers sing hymns from the other.
In the same way the victorious Israelites
looked back to the Red Sea from their positions on
the dry shore. The hanging mountain of water fell
down hissing at their heels and caught in its fury
the dark-skinned men of the Nile. The fish swam again
in the channel over the sand that had been dry.
God's followers beat drums in thanksgiving for what
he had given them. The deeds of almighty God
would be told again to every generation:
all men would hear how the sea reared up walls
so that a dry path was cut through the green waters;
the wind was stilled and the depths of the sea were poised
along each side of that miraculous highway.
With the defeat of vice, the virtues sing their psalms.
The victorious army at last reaches camp.
Suddenly a storm strikes at them. It is a storm

made by some evil to trouble Peace and disturb
this triumphal return with sudden disaster.
Concord is struck in the side by a lurking vice:
she is uninjured because the fabric of steel
repels the point and the blow does not reach her flesh;
yet an opening allows her skin to be scratched.
When the army of vices had been driven off,
Discord had slipped among the virtues in the guise
of a friend; she had left her torn cloak and her snakes
behind while she, with olive branches in her hair,
joined in the celebration. But she had a knife
hidden in her clothes because she wanted to hurt
Concord, greatest of the virtues, with her deceit.
But she fails in her intent. 'What has happened now?'
said Concord. 'What enemy's hand is hidden here
to injure victory and trouble our great joy?
We have reduced the passions to control and brought
goodness back to man. But of what use would this be
if one of the virtues is attacked in peace time?'

Her comrades turn toward her and see her blood dripping
through the armour. Fear betrays the attacker's face.
Her pale cheeks announce her guilt and her hands tremble
as she finds herself discovered. The armed virtues
surround her and demand of her that she tell them
her name, her race, her nation and faith, who sent her
and the name of the god she worships. In her fear
she cannot lie. She says: 'I am known as Discord
and sometimes men call me Heresy. I see God
in various ways: now smaller and now greater,
now in a twofold manner, now in a single.
When I desire, he lacks substance and is a ghost,
or he is my soul when I decide to mock him.
Belial is my teacher, the world is my home.'

Faith will tolerate no more of such blasphemy.
In a single thrust the queen of the virtues pins
with a spear the tongue of Discord and stops her breath.
Countless hands tear the deadly body of Discord
and each of the virtues throws a bit of her flesh

into the breeze or to the dogs or to the crows;
pieces of her body are dropped in the sewers
and flushed out to sea to be devoured by monsters.
At last the entire corpse is fed to unclean beasts.
Dreadful Heresy, torn limb from limb, has perished.
With this last skirmish all men become free to live
in the peace that has been given to all mankind.

All the virtues and he in whom they dwell are safe
and settled behind the protection they have built.
In the centre of camp they raise a platform high
on a hill, a place from which one sees every way
without any obstruction. The two sisters, Faith
and Concord, together stand there on the platform
united by their sworn allegiance to our Lord.
Since they share authority, they stand together
and from that place they summon all their followers.
The entire camp assembles in that place. No part
of man's soul lurks idly in some forgotten niche
of the body; all the tents are opened so that
no one can remain undiscovered and asleep.
All wait there eagerly. With the end of war they
wonder what it is that Faith will give to them now.
Concord speaks first: 'All glory has come to you now,
faithful children of the Father and his Son. You
have slaughtered the savages that attacked the men
who live in the holy city; you are victors.
But the peace of this nation demands that all men
in field and town live together in harmony.
Quarrels at home upset the good common to all;
difference from within will weaken us abroad.
Be watchful, brave soldiers: let there be no discord
among us; let none of us become foreigners
because of disputes that are hidden among us.
A will divided always assures disorder
and will place two at variance within one heart.
Let love unite understanding; let our one life
exist for one aim. Separation is not strength.
Just as Christ can intervene between God and man,

joining mortality and divinity so
that the flesh and God's Spirit are kept together,
so may it be that one spirit will form in us
and in the body be one action united.
'Virtues that are active will produce only peace.
Peace is the end of labour; peace is the prize won
in war and danger. Peace is the standard by which
the stars flourish and the earth is always at rest.
Without peace, nothing pleases God. He will not take
your gift at the altar if you hate your brother.
If you should die for Christ by leaping in the fire
and letting its tresses envelop you but still
you kept some unkindly desire, your sacrifice
would mean nothing. Merit is perfected by peace.
It is not swollen with pride, it has no envy;
it endures anything and believes everything.
It can be injured but will not bear resentment;
it forgives every offence and offers pardon
before the end of day for fear the sun will set
on its anger. If you wish to worship our God,
make your offering in peace. Nothing is sweeter
to Christ. Only a gift freely given in peace
pleases him with its sweet aroma. God gives
the dove the wisdom to see a snake in disguise;
the wolf wraps himself in the soft skin of a lamb
while he goes on with the bloody business of death.
By tricks just like these Photinus and Arius
have disguised themselves while remaining savage wolves.
This threat to my health and this superficial wound
show what danger to us rests in a stealthy hand.'
The assembled virtues all cry out in sorrow.
Then Faith adds these last words: 'Do not cry in sadness.
This is the hour of our glorious victory.
Concord has been hurt but Faith has been defended.
Indeed Concord stands by me and laughs at her wound.
Concord has saved Faith, you can be sure; Faith is safe.
There is only one remaining task, my captains.
The war is over and yours is Solomon's job.

He, though peaceful, was heir to a warring kingdom;
he became the unarmed master of an armed court.
Because his father reeked with the warm blood of kings,
Solomon began the task of washing the stain
from his father's house. A temple was erected
and an altar was set up in a golden place
to be the house of Christ, the Messiah to come.
That temple was the glory of all the kingdom.
The wandering ark was set in the holy place
and God himself resided in Jerusalem.
Let a holy temple be built here in our camp,
let us build a holy of holies for our God.
What good is it when we have driven back with steel
the great hordes of earthly sin if the Son of God
comes down in the city of the cleansed body to
find it barren and without a shining temple?'
Faith and Concord together lay out the building.
Her golden rod carefully measures the four sides
so that the walls will be square and the corners true
with no unequal side to break its symmetry.
On the east side, nearest the rising sun, they place
three gateways. To the south there are also three gates
and to the west as well and also to the north.
There is no building stone brought to that place, only
a single gem through which the passageways are cut.
That single stone spans the doors with a single arch
and the one stone forms the entire court of entry.
Over the twelve gateways are inscribed in gold the
twelve names of the apostolic senate. With these
labels the Spirit of God encompasses the
soul's privacy by giving sentiments of love.
Wherever we find the vitality of man,
we see that the strength of the body is fourfold
and approaches to the heart through the three gateways
that are found in only one side. With pure desires
the heart of man gives honour in its holy place.
Whether it be during the dawn of childhood or
in the strong burning heat of youth or the full day

of maturity or in the feeble winter
when old age is summoned to pray, three names present
their power at this place where the four entryways
meet and the power of the King is made real.
  The same number of precious stones set in the walls
sparkles; from their depths they pour into that temple
living colours that pulse and throb like breathing things.
A chrysolite of unusual size spotted
with gold nuggets is set between a sapphire and
a beryl so that their light is always changing.
An agate is filled with colour by its neighbour,
an amethyst, which scatters a flash of crimson.
This brilliant redness strikes the sardonyx, jasper,
topaz and carnelian which are side by side.
Scattered among these jewels are emeralds like grass
growing in the spring: their green light pours out in waves.
The bright chrysophase with its green and yellow bands
is conspicuous among that bright crowd of stars.
As these immense stones were raised to their high places
the crane creaked and groaned with the unexpected weight.
An inner chamber is also built in that place.
It stands on seven pillars cut from a boulder
of icelike crystal and it is topped by a stone
cut to resemble a shell holding a white pearl.
It is the pearl of great price bought by Faith after
she sold everything at auction and paid for it
with a thousand talents. Here is Wisdom enshrined,
and setting in place all her realm by framing laws
to be the safety of mankind. That sovereign holds
a sceptre that is a staff of green living wood.
Cut from its trunk, it draws no nurture from the soil
but bears leaves and roses red as blood with lilies.
That stem never withers, those blooms will never wilt.
This rod was suggested by the staff of Aaron,
a staff which forced buds from its dry bark and opened
a new life with the richness of hope bearing fruit.

*

To you, O Christ, most patient of teachers, we give
thanks and with our loyal lips we give the honour
that is your due, for our hearts have been fouled by sin.
It was your wish that we find the dangers in us
and recognize the struggle which our souls endure.
We know, now, that in our murky hearts conflicting
loves battle and as the fortunes of war vary
we become strong in the ways of virtue but then
we are weakened when virtue is captured and dragged
away in bondage so that we and they are slaves
to the most shameful sins and content to be damned.

How many times has sin been defeated and we
have felt ourselves glow with God's presence; how often,
then, have we cooled and given in to foul desire?
The war flares in our bones and man's double nature
is always in the throes of rebellion for flesh
oppresses the spirit like clay while the spirit
that was produced by the breath of God is always
hot in the bleak prison of the heart, rejecting,
even in its bondage, the filth that is the flesh.
The opposing winds of light and dark are at war
and we, body and spirit, have desires that are
at odds with one another until Christ, our Lord,
comes to help. He places the jewels of the virtues
in their proper places and in the place of sin
builds the courts of his temple; he makes for the soul
ornaments from its dark past to delight Wisdom
as she reigns forever on her glorious throne.

[I-24]

Hymns for the Various Hours and Days

(Cathemerinon)

THE FIRST HYMN: A HYMN AT COCKCROW

The bird that announces the day
tells us that daylight is coming;
Christ wakens our sleeping spirits
and like the cock calls us to life.

'Those beds', he cries, 'were only made
for sickness, for sleep and for sloth.
Be clean, true, sober and watchful
because I have come to you now.'

Unless the night was spent working,
one who waits to rise from his bed
until the sun has risen has
already waited much too long.

The shrill voices of the birds perched
just before dawn beneath the roof
are a figure prepared for us
of that Judge who will soon call us.

We lie in our awful darkness
covered up with our sluggishness.
He calls us away from our rest
for day is about to begin.

When the dawn scatters her sweet breath
across the sky she will make us
strong enough to embrace the light
which is the hope of those who toil.

The sleep that is given to us
each night is like the sleep of death.
Like the terrible night, our sins
make us lie asleep and snoring.

But Christ's voice comes down from the heights
because our souls have been enslaved
by drowsiness. He tells us that
daylight is near: he does not wish

that we sleep to the end of life
so that our hearts which are buried
in sin remain always asleep
and unable to see the light.

The demons who roam in the night
are struck with fear when the cock crows;
their happiness soon disappears
and they look for a place to hide.

The despised onset of new light,
salvation and divinity,
tears open the place of darkness
and routs the attendants of night.

They know that this light is the sign
of the hope that is promised us.
We hope for the coming of God
each time that we are freed from sleep.

What this bird means to us is seen
in our Saviour's telling Peter
that before the cock crowed, Peter
would have denied the Lord three times.

Sin is done before the herald
of daybreak announces the dawn
that enlightens all of mankind
and swiftly brings an end to sin.

For that reason he who denied
three times shed tears for the evil
that his lips spewed while his mind was
without guilt and his heart was true.

After that he kept a close watch
on his tongue lest it slip again.
When the cock crowed he became just
and from that day he never sinned.

For reasons such as these we know
that it was at this same moment,
when the cock was crowing loudly,
that Christ returned to us from Hell.

Then the vigour of death was crushed,
then the laws of Hell were thrown down,
and the greater strength of the day
forced the darkness into exile.

It must be now: let wickedness
lie dormant, let guilt fall asleep
and shrivel up, victimized by
the heaviness of its slumber.

Let the spirit be awakened;
may it use the time remaining
until the end of night to stand
watchful and alert in its place.

In tears, prayers and soberness let
us raise our voices to Jesus;
attentive prayers will keep the heart
from falling down in deadly sleep.

Profound oblivion has pressed
down on our senses long enough
and buried us while we wandered
in a country of empty dreams.

The things we have done for earthly
glory are false and frivolous
as the things we have done in our sleep:
let us wake up to what is true.

Gold, pleasure, joy, riches, honour,
prosperity and whatever
other evils that inflate us –
in the morning all are nothing.

Come, O Christ, and invade our sleep;
break the chains that darkness has forged.
Free us from our habits of sin;
fill us with the new light of day.

THE SECOND HYMN: A MORNING HYMN

Night and dark and the clouds of night,
the world's confusion and trouble:
be gone. The morning star appears,
the light shines, Christ is coming soon.

The murkiness of earth is pierced
by a stroke of the sun's spear; now
the colours return to all things
as the face of the sun rises.

The darkness in us will be torn.
The heart that has felt its own sin
will be cleared as the clouds break up
and be brightened in God's kingdom.

Then we will not be permitted
to hide the swarthy thoughts we think
but in the newness of morning
the heart's secrets will be opened.

In that time just before dawn
thieves have no fear of punishment
while light, enemy of deceit,
reveals theft in its hiding place.

Sly and expert deception loves
to be shrouded in darkness while
the lover prizes night's blackness
because it is right for his deed.

Behold, the flaming sun rises
to shame, to sadden and to judge
because there is no man who sins
easily under the sun's eye.

Can anyone refuse to blush
when he thinks of what he has drunk?
Desire is weak in the morning
when even the wicked are pure.

Now is the time to be austere.
Let no one take up foolishness.
Now all men put a serious
face on the follies they attempt.

This is the time when it is best
that all men be industrious,
whether soldier or citizen,
sailor, workman, ploughman or clerk.

One seeks fame in the courts of law,
another hears the bugle's call.
Both the merchant and the farmer
sigh greedily for their profits.

But we, ignorant of income
or interest or persuasive speech
or even the bravery of war,
are proud that we know only Christ.

We have learned to approach you on
bent knee with pure and simple minds
weeping and singing all the while
in our devout voices and songs.

This is the trade that makes us rich;
these are the deals by which we live.
These are the riches we begin
to work for when the sun appears.

Carefully inspect our feelings;
see every moment of our lives.
Many foul stains can be found there
much in need of your cleansing light.

Allow us to persevere and
let your light shine as you told us
when we were washed in the Jordan
and our uncleanness flowed away.

Whatever the night of the world
has darkened since then with its clouds,
we pray you, O King, brighten it
with the radiance of your face,

O Holy One. Just as tar turns
to milk and ebony turns to
crystal before your eyes, so can
you wipe away all stain of sin.

It was beneath the gloom of night
that Jacob wrestled so boldly
with an angel stronger than he
until the sun rose in the sky.

When the morning light touched his skin,
his knee buckled and he was lamed.
Defeated by that weakness, he
was no longer able to sin.

His thighs were deprived of that strength
which lurks in the lower body,
in the place where lust is enshrined,
far away from the heart's control.

These stories tell us that all men
buried in darkness lose their strength
to keep up the struggle with sin
unless they give in to God's strength.

That man whom the daylight revealed
crippled and severely weakened
after his nocturnal struggle
is the man who is more blessed.

May the blindness which has allowed
us to fall in danger and led
our feet away from the footpath
be gone; may our vision be clear;

may this morning light illumine
our day and purify our souls.
Let our tongues form no devious words;
let our minds harbour no dark thoughts.

May all of this day pass so that
neither our tongues nor our hands nor
our shifty eyes may commit sin.
May our bodies be free of guilt.

There is one who sees from above
and stands there watching everything
that we do and are through the day.
His lonely vigil has no end.

He is both our witness and judge.
All things that a man's mind conceives
he is careful to consider
because he is never deceived.

THE THIRD HYMN:
A HYMN BEFORE FOOD

Bearer of the cross, spreader of light,
source of all things and born of the Word,
you came from a virgin's body and
in the mighty Father you were first
before the stars, the world and the sea.

Turn the brightness of your face to us
and let your joyful light shine on us
so that we may enjoy this small meal
under the grandeur of your name and
under the honour which you give us.

Without you, O Lord, nothing desired
by the mouth can have a good flavour
unless you, O Christ, before the food
is served, season both food and dishes
just as faith makes everything holy.

May our platters be freshened by God;
may Christ be ladled into our bowls.
May everything that we are and do –
our talk, whether grave or slight, our jokes –
be ruled by God and his triple love.

Nothing that has been found in the rose
and nothing spicy to tease my taste
is here but a heavenly liquor
flows through me with the smell of faith, sweet
as nectar, flowing from the Father.

Come my muse, put away the ivy
that men have woven about your head.
Learn to weave nuptial garlands tied up
by dactyls so that your flowing hair
will be wreathed in strophes made for God.

What more could a generous soul do,
one who is a native of Heaven,
than tell of what she has just received,
always singing her Creator's praise
in carefully structured lines of verse?

Our God has given all things to man
and made him master of all the earth.
All that the sky, the earth or the sea
produces in air, or field or flood:
all these are mine just as I am his.

Birds are caught in nets by cleverness
and twigs smeared with a glue made from bark
catch a row of brightly feathered things
and will not release them in the air.
God has given all of this to man.

See how schools of fish are caught in nets
that slowly draw together; notice
how hooks tied to rods capture the fish
who takes the barbed steel into his mouth.
They are pierced and injured by their trust.

The soil pours out the riches it holds
in a crop of grain that bursts the barns
while in another place the vineyards
are heavy with new shoots and the grape,
which is the first nourishment of peace.

All of this wealth is given to us,
the followers of Christ, to supply
all of our needs. We have no desire
for slaughtering cattle and carving
their flesh to make us a feast of blood.

Let barbarians and savage tribes
get their food from the four-footed beasts;
all that we need are a few green leaves
and the pod that is heavy with beans.
These alone are enough for a feast.

Buckets brimming high with foamy milk
that has just come from a full udder
are emptied and a liquid is mixed
with the milk to make it solid. Then
the curd is pressed in a wicker frame.

The new wax comb oozes with honey
as fine as that found in Greece. The bee
who has no time for marriage gathers
this essence from the crystalline air
and the dew which collects on the thyme.

The orchard's ripeness comes from the soil.
The tree is shaken and its burden
falls like a sudden shower of rain
so that all of the ground is covered
by a precious carpet of red fruit.

What ancient instrument – horn or lyre,
with its music made by wind or strings –
could ever make songs to thank our God,
who is all rich and all powerful,
for the gifts that we enjoy so much?

To you, O most excellent Father,
shall we sing when the morning is new,
when the sun has gone through half its course
and when the sun sinks into the west
and we know that it is time for food.

Let me praise the Father on high for
the moist breath of life that is in me,
for the blood that throbs in my heart and
for the tongue which beats within my mouth
against the walls of its resonance.

It was your hand, O Holy One, that
took the moist earth and gave it our shape.
He made us to the form of himself
and to assure our perfection, breathed
from his mouth the warm breath of our life.

Then he commanded man to reside
in a grassy place with meadows
where the sweetness of spring had no end
and the green level ground was watered
by a stream flowing in four channels.

'All of this is to be used,' he said.
'Everything is for your enjoyment.
But you must not pick the bitter fruit
that hangs from the branches of that tree
growing there in the garden's centre.'

Then a treacherous serpent enticed
the maiden's simple heart to seduce
her companion and force him to eat
just a bite of that forbidden fruit
because she had already eaten.

After they consumed the fruit their eyes
were opened and they saw their bodies –
a criminal deed – naked. The sin
brought shame to their cheeks and they covered
themselves to hide the flesh that they found.

In the presence of God they trembled.
Driven out of that innocent place,
they discovered the burden of law
and the woman came under the rule
of the husband to whom she was wed.

The evil snake who plotted their fall
was condemned to have his three tongued head
bruised and crushed by the woman's sharp heel.
The woman became the snake's sovereign
just as man became the woman's lord.

Like those two, all generations now
are sunk in depravity and sin.
As men copy their parents they push
good and evil together until
death must end their rebellious ways.

But now, a new kind of heir is born:
a man from Heaven, free of the world,
God himself has put the shape of man
on his own divinity without
becoming in any way sinful.

The voice of the Father became flesh.
Bent over with divinity's weight,
the flesh is pregnant out of wedlock.
But a virgin bears the holy one
who will be born free of guilt and shame.

It was this that the ancient curse meant.
That blood feud between the snake and man
finally reached a kind of conclusion
when the devious evil serpent
was crushed by the heel of a woman.

The virgin worthy to bear this child
overcame the poison of the snake
and the snake, twisted tightly in knots,
spat its green venom on the green grass
and conceded victory to God.

All of nature is now overturned.
The beasts tremble at the sight of sheep,
the frightful wolf prowls among his prey
and sees that they have become fearless.
The stalking mouth has been closed at last.

A wonderful change makes the lion
subject to the lamb while a small dove
glides along through the upper air and
compels the eagles to take to flight
through the restless clouds and gusty winds.

You, O my Christ, are the mighty dove
to whom the eagle nurtured on blood
gladly gives way. You are the white Lamb
who keeps the wolf from harming your flock.
It is you who shuts the tiger's mouth.

Powerful God, hear our fervent prayer
and grant that with this modest meal, we,
your servants, may sustain our bodies
and keep from our stomachs the burden
of those feasts which weaken the body.

May the wine of bitterness be gone,
may we not enjoy poisonous things.
May our eating be always restrained
so that we avoid things forbidden
and save our bodies from injury.

Let the dreadful serpents be content
with knowing that the sadness of death
was brought to man by forbidden food.
It has already happened once: by
eating in sin, God's offspring must die.

The breath that came from the mouth of God,
the radiance of life, will never die
because it has come to us from God.
Flowing down from his heavenly throne
it comes with all the force of reason.

So mighty is its power that it
will restore life to flesh that is dead.
Once again the old bodily forms
will be reborn in the airless tomb
when God's breath blows the dust together.

Indeed – I am no fool – I believe
that bodies have a life like the soul's
because I remember now that Christ,
when he returned from the Phlegethon,
walked into Heaven with easy step.

In that same hope my own body waits.
Though we know that our limbs must first rest
perfumed by spices within the tomb,
Christ our exemplar who rose from death
will call us to live among the stars.

THE FOURTH HYMN: A HYMN AFTER FOOD

Now that we have fed our flesh with the food
which the weakness of our bodies demands,
let our tongues repay the Father with praise.

He is the Father who, enthroned on high,
rules the Seraphim and the Cherubim
and all other things that are beneath him.

It is he who is called the Lord of Hosts.
His life lacks any beginning or end;
maker of all things, he devised the world.

He alone is the fountain of that life
flowing from Heaven's brightness. He injects
faith and goodness, he halts death, he saves us.

He made us live and he makes us flourish.
The Spirit of God will rule forever
because both the Father and Son send him.

His purity goes into the chaste heart
which, consecrated as his temple, laughs
when it has drunk deeply of the godhead.

But if he should discover some deceit
growing in the organ in which he lives,
he will depart as though it were unclean.

The guilty conscience gives off a dim flame
and heavy smoke while the fires of sin burn.
Its foulness evicts all things that are good.

Not only modesty and clean desires
make our hearts a proper temple for Christ,
other things as well must be considered.

We must not become intoxicated
because such excesses will damage the place
where faith takes up its residence in us.

Hearts left unencumbered by clean living
are more fit to receive God's inpouring.
He is the spice and food that gives us life.

But you, O God, make double provision
for our growth: you strengthen and enliven
both body and soul with two kinds of food.

Once your pre-eminent power strengthened
a man in a lion's cage by bringing
him a meal from a very great distance.

He had been exposed to this cruel death
by the king and people of Babylon
because he spat on their metallic god

and thought it a sin to lower his head
before a statue made of polished bronze.
You saved him from death in those noisy jaws.

Faith and goodness are always a defence;
the untamed lions licked that brave man and
they trembled at the sight of your power.

Like gentle kittens, their hair was laid back,
their rage and hunger were gone and they sought
his favour by walking around his feet.

When the lion's den had become silent,
he lifted his hands to you. It was he
who gave witness before to your great strength.

Because he had been imprisoned without
any relief and was now without food,
you sent an angel to serve his desires.

The heavens opened and your messenger
descended to earth where he found a meal
cooked by the holy prophet, Habakkuk.

Though this simple food was meant for farm-hands
your angel took the prophet by the hair
and carried him and the meal through the air.

The kidnapped prophet and his food floated
to the lions' den and he served the feast:
'Eat the banquet that God has sent to you.'

Daniel did as he had been told and then,
strengthened by food, turned to Heaven and then
gave praise to God: 'Amen, alleluia.'

In this way, O God, giver of all things,
are we refreshed by you and now we give
you thanks and consecrate hymns to your name.

This is the feast that is prepared for all
who remain faithful to the laws of God
the Father and his Son who is our Lord.

We are confined here by a cruel tyrant,
the world's harshness, but you give us guidance
and save us from the beast that roams about

us roaring and gnashing his teeth in rage
because he desires the taste of our flesh.
We beg you, mighty God, save us from him.

Annoyed, weighed down and tossed by evil we
are despised by those who injure us and
imprison us; faith is our punishment.

Yet in our trouble you give us comfort
for nourishment seems to come from on high
and the enraged beast soon becomes tranquil.

Food that is prepared for virtuous men
is given to those who gulp it down
rather than taste each delicate mouthful.

Such men make this food a substantial part
of their innermost selves. Only such men
will have the strength to reap the Master's crop.

There is nothing sweeter or more tasty,
nothing more helpful to man than the words
of the prophet telling what is to come.

Once we have tasted this wisdom, haughty
powers may pass corrupt judgements and lead
us away to die; the hungry lions

may attack us but we will always see
as we bear our cross that you, O Christ, and
our Lord, the Father, are together one.

THE FIFTH HYMN: A HYMN FOR LIGHTING THE LAMPS

First maker of the light and our kindly guide,
you who measure all of time into seasons,
now the sun has gone and darkness is with us.
Give light again, O Christ, to your faithful ones.

Even though the heavens are filled with bright stars
and the moon is hung there like a lamp, still you
expect us to seek light by striking the flint
until fire jumps from the body of the stone.

In this way man knows for certain that his hope
of ever attaining the light rests on Christ
who called his body a rock and established
himself as the source from which our light is drawn.

With lamps sprinkled by rich oils or with torches
dry as summer grass we feed those little flames.
We make tapers too of flax smeared with bee's wax
which still smells like the flowers from which it came.

However we feed it, the little flame grows:
in a clay dish with oil and a linen wick
or on pine knots dripping with pitch or on hemp
that draws the warm wax up so the flame can drink.

All the while, the bee's hot nectar falls in sweet
teardrops for the steady heat of the flame sends
it dripping around the base of the candle
in a rich shower of fire from the summit.

Now the walls of our houses gleam, O Father,
with your gift of fine flickering flames. Their light
imitates the vanished light of day while night,
defeated, hides in its torn mantle and flees.

Who is so blind that he cannot see this light
coming so swiftly down from its source on high?
We must never forget that Moses saw God
show himself in the blaze of a burning bush.

Blessed is Moses who was able to see
the Lord of Heaven in those sacred brambles;
blessed is the man who untied his sandals
lest he pollute a holy place with his shoes.

It was this same blaze that the chosen nation
followed across the empty desert after
they had been set free from heathen tyranny
because their fathers had been strong men and good.

Wherever their column turned, moving by night
they followed a beacon brighter than the sun
which led them always watchful and unsleeping
through the oppressive darkness in which they walked.

But the king who ruled the lands about the Nile,
consumed by jealousy and hatred, ordered
an army in pursuit. These men were formed
in fast moving columns with the finest arms.

Answering the bugle's call, his men took shields,
buckled their bodies in sword belts and waited.
One took a spear, another fastened steel heads
to oak shafts that came from the island of Crete.

The horde of foot-soldiers made orderly ranks
while others mounted the terrible chariots.
The banners of war, emblazoned with dragons,
were unfurled and Pharaoh's army was ready.

While this happened the nation that had suffered
in Egypt's burning heat was free of bondage.
They halted their weary march in a strange land
that is found along the coast of the Red Sea.

Without warning the army of the tyrant,
in spite of his promise, appeared at their heels:
without a moment's pause the attack began
and Moses led his people into the sea.

The tide pulled apart and left them in a dry place
while the crystalline waters became like walls
on either side. Without hesitation they
forgot their fatigue and hurried to safety.

Then the African soldiers, filled with hatred
and thirsting for Hebrew blood, followed their prey
recklessly into that watery trench and
obeyed their king without thinking of injury.

Like a great storm on the ocean that army
swept into the open inviting flood, but
then the walls fell together and the tides flowed
again back and forth in their usual place.

The Hebrews looked back to the way they had come
and saw, left on the waves like a storm's debris,
the wreckage of chariots and weapons and dead
horses tossed together with princes and men.

It was a sad day for the tyrant. But you,
O Christ – what tongue can sing your praise – overcame
Egypt by the strength of many plagues that forced
her to make a path for the rule of justice.

A sea which cannot be crossed by man was calmed
when you forbade it to rage; a highway spread
across its breadth so that your people could walk
in safety while their enemies were destroyed.

When you commanded, the desert's sterile rocks
burst with bubbling springs that flowed on the dry sands
in streams so that all of your people could drink
beneath the dry, unflinching heat of the sun.

They came to a place with pools of water that
was too bitter to drink. Moses was given
a log which made those waters sweet as honey:
wood sweetens bitterness; the cross gives us hope.

They became hungry and food filled their campsite:
it came like snow, it showered on them like hail.
With this meal, this banquet, given them by Christ,
they spread their tables and forgot their hunger.

Then a windstorm with sheets of rain brought a cloud
of birds to their camp. When the wind and rain died
the birds remained on the ground and would not fly
away to the skies. All of this was given

to our fathers by God's stupendous power.
With his constant support we are always fed
and our hearts are filled with his heavenly food
which nourishes our souls and makes us stronger.

Through the age-long tempest he calls out to those
who are weary; making a path through the storms,
he guides those who are his: he is the refuge
for those who have known a thousand distresses.

He calls them to enter the land of the just
which is covered and sweetened by roses and
watered by many running streams that freshen
the marigolds, the violets and crocuses.

Rich balsam flows from its slender twigs, precious
cinnamon pours its scent and the leafy nard,
a most exotic scent, is carried along
the river which has seen the place of its source.

The souls of the blessed sing their pleasant songs
in the grassy meadows; the sound of their hymns
comes in a concert of harmony sweet as
the lilies that grow beneath their holy feet.

And it must be said that even the damned souls
in Hell are free from the pains of their torment
during the night on which God returned from Hell
and Acheron's dark shores to the world of men.

His coming was not like that of the morning
star rising from the ocean's pit but rather
he came as one greater than the sun bringing
a new day to a world saddened by his death.

On that night the fury of Hell is lessened,
its pains become mild and the souls of the dead,
freed from fire if only for a time, rejoice
while even the sulphurous rivers are cooled.

We, however, keep that night in holy joy.
Praying without rest, we make petitions and
on the altar that is set up among us
we make a humble offering of ourselves.

The lamps that hang from every part of the roof
blaze brightly and the flame which floats on its oil
casts its light through the clear crystal of the glass.
The place of our prayer is so brilliantly lit

that one might think the stars of Heaven itself
were burning there in the ceiling. It seems that
all the stars were scattered there above our heads:
two bears, the evening star and the oxen.

What a perfect gift we have prepared for you:
at the beginning of night we offer light,
your most precious gift to us, the gift by which
we recognize every blessing you give us.

You are the light of our eyes and of our minds;
with this light we see as through a glass clearly.
Accept the light we offer to you; accept
this light which brightly burns in the oil of peace.

Accept it, most holy Father, through your Son
in whom your glory has been revealed to us,
through Christ our Lord, your only Son, through him who
from his Father's heart exhales the Comforter.

Through him your splendour, your honour, your wisdom
and praise, your majestic goodness and concern
continue the reign of your threefold godhead
joining the ages together forever.

THE SIXTH HYMN: A HYMN BEFORE SLEEPING

Be near us, highest Father,
whom no man has ever seen;
and Christ, the Father's Word and
you, beneficent Spirit:

who in this one Trinity
are all one strength and one light,
God of everlasting God,
and God sent each by other.

The labours of day are past
and the time for stillness comes;
the caresses of slumber
relax our weary bodies.

The mind when tossed by the storms
of worry and care will drink
deeply out of the precious
goblet of forgetfulness.

The waters of Lethe wash
over the body so that
no sensation of soreness
remains to bother the mind.

This is the law which God made
for our feeble bodies: that
our labour be tempered by
the healing pleasures of sleep.

But while rest spreads over us,
and sleep flows through the body,
lulling the heart into peace
and bringing quiet to us,

our spirits roam through the air
with all their vigour intact
and in various ways see things
that are hidden from our sight.

The mind, which came from heaven
and whose strength is in the skies,
cannot rest in idleness
when it is freed from worry.

By imitation it makes
images of different shapes
and enjoys that ghostly art
while it lives among those things.

But on the other hand fear
can trouble our restful dreams,
while even a brilliant light
comes to tell us what will be.

The world of things is scattered
and a lying shadow makes
our minds fearful and deceives
us with a cloud of darkness.

If a man's guilt is but slight,
this brilliant clear radiance
will teach him many secrets
about things no man should see;

but a man whose heart has been
polluted by sinfulness
will find himself afflicted
by fear and terrible dreams.

This was proved by Joseph who
told to Pharaoh's two servants
who were imprisoned with him
the meaning of their visions:

one would soon return to court
and be cup-bearer again
while the other would be hanged
and then eaten by the birds.

Then he warned the king himself,
when the king had told his dream,
to make provision for drought
by filling his storage bins.

Soon he became protector
and a prince in the kingdom;
he carried a sceptre like
the king's and lived at the court.

How deep are the mysteries
that Christ reveals to the just
while they are sleeping soundly,
how clear and quieting.

The best-loved evangelist,
when Christ threw open the clouds,
saw many things that were dark
before his teacher taught him.

The Lamb of God, Thunderer,
stained with the blood of his death,
alone has strength to open
that book which tells the future.

In his strong hand he carries
a double edged blade threatening
two strokes at once: it flashes
as he waves it in the air.

Only he can see into
both body and soul. The blade
which is doubly fearful is
death for both body and soul.

The Father has given him
the seat of lasting judgement;
his name is given first place
before every other name.

Yet he is moved by kindness
which softens his judgement and
assures that only a few
will be allowed to perish.

He is the great destroyer
of Antichrist and over
that monstrous being he wins
a victory easily.

This is the beast whose hunger
devours all peoples, he is
that most bloody Charybdis
whom John's writings have condemned.

It is he who tries to wear
the holy name of Christ: but
then he is slaughtered by Christ
and thrown to the depths of Hell.

In such a sleep honest men
rest their minds without worry
so that their souls can travel
across Heaven's length and breadth.

But we deserve none of this
because error fills our hearts
and we are corrupted by
our fixed desires for evil.

We must be content to rest
the body and hope that we
will never be bothered by
those shadows of emptiness.

Take heed, worshippers of God:
remember that you were washed
by immersion in water
and marked with the holy oils.

Be sure that when you lie down
at sleep's call you mark your brow
and the place where your heart beats
with the blessing of Christ's cross.

Be sure that your couch is pure
so that you will always rest
both safely and securely
in the great love that is Christ's.

The cross will drive out all sin;
darkness will flee from the cross;
when the spirit has this sign,
nothing can keep it silent.

Let every wandering dream
be kept away; may the guile
of the lying one be gone
with all of night's ugliness.

O winding serpent, depart.
Christ is here. Take your thousand
deceptions; do not disturb
these hearts that belong to him.

Though our bodies are asleep,
even in sleep will we think
of Christ and the sign that drives
the foul enemy away.

THE SEVENTH HYMN: A HYMN BEFORE FASTING

Nazarene, Bethlehem's light, the Father's Word,
born out of the womb of an untouched virgin;
be present, O Christ, at our chaste abstinence
and, as King, be pleased with these our holy days
which we offer to thee as a sacrifice.

Surely there is nothing purer than this rite
by which the heart's tissues are cleansed and revived
and the undisciplined body is compelled
to sweat so that fat will not constrict our minds
and choke our souls with the foulness of its stench.

In this most efficacious way we conquer
luxury and appetite. The awful sloth
that comes from wine is put away with passion,
frivolous talk, and the plagues that dull our minds
and keep us from the radiant fire of God's love.

If any man eats and drinks without restraint,
the noble soul will waste away without fasts
to defend its spark of life. In such a man
the mind will sleep heavily in the slow heart
while both the body and soul live with less heat.

May the desires of our bodies be reined in;
may the smokeless blaze of wisdom shine in us.
The soul will see clearly and it will be free
to breathe and offer its prayers to the Father
without the constriction of any slavery.

It was by such a method that Elias,
that ancient priest, renewed his strength while he lived
in a Syrian desert. Many men say
that in his quiet, remote retreat he stripped
from himself a multitude of heavy sins.

Soon after, Elias was taken away
in a flying chariot with horses of fire.
He soared into the heavens so that the world
and its filth would not touch a holy man whose
lengthy fasts had given him such a freedom.

Moses, who was the messenger of God, could
not see the Lord of the seven heavens till
he had fasted through forty turns of the sun.
When that heavenly body saw the prophet
free of all sustenance, his prayers were answered.

While he prayed he wept. Those falling tears fed him.
He wept through the night and his tears wet the dust
where he laid his face. Finally God spoke to him:
the majestic voice of the Lord touched him and
he trembled at the fire his eyes could not see.

No less than Moses was John, too, a master
of such might. He preceded the Son of God,
he straightened the crooked paths and made a way
for Christ to follow; like all the prophets, he
went before the Word making preparations.

This was done at the beginning because God
was about to reveal himself among men.
The steep places were levelled and rough places
were smoothed so that when Truth had come to this earth
there would be nothing to hinder its passage.

There was nothing usual about John's birth:
he was a first child who came late and then pulled
at the breasts which had shrunk as his mother aged.
Before he was born, while still in her body,
he saw a virgin bearing the Son of God.

When he was a man he went to the desert.
Wearing only untanned skins and his own hair,
or garments made of the coarsest wool, dreading
the corruption and defilement of his flesh,
he shunned the unclean habits of the city.

There, in the rigorous ways of abstinence,
he lived a life of hard, unbending strictness.
Until late in the evening both food and drink
were kept away from his mouth. He fed himself
locusts and the strong sweetness of wild honey.

He was the first to preach and teach the new law.
In the holy river he washed sin away
so that after the filthy bodies were washed
the flesh was clean and the bodies were ready
to receive the shining Spirit from Heaven.

From this washing, which removed all stain of sin,
men came renewed and resplendent like raw gold
when it has been refined in a furnace, and
bright as the brilliance of silver when it is
purified of dross and polished with soft cloths.

Let me tell, now, the tale of an ancient fast,
a story which is found in the sacred book.
The angry bolts of the Father were appeased
and his fury was immersed in love so that
all in the city were saved from destruction.

Once there flourished a proud and haughty people
who had given themselves up to indulgence:
in its wickedness the entire nation passed
beyond every restraint. Stiff necked and stupid,
it soon disregarded the worship of God.

Justice, which is always merciful, at last
was offended and moved to righteous anger.
It took a flaming sword in its right hand and
brandished over that city the noise of hail
and cyclones in a cloud of fire and thunder.

He is always more anxious for repentance
than destruction: he waited for them to stop
their lust and the folly of established vice;
the awful Judge who listens to any plea
restrained his anger for a little more time.

Then the merciful one called Jonah to go
and warn that people that punishment was near.
But because he knew that the Judge would rather
save than strike as he had threatened, secretly
he prepared to flee to avoid that mission.

He found a huge ship ready to leave; he crossed
the plank; the wet lines were cast off and they sailed.
When they were far from land a great storm came up
and every sailor sought the cause of Heaven's
rage. Jonah's guilt was revealed by casting lots.

Accused, he confessed; arraigned, he was condemned.
A simple turn of the jar had shown his guilt.
They, as one man, threw him over the railing
and into the open jaws of some monster
who swallowed Jonah into his dark belly.

The beast's hunger rushed him unhurt past his teeth
so that he flew across the tongue without loss
of blood. The dripping white molars could not hold
that morsel in their bite; he passed through the mouth
and beyond the palate into the gullet.

For three days and nights he stayed in the whale's gut
wandering among the monster's organs and
exploring the tightly twisted paths, his breath
choking and coughing within him all the while
because of the animal's great heat and stench.

Then, at the end of the third night, the beast retched
and he was spat out unharmed. Quite astounded
to find himself both alive and uninjured,
he was washed ashore where the waves break loudly
and the ocean's spray falls on the salty rocks.

Without a moment's hesitation he turned
and walked to Nineveh. After scolding them
for the shameful lives which they had led, he said:
'The wrath of the almighty Judge hangs above
you and will soon descend upon everyone.'

His mission finished, Jonah left that city
and went to the peak of a near-by mountain
so that he, in safety, could watch the ruin
of a city. While he waited he enjoyed
the shade of an ivy plant that flourished there.

But then it happened. The people, touched by shame,
were suddenly in an agony of grief
which came to them with the fear of death. Each one
of them – commoners, officials, citizens
of all ages, pale young men, weeping women –

was rushing about in crowds through the city.
They agreed to public fasts and stopped eating.
Mothers exchanged their jewels for coarse garments
and then sprinkled their heads with ashes rather
than powdered gold and thin veils of precious silk.

Fathers wore robes of mourning without belts and
people of the city, lamenting their guilt,
put on tunics made of haircloth. The maidens
left their hair uncombed and covered their faces
with black veils while their children wept in the dirt.

The King of Nineveh himself broke the clasp
that held his robes and tore the cloth into shreds
which glowed still with the purple purchased on Cos.
He put aside his jewels and the precious crown
and he sprinkled ashes on his scented hair.

Not one of them thought of eating or drinking;
every man had left the table for fasting.
Indeed the cradles were wet from the weeping
of the city's infants who were hungry; since
even the nurses fasted, there was no milk.

The shepherds and herdsmen put their flocks in pens
so that no cattle or sheep could crop the grass
or plunge their muzzles into a mountain stream.
The noise of their hunger and thirst filled the place
with the sounds of a nation doing penance.

The anger of God – short-lived as it is – was
soon appeased by the sight of that conversion.
His wrath was softened and his justice exchanged
for mercy. He will always forgive men's guilt
when they humble themselves and weep for their sins.

But why should I tell such an ancient story
when Jesus, weighed down by a mortal body,
fasted to purify his heart? It was he
whose name, Emmanuel, which means 'God with us',
was given by a prophet before his birth.

This body, weak by nature and held captive
under the lawless tyranny of pleasure,
was freed by being subjected to the law
of virtue. He endowed the flesh with freedom
and conquered the passions that kept it a slave.

He lived in a distant and unfriendly place
for forty days during which time he never
tasted the pleasantness of food. He strengthened
his body with a wholesome fast that conquered
the weakness remaining after pleasure goes.

The enemy saw him and wondered that he
in his feeble body endured such hunger.
Then he tried to discover by artifice
whether God had been received by that body
but Christ revealed his trick and forced him to flee.

Let each one of us, O Christ our teacher, go
each as he can in the way you have shown us.
Put the Spirit in command of our affairs
so that we, as the lust for food is conquered,
may take the battlefield and be triumphant.

For this will we earn the enemy's hatred;
for this will we earn God's approval, who rules
Heaven and Earth. It is he who makes the gift
acceptable; he wakens the heart to faith
and clears away the plagues that threaten our lives.

When joined with generosity, a purging
fast destroys a thick crop of mutinous sins
more surely than fire is put out by water
and more surely than a snowdrift is melted
by the sun's heat coming on a winter day.

To clothe the naked, to feed the hungry and
to give generously to those who beg for it
are all, indeed, noble forms of virtue, for
all of us, whether we be rich or poor, share
the lot common to all of humanity.

A man whose right hand seeks fame but is lavish
with money for other men while his left hand
knows nothing of the kindly deed is a man
whose loan will be repaid a hundred times when
he is enriched with an everlasting wealth.

THE EIGHTH HYMN: A HYMN AFTER FASTING

Christ, who give guidance to your servants,
who govern us with a gentle rein
and curb us and always direct us
with easy laws,

you, while still carrying the burden
of this clumsy flesh, endured hardships
so that we might see your example
and your teaching.

The ninth hour, when our fast must end,
comes as the sun wheels into the west.
Three parts of the day are gone and now
the fourth remains.

We, as we take the food allotted,
end the short observance of our vow
and our appetites enjoy this taste
of our repast.

We have known such kindness from Heaven,
we have been led with such friendly words,
that this obedience is easy
for our weak flesh.

He demands that none of us must wear
unpleasing garments or soil his face.
We must comb our hair because it is
our head's glory.

'Wash all of your body when you fast,'
he said, 'Do not become pale and wan,
do not let the bones of your face show
in haggardness.'

All things done for the Father's glory
should be covered up by modesty.
God knows every secret and rewards
the hidden gift.

When a sheep sickens and falls behind
and its wool is torn on the brambles,
he, the unsleeping shepherd, will search
in every place

until he has found that which was lost
and returned it to the healthy flock
where all are always safe from the wolves.
He will return

that sheep to its own grazing place where
there are no rough burrs and no thistles
armed with needles. It is a shady
well-watered place.

The grove into which the shepherd takes
his flock is filled with palm trees and grass
and over the running waters bend
branches of bay.

How can we, devoted Shepherd, pay
for such marvellous gifts? Nothing that
we might give will pay you for the gift
of salvation.

Even if we never ate again
and spent every minute at our prayers
until we had mortified the flesh
and become weak,

still we alone with all our efforts
would be inferior to that gift
which the Father has so easily
given to us.

As a result, lest we be ruined
and our strength leave these bodies of clay
and our whitened veins fill up with blood
to weaken us

and take our virility away,
our rule about fasting is not harsh.
We are not driven by fear, each one
does what he can.

It is enough, whatever one does,
to do it after asking that God
bless his intention, whether he fasts,
or eats his food.

God is always kind and will consent
to bless whatever good that we do
as now we presume that it is wise
to feed ourselves.

I beg that this act be good for us;
may this food spreading into our veins
strengthen the worshippers of Christ who
offer this prayer.

THE NINTH HYMN: A HYMN FOR ALL THE HOURS

Come boy, bring the poet's plectrum and I will write
in pleasant trochees songs about the deeds of Christ:
of him alone will my lyre and the muses sing.

A man, priest and king in vestments, sang of his birth
in a rich voice with stringed instruments and drums.
He was drunk with a heavenly inspiration.

We will sing about miracles that have been proved
by the witness of a world which does not deny
what it has seen: God revealed in his Son to men.

Born of his parent's love before the world began,
the Alpha and Omega, he is the fountain
and end of all things whether they are or will be.

He gave the order and all things were created;
he spoke and the earth, the heavens and the ocean,
the three layers of earth and all that lives came to be.

He took for himself a human body so that
we – because all men must die – would not be buried
in the pit of Hell for the sin of our fathers.

O blessed birth: a virgin's labour after she
conceived by the Spirit produced our salvation.
The child who has redeemed the world revealed his face.

Let the heights of Heaven sing; may the angels sing;
let all the powers everywhere sing his praises.
May no tongue be silent; let every voice sing out.

Behold, it is he whose birth the ancients foretold;
it is he who was announced in the prophet's words.
Let all things together offer praises to him.

Water poured into mugs becomes Falernian
and the steward tells how wine came from water jugs;
the host is amazed to taste such a fine vintage.

'Limbs diseased and ulcerous and festering flesh
I command to be cleansed'; it was done as he said
and the swollen, discoloured tissues became pure.

To eyes buried in darkness you have applied clay
softened by the sweetness that wets your holy tongue;
by this cure their eyes are opened and light returns.

You scold the torrent of wind for tossing the sea
up from its deepest parts so that the fishing boats
are threatened; it obeys your word and becomes calm.

A woman secretly touches the dusty fringe
of your garment and is healed; the flow of blood stops
and at that same instant the paleness leaves her cheeks.

He saw a young man dead just at the end of youth
with only his mother to bear him to the grave;
'Arise', and he stands, a healthy man, at her side.

To Lazarus, who has been entombed for four days,
he restores breath and commands that he be alive;
with a gasp, the decayed flesh is restored to life.

He walks on the waters of the sea and he steps
across the tide; the churning sea becomes a path
and the waves do not part beneath his holy step.

One who has been a madman chained in a cavern,
grinding his teeth together and beset by fears,
falls to his knees when he sees Christ passing by him.

The plague of wily devils in its thousand shapes
seizes a herd of unclean swine and leaps into
the black waters destroying its hosts and itself.

'Take twelve baskets and gather the pieces of food
left over from the feast'; five loaves and two fishes
have amply filled a thousand or more disciples.

You alone are our food and our bread; you alone
are the seasoning that never fails: he who eats
this food is filled, not in his flesh, but in his soul.

Ears whose boulevards are closed open at his call;
when he speaks all obstructions are cleared away and
the ear again enjoys both whispers and voices.

Every sickness yields, every weakness is destroyed:
tongues that had been tied speak; a man who had been lame
joyfully carries his cot through the city's streets.

He even enters the gates of the underworld
so that those who died before his time can enjoy
the goodness of that salvation that he has won.

The door is forced to open as he approaches,
the bolts are broken and the hinges pulled apart;
the gate that opens only inward freely swings

so that the dead may flee through the door they entered:
the law of Hell is overturned and that threshold
stands open to all who wish to cross its black sill.

But while light flooded the darkness the sky was black
and the stars dimmed; the sun, wrapped in robes of mourning,
fled from the heavens and in sorrow hid himself.

They say that the world trembled when it recognized
the chaos of eternal night. Release your voice,
my heart, release your tongue and sing of victory:

sing of the passion, sing of the triumphant cross,
sing of the sign burned on us. What a marvellous
wound, how strange the death. Blood wins a crown for us while

water washes us. The snake saw the sacrifice
of that holy body and at once his venom
lost its bitterness and he was struck by anguish.

With your long hissing throat shattered, wicked serpent,
what have you won by your ruin of the first man?
By receiving God, human flesh has lost its guilt.

Our Saviour has permitted himself to feel death
for a little while so that he can lead the dead
back to life by breaking the chains of their old sins.

Many holy fathers and saints did as he did
and returned with him putting on the cloak of flesh
so that they walked out of their tombs on the third day.

Arms and legs were formed again out of dust while veins
grew warm as the bones and tendons and inner parts
each found its place beneath the cover of the skin.

When he had condemned death and returned man to life,
he ascended in victory to the judgement
seat taking with him the glory of his passion.

May you always be glorified, Judge of the dead;
O King of the living, may all glory be yours.
Seated at the Father's right hand, you are well known

for the great power which will come to us from you
to avenge all sins: old men and young, small children,
mothers, maidens and young girls all sing your praises.

Let the flowing waters of the rivers, the shores
of the oceans, rain, drought, snow, frost, timber and wind
unite by day and night to praise you forever.

THE TENTH HYMN: A HYMN FOR THE BURIAL OF THE DEAD

God, the blazing fountain of our souls,
who joined two elements, one living
and the other dying, to create
man out of your divine fatherhood,

remember that both are yours. For you
they were combined, it is you they serve
while together they cling, flesh and soul,
stirred and moved by the life you give them.

When they separate man is finished:
the thirsty earth welcomes the body
and a breath of air takes the spirit;
each part of man goes back to its source.

All created things in time weaken
and waste away: things joined together
must be separated; things composed
of contrary parts must come undone.

But you, O God, have shown us that death
can be conquered; you show us a way
by which those men who have died will rise
again. So long as nobility

is cut down by our mortality
as though it were locked in a prison,
that part which came to us from Heaven
will always prove itself the stronger.

If, by chance, a worldly longing wants
to taste the mud and enjoy the earth,
the spirit too will be deflected
and follow the body's direction.

But if the fire remembers its source
and rejects the stifling contagion,
it will take with it all of the flesh;
body and soul will live in the stars.

We see this body without its soul,
resting before us; but before long
it will seek to be joined to its soul
so that they together live on high.

The time is coming when the bones' warmth
will return to this flesh and be clothed
again by its old house which will stir
with the life that comes with living blood:

bodies that have long been dead and still
in their foul tombs will be carried high
into the fresh heavenly breezes
together with the souls they once knew.

For this reason do we take such care
of graves; for this reason do we give
these honours to a lifeless body
which we carried here in procession.

For this same reason do we spread white
linen cloths over it and sprinkle
it with a precious preservative,
myrrh, which has been carried from Saba.

What do the carved tombs and monuments
mean if they do not say that something
precious, something sleeping, has been placed
in them for safety as in a vault?

This far-seeing care is expended
by the followers of Christ because
they believe that all who are asleep
and cold will one day return to life.

Whoever finds bodies unburied
and in kindness covers them with earth
makes a gift of his kindly concern
to Christ, our all-powerful master.

The same law demands that all men mourn
the death of another man whether
he be cousin or stranger because
the death of man is the common fate.

The father of holy Tobias,
a saintly man, though his meal was hot
left it to cool while he went away
to help at another's burial.

Though his servants stood by the table,
he left the utensils of eating
and turned his mind to death and the grave.
With tears, he laid those bones in the earth.

Before long his reward came to him
and he was given a rich prize: when
his blind eyes were massaged with fish oil,
they were opened to the light of day.

Even then the Father of the world
taught him how harsh is the cure for those
who desire a reasonable life:
the new light burns both body and soul.

Our Father also taught the old man
that no one sees the kingdom of God
before he has suffered in darkness
the bitter enmity of the world.

Death itself is better than living
because the pain of death opens up
a heavenly road for the just man
so that in suffering he is saved.

Bodies that are dead now will return
in a better age, and the body
which warms again after being dead
will not ever again suffer death.

The cheeks which now are white and wasted
will have skin coloured by the red blood
so that they will be more beautiful
than the blossom of any flower.

In that day the jealousy of age
will not rob the forehead of its grace,
nor will the arms be lean and consumed
so that all the body is shrunken.

Disease, which comes from Hell, will suffer
the pain of his torment as he writhes
in chains and sweat. He wears our bodies
with fevers now; he will suffer then.

From the highest most remote Heaven
the immortal and victorious flesh
will see him afflicted with the pain
that he himself had, once before, caused.

Why should you who are living lament
with these loud and silly noises and
rail against the eternal laws in
such a senseless display of mourning?

Let your doubting sadness be silent;
let your flowing tears be dried, mothers.
Let this mourning come to a quick end
because death is not the end of life.

When a dried seed is dead and buried
it comes to life and produces shoots.
When the seed is returned to the earth
it repeats the harvest of the past.

Receive now, Earth, our brother's body.
Take him to your bosom; care for him.
It is a man's body we give you;
he was nobly born, look after him.

In this flesh lived a soul created
by the breath of God; in this body
Wisdom, whose head is Christ, had a home.
He who planned and made this man will not

forget him. Cover and protect this
treasure which we now place in your care.
Soon our Father will seek what he gave,
the image of his most divine face.

When that time of justice comes, that time
when God will fulfil all hopes, this grave
will be opened and it will return
the form which today we give to it.

Even though time turned these bones to dust
and that dust became but a handful
of ashes, still the man that he was
will never be allowed to perish.

Even if the fickle winds that blow
in the void were to carry this flesh
away until nothing remained, still
the man we have known would not be gone.

But until you, O God, have summoned
this body and made it new again,
where will you send the soul? In what place
will the spirits of men take their rest?

Lazarus rested in the bosom
of the patriarch among flowers
while the rich man, burning in the pit,
looked up and saw him from a distance.

We will do as you have told us, Lord.
In your defeat of death's blackness you
advised your companion on the cross,
the thief, to follow in your footsteps.

For those who are faithful to your word,
there is a well-lit road to the gates
of Paradise; those who follow you
will enter the garden Adam lost.

I pray you, our Leader, give orders
that your servant, this spirit, be drawn
to you in the place where it was born,
the place from which it went to exile.

We will attend to these buried bones
with sweet violets and green branches;
we will sweeten the stones by sprinkling
precious perfumes on the epitaph.

THE ELEVENTH HYMN: A HYMN FOR CHRISTMAS DAY

Why does the sun return and leave
his restricted circle behind?
Is not Christ who opens the path
of light born among us today?

How brief was the light this day left
as it rolled through the sky. Its light
at last was nearly extinguished
as it shortened from day to day.

But now the sky shines joyfully;
the earth is glad and rejoices,
for the grandeur of the sun climbs
up again to its former place.

Come out among us, little boy.
Your virgin mother is herself
Chastity; because of her, you
have become our mediator.

Though you came from the Father's mouth
and are the Word of God in flesh,
still before time began you were
in the Father's heart as Wisdom.

Wisdom established the heavens,
the sky, the day and all that is.
All things were made by the power
of the Word for the Word is God.

But when time had been established
and all things were set to order,
the Creator himself remained
hidden in the Father's bosom

until many thousands of years
had passed and he himself would deign
to come into a sinful world
which had been corrupted by men.

Men in their blindness listened to
some idle chatter and assumed
that a piece of bronze or cold stone
or even wood could be their god.

In listening to these prophets
they found themselves under the sway
of the robber who took their souls
to himself and threw them in Hell.

But Christ did not let his people
fall and be destroyed in this way;
he put on the garment of flesh
so that the Father's work would not fail.

By taking a mortal body
and making the flesh live again
he destroyed the bondage of death
and returned men to the Father.

This is the day when God on high
breathed you forth and set you in clay
so that the flesh of all mankind
was united with his own Word.

O noble virgin, does it seem,
now as your long weariness ends,
that your unspotted purity
brightens for the child that you bear?

Oh what wonderful joys are held
in the purity of that womb;
from that virginal body comes
the brightness of a better age.

The infant drew breath and he cried
and with that spring had come
for at that same instant the world
threw off its old sluggish manner.

All the countryside was sprinkled
with flowers and the desert sands
became sweetened with the perfume
of precious nard and sweet nectar.

Child, the world's coarseness felt your birth:
the grey hardness of granite was
overcome and all the boulders
were wrapped in a cushion of grass.

Honey flowed from the earth's fissures
and the dry branches of the oak
dripped perfume on the ground; even
the tamarisk tree gave balsam.

How holy was the manger that
was your cradle, eternal King.
The beasts who ate from it and all
nations will revere its rough planks.

The cattle, beasts without knowledge,
adore it: they are foolish beasts
whose only wit is cropping grass
and whose strength is spent in chewing.

Even though heathens and cattle
come faithfully to the stable
and show that they, though they are dull,
can still have some understanding,

the children of the patriarchs
deny him and hate God present
among them. They act like men drugged
or made insane by the furies.

Why must you hurry down the path
of sin? If any sense remains
in your heads recognize the Lord
and Master of all your princes.

Look at this child who is given
to all people as their King; see
his hiding place, his mother and
her midwife, see his infant bed.

This is he on whom all sinners
look when he is seated among
the flickering clouds: then you will
weep and shed tears for your evil.

While that trumpet gives the signal
for the earth to burn, and the poles
of the universe collapse and
everything crashes in ruin,

he himself, raised over all else,
will reward each as he deserves:
giving to some unending light
and to others the pains of Hell.

Then, Judaea, will you have felt
the lightning that comes from the cross;
then will you know that he whom death
had swallowed up has been spat out.

THE TWELFTH HYMN: FOR THE EPIPHANY

Whoever tries to find Christ
should look in the high places:
it is there that one can see
the signs of lasting glory.

This star whose bright globe subdues
even the light of the sun
announces that God has come
to earth in the flesh of men.

This star does not serve the night
and wax and wane with the moon:
it shines alone in the sky
and times the progress of day.

Though the Bears turn on themselves
and in their motions refuse
to set, still they are often
hidden behind the storm clouds.

But this star always remains.
This star never sets nor is
it hidden by passing clouds
which draw veils across its face.

May the woeful comet die;
may the heat of every star,
even Sirius, sink now
destroyed by the heat of God.

Look there! From far off Persia
out of which the sun rises
wise men, diviners, observe
this sign of royal presence.

As soon as its light shone out,
all other stars dimmed their glow
and even the morning star
would not compare his beauty.

'Who', they say, 'is this ruler
who masters the stars? Who is
it that makes the stars tremble
and commands all of Heaven?

'We have seen a brilliant thing,
something that can never end,
something sublime, limitless,
older than sky or chaos.

'This is the King of the world
and the King of all the Jews
the birth of whom was promised
to the father, Abraham.

'That father of the faithful
who sacrificed his first born
was told by God that his sons
would one day equal the stars.

'Now we see David's flower
sprung from the root of Jesse
blooming high on the sceptre
and being first in the world.'

Turning their gaze again to
the star, they charted the path
which the blazing trail of light
indicated they must seek.

The beacon hung in the sky
above the infant's head and,
turning its light to the earth,
it revealed the sacred head.

When they saw him, the wise men
unpacked rich gifts from the east
and bowing themselves, they gave
incense, myrrh and royal gold.

'Take these, the insignia
of your strength and royalty,
O child for whom the Father
made a triple destiny.

'These treasures and the incense
announce that you are both God
and King, but the powdered myrrh
foretells the fact of your death.'

In the tomb broken by God
because he let the flesh die
and then raised it up again,
are chains forged for men by death.

Bethlehem, you are the first
among all cities of men
because you have given birth
to the Saviour of the world.

You have nurtured the Father's
only heir, born of the breath
of God the Thunderer but
also God living in men.

He is witness to the Word
of God, as the prophets said,
and is invited to come
into his kingdom and take

possession – a kingdom that
includes all things in Heaven
and on Earth from east to west,
the depths of Hell and the skies.

An anxious tyrant, Herod,
heard that the King of all kings
had come to rule Israel
and claim the throne of David.

Distracted by this he cried:
'He that pretends to my throne
has been born in my kingdom.
Let all of you take up swords.

'Every male child must be killed;
drench every cradle in blood;
search the bosom of each nurse.
When the mother takes the boy

'to her breast let his male blood
redden your blades and splash down.
Every infant is suspect;
none must escape my judgement.'

They obeyed the tyrant's word
and tore through the countryside
like madmen stabbing each boy
and ripping life from the flesh.

The bodies were so tiny
that there was almost no space
for the gaping wounds; the blade
was much larger than the throat.

A barbarous thing to see!
A head was broken on stones
and the milk white brains splashed out
as the eyes fell from their pits.

A child's quivering body
was thrown in the raging stream
where, in his constricted throat,
water and air caused spasms.

All honour to you, martyrs,
destroyed at the gate of life
almost like roses withered
in the bud by stormy winds.

You are Christ's first offering,
a flock slain in sacrifice;
before the altar of God
you play in your innocence.

Who profits from such evil?
Could such a crime aid Herod?
Among such slaughter only
Christ survived to grow older.

While the blood of his peers flowed,
the virgin's son was untouched
by those who robbed so many
mothers of their newborn sons.

In a similar fashion
Moses, guardian of his race,
became a figure of Christ
by escaping Pharaoh's law.

A decree had been issued
which ordered that all mothers,
when their children had been born,
were forbidden to raise boys.

But the sly midwife whose mind
could not obey such a law
stole the baby in the hope
that he might live in glory.

In time he grew and became
a priest and servant of God.
The hands of Moses carried
God's commandments down to men.

Do we not recognize Christ
in the life of this great man?
After he killed his master
he lifted his people's yoke.

But we, always ruled by sin,
have been given our freedom
by our leader who ended
the darkness of death, our foe.

When they crossed the sea, Moses
washed his people and cleansed them
with sweet waters while a shaft
of light marked the way for them.

While his men fought a battle
he stretched his arms over them
and Amalek was subdued
by this figure of a cross.

After their long wanderings
a victory was secured
and Joshua divided
the land for his followers.

At the end he put twelve stones
in the river to divert
the flood: these are the figures
of Christ's chosen apostles.

The wise men said they had seen
the King of their race because
they had seen his deeds figured
in the lives of their heroes.

He is the King of those men,
the Judges, who ruled the sons
of Jacob and is the King
of the Church. He is the Lord

of the old and new temple.
Ephraim's sons and the house
of Manasses worship him
with the sons of the twelve tribes.

Even the families who fell
into a barbarous cult
and fired an idol of clay
now break their statues of Baal

and abandon the sooty
gods of their fathers whether
of stone or metal or wood
to follow the words of Christ.

Let all the peoples rejoice,
Judaea, Rome and Greece, Thrace,
Persia and Scythia: one
King is now the King of kings.

Let everyone praise the Lord –
all the blessed, all the damned;
the living, feeble and dead –
from this time no man will die.

Epilogue
(Epilogus)

He who is devout, faithful
and without guilt offers to God the Father
the gift of that pure conscience
which the blessed soul contains in great plenty;
while another man scatters
wealth so that the poor receive the gift of life.
I however consecrate
these racing iambics and spinning trochees
for I have no holiness
and have not riches enough to aid the poor.
However, God will approve
my prosaic song and in kindness listen.
The rich man's house is adorned
with many beautiful things set all about:
goblets of the brightest gold,
basins of hammered bronze, polished copper bowls,
plain jars made of earthenware,
great heavy trays made of the purest silver,
delicate things patiently
carved from fine ivory and serving dishes
whittled out of oak or elm.
All things there, whether precious or cheap,
are there because the master
has bought them and set them aside for his use.
I am in the Father's house
because Christ desires only humble service
from me, a lowly vessel.
My place is in a corner out of the way,
I am as cheap earthenware
in the house of salvation, my job is slight.

But I am proud to have made
even the least service to our Father, God.
Whatever my songs are worth,
it will be my pleasure to have sung of Christ.

RUTILIUS CLAUDIUS NAMATIANUS

INTRODUCTION

RUTILIUS CLAUDIUS NAMATIANUS was born late in the fourth century A.D. at Toulouse. His father, whose statue was later erected at Pisa, enjoyed a career as a distinguished public official. Rutilius Namatianus himself held high positions in the court of Honorius (r. A.D. 395–423). Though these positions are not very clearly known, it is a certainty that he was Prefect of the City in A.D. 412.

A man of wide education and experience, he was well versed in the literary and philosophical traditions of his day. The times in which he lived were anything but tranquil. In A.D. 410 Alaric the Visigoth had sacked the city after laying siege to it. By A.D. 416, when Rutilius Namatianus began his journey back to Gaul, much of that land as well as the Italian peninsula had seen the repeated movements of various barbarian armies. There is no reason to think that Rutilius Namatianus was exaggerating his awareness of the misery which he saw wherever he turned. Indeed it may well be that he diminished in his description the degree of misery which prevailed.

He began his journey in the fall of A.D. 416. If our awareness of the distances is correct, it is safe to argue that about two months would have been required for a journey such as he describes. It is most probable that he began the poem shortly after the completion of the journey. However, with the poem's ending we have also the termination of his career as we know it. He clearly announces his intention to continue, yet only six lines later the work ends.

The poem opens with an exordium (164 lines) of extravagant praise for the grandeur which is Rome. The reader, however, cannot avoid the shock of recognizing that while the poet is heaping praise on Rome and her achievements, he is in fact beginning his account of a sea voyage because the land routes are no longer passable and the provinces of the Empire are no longer secure. Six years after the sack of Rome the barbarians are again, literally, at the gates but Rutilius Namatianus, at least, persists in his belief that Rome despite every adversity is so great and so powerful as to transcend the ordinary norms of victory and defeat.

The poem does more than recount a journey. There are at least three major departures from the narrative line. Each digression, however, is significant and valuable because it reveals something of this man who claimed Roman citizenship as his birthright and passport to every point of the compass. Yet Rutilius Namatianus is not our ideal of an urbane and sophisticated man of the world. He clearly and most vehemently gives expression to his disdain for both Christian and Jew. He recognizes both as alien to Rome and certainly foreign to what he considers to be his own cultural standards. Yet it must be remembered that Rutilius, like most of his contemporaries, enjoyed a Roman citizenship of relatively recent invention. While he accused the Christian and the Jew of being anti-Roman, he barely referred to the fact that his own claim to Roman citizenship was tenuous.

This, however, is not a substantive issue as it is incontrovertible that Rutilius Namatianus, like his alleged enemies, was indeed a Roman citizen. The important realization that should derive from his invective is that he most assuredly represented an old order which was rapidly passing out of the present. For Rutilius, the Christian and the Jew represented only annoyances while he saw the barbarian presence as the primary threat. Yet, ironically, there is a process of ultimate assimilation which preserved much that was both Roman and barbarian. Rutilius was convinced of Rome's essential nobility and immortality; yet he could never have imagined that Rome would survive not by defeating her enemies but rather by the fact that her enemies gradually became Romans, just as the ancestors of Rutilius Namatianus had themselves become Roman.

The poem is a charming account of a man whose feelings have been assaulted by adversity. We find him describing the coast of Italy with genuine warmth and affection while we recognize his real grief at being compelled to leave Rome. Yet he was an honest man who could admit that his love for Gaul is at least as much concern for the assets of his inheritance – vineyards, flocks and fields – as it is a filial concern for the countryside out of which his family was born. He expresses joy at the chance to renew old friendships, and he is saddened by the inexorable progress which his journey demands. One cannot help but feel pity for a man living in an age of such transience when the joys of friendship are unusually brief and the sorrow of parting is so inevitably linked to every introduction. He admits to all the weakness engendered by love; he honestly admits to hatred.

Rutilius Namatianus could not have known that his optimistic praise of Rome's vitality was in reality a praise of past rather than future greatness. He could not have foreseen – and probably would have found it most distasteful if he had been able to see – that Rome's pre-eminence would pass from the world of politics and military triumph to a more restrained cultural pre-eminence. Once an Empire's hub, Rome became the centre of a new ecclesiastical polity, a state which fell heir to weaknesses amazingly analogous to those of her imperial predecessor. Still Rome endured and the work of Rutilius Namatianus endured with the city he loved so extravagantly.

A SELECTED BIBLIOGRAPHY

Baehrens, E. (ed.), *Poetae latini minores*, Leipzig, 1883, vol. V.

Burman, P. (ed.), *Poetae latini minores*, Leyden, 1731, vol. II.

Duff, J. Wight and Duff, Arnold M. (eds. and trans.), *Minor Latin Poets with Introductions and English Translations*, London, 1961.

Keene, Charles Haines (ed.) and Savage-Armstrong, George F. (trans.), *De reditu suo, libri duo, The Homecoming of Rutilius Claudius Namatianus from Rome to Gaul in the Year A.D. 416*, London, 1907.

Vessereau, J. and Préchac, F. (eds. and trans.), *Sur son retour*, Paris, 1933. Collection des Universités de France, publiée sous le patronage de l'Association Guillaume Budé.

Wernsdorf, J. C. (ed.), *Poetae latini minores*, Altenburg, 1788, vol. V, part 1.

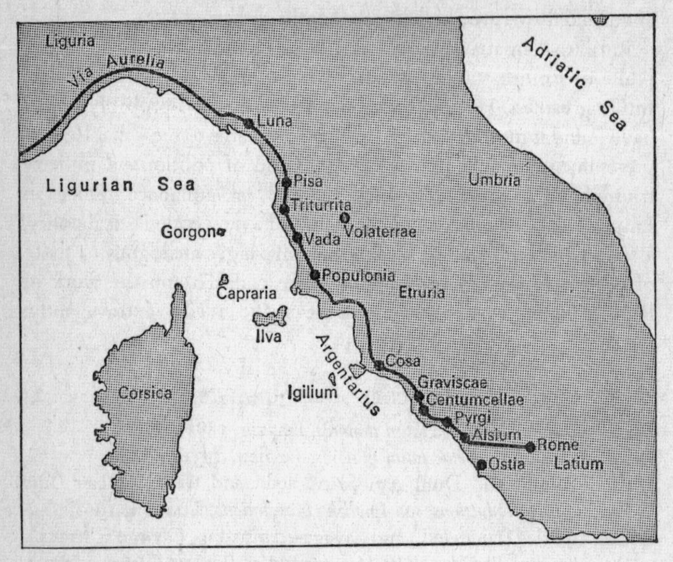

Ancient Italy showing sites mentioned in Rutilius Namatianus: *De reditu suo*

Concerning His Return

(De reditu suo)

BOOK I

Perhaps, reader, you wonder why this return trip
gave up the niceties that go with Rome.
A city like Rome cannot be praised too strongly;
no veneration could bore us with length.
I wish I could spend my time congratulating
those who deserved to be born on its soil.
The mighty sons of the great families crown their
strength with the glory of the capital;
no other land could have been so finely endowed
with the rich seeds of heavenly virtue.
Those others who have come under the rule of Rome
are happy with their Latin fields and homes.
The house where the Senate gathers, though surrounded
by the holiest traditions, opens
to all, even foreigners, who come with merit:
it welcomes those men who belong to it.
Those who sit there share senatorial power
and receive a portion of the sacred
genius which makes this council like that heavenly
council which governs all the universe.

Unfortunately I must leave that favoured land;
Gaul, where I was born, summons me away.
Long wars have ruined the fields of my native land;
pity takes me from the land that I love.
It is nothing to neglect men who are at ease,
but suffering compels our loyalty.
An ancestral home needs our presence and our tears;
labour which grief has urged is often best.
It is sinful to neglect ruin already
compounded by neglect: now is the time,

after the fires have cooled, to rebuild, even if
 we are rebuilding only shepherds' huts.
If the waterways spoke, if our trees uttered words,
 I would be spurred, my wishes would have sails.
My favourite city has relaxed her embrace and
 my native land has won. I cannot wait:
I will travel by water because roads can flood
 or be littered by slides and falling rocks;
Tuscany and the Aurelian Highway have
 already fallen to the Goths. It is
best to trust the sea because the rivers are not
 bridged and the land has become wild again.

Again and again I kiss the portals of Rome,
 slowly my feet cross the sacred threshold,
I beg forgiveness for my leaving, I offer
 a sacrifice in words garbled by tears:
hear me, Rome, queen of the world and brightest jewel
 in the vault of Heaven. Hear me, mother
of men and the gods: your temples bring Heaven near;
 we chant your praise as long as we have breath.
No man will ever be safe if he forgets you;
 may I praise you still when the sun is dark.
Your power is felt wherever the sun's light shines,
 even to the farthest edge of the world.
The sun god revolves only for you, his horses
 that rise from your soil sink down to your soil.
The parching death of Africa has not stopped you;
 the stiffening cold of the north made way for you.
The earth has opened a path for you; wherever
 there are living things, there are you also.
You have united the distant nations; under
 you, captivity has become profit.
Men who have never known justice have been conquered
 and then been given rights under your laws;
what was only a world you have made a city.
 All things have been drawn to you and made good.

Our great race is descended from Venus and Mars:
  he sired Romulus and his line, she bore
Aeneas and his line. The two gods left their mark:
  even today Rome mingles victory
with mercy; her enemies become her allies.
  The gods are worshipped for their gifts to you:
Minerva, who gave us the olive tree, Bacchus,
  who taught men the art of making wine and
Triptolemus, who was the first to plough the soil –
  these are gods especially dear to Rome.
Altars are raised to the healing arts and the god,
  Paean, who fathered those skills. Hercules
is worshipped for his strength while Rome has brought all things
  together beneath the rule of one law.
Venus, you are praised in every corner of Rome's
  dominion where men live without fetters.
The stars, which know all that has been, have never seen
  a more beautiful Empire: Assyria
attempted but failed to unite the world; Persia
  conquered only her neighbours; the empire
of Alexander was torn apart by endless
  wars and rivalries. Rome was not larger
at her birth, rather she had wisdom and judgement.
  War and peace alike were prudently used
to enhance a position that never weakened.
  Rome deserved to prevail but that she has
prevailed to this extent is a mark of her strength,
  rather than a mark of her destiny.

To count up the glories of Rome is like counting
  the stars in the sky: the temples of Rome
are so fine that the gods themselves might live in them;
  streams that flow over my head on arches
are grander than even the highest rainbow's arch.
  Those structures are like mountains in the streets;
the Greeks would say the giants had built those arches.
  Rivers are channelled within the walls, lakes
vanish in the baths; rivers flow in the gardens

and the walls echo the sounds of water.
The heat of the summer is tempered with coolness
and a pleasant thirst is quickly relieved.
Once an enemy approached but boiling waters
burst out of the ground and forced his retreat.
When the city was saved, the water disappeared
and is remembered as a miracle.
Why should I tell of woods that grow in your houses
or the birds that always sing in those limbs?
Your spring never fails to be mild, even winter
is curbed by your beauty. Hear me, O Rome:
freshen your brow and let it wear again the wreaths
which are marks of your greatness, let a crown
of gold flash on your towering helmet, let your
bright armour flash the light of perpetual fire.

May misfortune be forgotten; may your wounds close
and heal because you have ignored the pain.
Surrounded by failure, hope for prosperity;
may you be enriched by all your losses.
Even the stars must set before they rise again;
you know the moon wanes before it waxes.
You were defeated by Brennus along the shores
of the Allia, but it betrayed him.
The Sabines forced you to sign a cruel treaty
but eventually they became your slaves.
Even Pyrrhus won the battle but lost the war;
Hannibal lived to mourn his victories.
Things which must be held under water rise again
with vigour and strength greater than before.
A torch which is pointed downward only regains
the flame it had begun to lose. Fortune
which is cruel today will be kind tomorrow.
Let your law extend to all the known world;
it will not die. You have lived a millenium
plus sixteen decades and now nine more years.
You need not fear the furies; the years that remain
have no limit but the earth's firmness and

the strength of Heaven supporting the stars. Your strength
is the weakness of all other empires:
you are strong because you can learn from misfortune.
Let an unholy race admit your might;
let the Goths in panic expose their necks to you;
let the peaceful lands pay bounties to you;
may your lap be filled with barbarian treasures.
Let the lands of the Rhine be ploughed for you;
let the Nile overflow to enrich your people.
May a fertile world give food to its nurse;
may the fields of Africa watered by northern
showers give you their harvests. May the fields
of Latium fill your granaries full and may
the wine presses burst with floods of nectar.
Let the Tiber, crowned with reeds, serve your royal sons
and bear the wealth of commerce on his stream.
Finally, Rome, I pray that your power will smooth
the seas for me as I travel beneath
the sign of the Twins. If I pleased her when I served
as prefect and gave my respect to the
senators and asked their advice, may Venus guide
me today along my watery path.
That I never punished a crime is not my boast
but rather a tribute to the people.
Whether I will take my last rest in my native
land or whether I shall see you again,
I will consider myself lucky indeed if
you will always deign to remember me.

That is enough. Our friends were waiting; it was time.
With sadness, each one of us said farewell.
One by one they began to return to Rome but
Rufius, the son of Albinus, stayed.
He claims descent from the ancient prince, Volusus,
and he cites Virgil as authority.
This man has such eloquence that as a young man
he became spokesman for the emperor.
Before that, he had been pro-consul in Carthage

and he ruled Tyre with both terror and love.
He was a young man of great promise: he will be
a consul, nothing can prevent the fact.
At last I compelled him to leave me on the road.
Sadly he turned back; we were of one mind.
I boarded a ship at the point where the Tiber
forks: the channel to the left has many
sandbars, while the channel to the right is quite safe.
Aeneas made that treacherous channel
famous for it was on its shores that he landed.
The sun had entered the Scorpion's claws,
the nights were long and our pilot was reluctant
to begin the voyage. We waited there
consumed by impatience and annoyed by the heat.
We did not wish to risk our fortunes on
the sea until the Pleiad had finally set.
We could see the distant splendour of Rome:
while our eyes could pick out the highest places we
saw the rest of the city in our minds.
There is the place of the imperial fortress
and there is the government of the world.
Homer tells us that it is the rising smoke which
marks a well-loved place, but this is not true.
The air over the city is clear and the heights
glow serenely in the light of the sky.
On those seven hills the sun's light is purer than
anywhere else; Rome herself makes daylight.
Again and again we heard the shouts from the games:
a flood of cheers means that the crowd is large.
The echoing air sent those sounds and we heard them
as though we were there rather than wishing.
For fifteen days we studied the sea and waited
until the new moon brought a better breeze.
The night before we sailed I dismissed Palladius,
my cousin, who was a native of Gaul.
He had come to Rome to study law in our courts.
More than cousin, he had become my son.
Even today his father is the governor

of the northern coast of Gaul. He returns
freedom to those who are free and he guarantees
that slaves will never enslave their masters.
Because he has established a respect for law,
Exuperantius is a great man.

In the half light of dawn the anchor was lifted.
As we left the shoreline the colours were
returning and we could see the fields on the hills.
Our little vessels stayed close to the shore
so that safety was always near. The cargo ships,
with their huge spread of sail, can plough the waves
of summer but we chose autumn for its still air
because it permitted us to escape
the land without in the least impeding our haste.
We sailed north past Alsium, and Pyrgi
was soon behind us. Today these are large estates;
at one time they were little villages.
Caere, once called Agylla, passed on our right,
and then we passed Castrum, a ruin now,
destroyed by wind and water: only a gateway
marks the place where men lived. Over that gate,
like a guardian, is the figure of a shepherd
with horns on his brow. Time has forgotten
his name, though legend associates it with Pan.
It may be that this is the place known as
Castrum Inui. If so, it was sacred then
to an excess of love and many births
since its patron was the god of reckless pleasure.
Then we moored at Centumcellae beneath
the towers that stand over the harbour and docks.
We put in to shore at this place because
a strong south wind was making our progress too slow.
The city has been built on piers so that
ships can dock and be safe from the wind. Like a bath
at Cumae, these waters are calm enough
for a weary swimmer to relax without fear:
the piers enclose a harbour which is like

the floor of the circus; an island built by men
is placed to guard and shelter the entrance.

Even in the city waterways have been built.
While in that place we saw the famous springs
which are only three miles from the city: those wells
are not bitter and the water is clear.
The pure and delicate taste makes the swimmer think
the water would be better for drinking.
The legend says – if one can believe what one hears –
that a bull, while tossing pieces of sod
over his head as a prelude to a fight, found
these springs when his horns struck a hard tree stump.
Another version says that a god in the shape
of an ox would not let the springs stay hid.
There is precedent for such disguise: Jupiter
took the form of a bull and then used it
to steal Europa from her father's house. We too,
like the Greeks, have a land of great legends.
If Pegasus revealed the fount of Helicon,
let us believe that these waters were found
just as the hoof of a horse dug the muses' well.
This land, the subject of Messalla's verse,
is the equal of the Pierian mountain,
the home of the muses. Messalla's lines
are over the gateway to the fountain and they
capture the visitor's eye as he leaves.
This man, Messalla, traces his family to
the first of the consuls: he was prefect
and commanded the praetorian guard, but he
is more famous for his witty sayings.
He has shown the habitation of eloquence:
oratorical powers depend on
a man's most profound desire to live a good life.
We must go; it was only a visit.

Dawn came to a purple sky, the sails were spread out
in curves to catch the wind; we sailed far out

to miss the sandbars around the Munio's mouth
which is well known for its dangerous surf.
Next we saw the roofs of Graviscae which is thought
to be unhealthy during the summer;
still, the area around the town is wooded.
Next we passed the stone ruins of Cosa:
one should not laugh at the misfortunes of others,
but it is said the town was abandoned
when rats invaded the place. I am reminded
of Homer's tiny soldiers and I think
of cranes forming alliances to fight their foes.
Soon we saw the port of Hercules where,
as the light of day faded, a gentler breeze blew.
This is the place where Lepidus made camp
before he fled to Sardinia. From this port
which serves Cosa, Rome, under Catulus,
drove off the enemy that had once been Roman.
Walking through the few traces of his camp,
we remembered the accounts of Lepidus and
how he had become the perfect villain:
one of that man's sons waged civil war and allied
himself openly with Rome's enemies;
a third Lepidus plotted against the city
and very quickly received his reward;
a fourth, of that same name, tried to achieve power
but was caught in his adulterous scheme.
That family as we know them today will be judged
for what they are, not for what they have been.
Their reputation today is another thing;
it seems that they have put away the past.
Must we believe that names can create character?
Only our children can make that judgement.
Whatever the case may be, is it not strange that
so much misfortune has come from this line?

The shadows of night were still heavy on the land
when we returned to the sea; a kind breeze
came down from the hills and our ship struggled around

the jutting point of Argentarius.
The road takes a shortcut over this point but we,
because we sailed around it, lost much time.
It reminds me of the Isthmus of Corinth which
is pounded by the tides of two oceans.
We barely made it around that place: the helmsman
with his labour forced the ship to obey;
it seemed the wind changed direction every minute
and all the crew was forced to be nimble.
The sails which bellied out so nicely suddenly
went slack then bellied again with the wind.
Far off, in the distance, I saw Igilium
and its forests. It is a famous place:
recently it was nobly defended either
by its cunning or the emperor's strength.
Though surrounded only by a narrow channel,
it defied the enemy; it welcomed
refugees from a wounded Rome and it gave rest
and safety to men who had lost their homes.
Soldiers on horseback had brought terror from island
to island by travelling on ships. This place
was near Rome but far indeed from the enemy.
We put in at the mouth of the Umbro.
It is a large river with a safe entrance for
the tired and frightened sailor who comes there.
I was more than eager to leave the ship and spend
at least some time ashore, but the sailors
were anxious and I could only go where they went.
As we went on, the breeze died with the sun.

We anchored near the shore and measured out the beach
for camp. A grove of myrtle gave us wood,
we pitched our tents on oars that we used for tent poles.
Daylight returned. We pushed on in the calm
and, though it did not seem to move, the fading shore
proved that our bow was slowly progressing.
Soon Ilva came into sight. It is a rich place
with more iron in its rocks than Noricum.

Iron from Ilva is even purer than that made
in Gaul by the Bituriges although
the island has fuel for only the smallest hearths.
Sardinian ore is also poorer.
The earth does more good by giving birth to iron
than it does with all its rivers of gold.
Gold begets vice; the desire for gold leads to crime.
Golden gifts make brides of unwilling girls;
loyalty tainted by gold can betray a town;
gold frees ambition to do as it will.
But this is not true of iron: iron ploughs barren fields;
iron provided man's first occupation;
the demi-gods mastered nature with iron weapons;
iron gives a man the strength of many men.
With thoughts like these I passed a quiet time while we
listened to the chief oarsman calling strokes.

Before noon Faleria came into our sight.
On that day a fair was in progress and
the country people had come into town because
it was the day when Osiris wakes and
gives new life to the autumn seeds. We sought lodging
and strolled in a pleasant grove with small ponds.
There were fish in that water and we watched them play.
But we paid a high price for our short rest:
our host was harsher than Antiphates. He was
a miserly Jew, one of that strange race
who refuses to eat what is perfectly good.
The noises he made were quite unpleasant:
he charged us for damage to his plants and complained
about the amount of water we drank.
We paid him but despised him because his kind trims
most disgracefully the genital's head.
They are utterly silly: their sabbaths are cold
and their hearts are colder than their beliefs;
they spend the seventh day as though their god were tired.
No child could believe the things they believe.
Pompey's wars should have been elsewhere; Titus should not

have bothered to lay siege to their city.
Their belief is a plague that creeps back again after
it has been rooted out. A conquered race
has now subdued its conquerors. A north wind came
and we with our oars sought out some haven.

The coast of Populonia opened into
a safe harbour. Unlike Pharos, there is
no lighthouse, but men long ago built a castle
on a cliff that rises out of the surf.
This place served two purposes: from the landward side
it was an armed fort, from the seaward side
it was a beacon light that shone for the sailor.
But the years will crumble even stone. Time
has worn its turrets down, only traces remain;
the ancient houses are buried under rubble.
We must not complain if our bodies decay, we
can see that cities also must decay.
At this place we heard good news: a friend, whose great name
escapes the laws of metre, had become
prefect of our sacred city. Moved by joy, I
nearly returned. Once I sang the praises
of Rufius, my friend; I will do it again.
Nothing can be too good for one like him;
may there be celebrations such as there were when
I found my hopes become reality.
Give us garlands for our joy; a part of my life
has achieved greatness; may those great duties
always bring pleasure to me. I have new merit
through one who has achieved this dignity.

The north wind changed at dawn and we ran with the wind.
The hills of Corsica rose before us
and as we watched, the grey masses of rock blended
with the dark clouds until they seemed nearer.
Similarly, the moon tricks our eyes: when we think
she is entirely gone, we see her still.

It is said that Corsica was discovered when
  a herd of cattle with their cowherd swam
out to sea until they found this fertile island.
  It is always good to know those legends.
Midway between the island and the mainland we
  passed Capraria, a dreary place, where
there are men who shun the light and call themselves 'monks'.
  They have taken their name from the Greek which
means 'alone' because they wish to live with no one;
  they fear fortune, whether good or evil.
Would a man live in misery to escape it?
  Because of their fear, they shun what is good.
Such reasoning is the raving of a madman.
  Whether they are evil men who demand
punishment for their sins or whether their sad hearts
  are burdened with black bile, I cannot say.
Homer ascribes Bellerophon's melancholy
  to an excess of black bile, for men say
that sorrow caused him to hate the sight of all men.
  Whatever their reasons, I find them strange.

As we approached Volaterra we passed Vada,
  a place where the channel is quite shallow.
A watchman sat in the bow guiding the helmsman
  by his shouts into deep and safe water.
The narrow places are marked by trees and timbers
  driven into the sand: the laurel tree
is used because the branches are thick and will stand
  over the mud banks that shift back and forth
like the Symplegades. Suddenly a storm blew
  from the northwest. Such a wind tears the trees
and quickly compels the mariner to tie up.
  We were no sooner under shelter than
the hard rains came down. The fine hospitality
  of Albinus' country estate was mine.
It was he who followed me as prefect, in him
  did my own authority continue.

Though young, he bore well the burdens of that office;
  though young, his dignity was that of age.
We respected one another and friendship grew
  as he took the power that I once held.
He took my place reluctantly. His affection
  for me has made him now a greater man.

Next we inspected the salt flats that are the wealth
  of this estate: the sea runs through channels
into many small ponds; the gates are closed
  and while the summer's heat advances and
the grass turns brown, the land is parched and then
  the heat solidifies the sea water.
Like the Danube freezing in winter, the salt cakes
  in the summer sun and what was a pond
looks now like sheets of ice. Who understands?
  Let one who worries about causes think
of this: ice and frost are melted by the sun while
  water can be hardened by the same sun.
This phenomenon happens again and again
  whenever the sun pierces the water.
How often it happens that good things come from bad.
  The weather gave us a delightful rest:
Victorinus, my dear friend, met me at that place.
  His fine home in Toulouse had been captured
by the Goths and he had come to Etruria.
  His wisdom and good sense were evident
in adversity and prosperity alike.
  His great abilities were known to both
the ocean and the north: the unploughed British lands
  remembered the restraint of his power
when he had been vicar; all men in that country
  recall his stay with the highest regard.
That place is one of the most remote of our lands,
  but he ruled it as though it were in Rome.
It is best to have become popular among
  those who should ordinarily hate one.
Though he had every right to enjoy life at court,

he so loved the country that he refused
to improve himself by living in the bright light
that shines on those seeking to be advanced.
I embraced him and laughed at the contrary winds
because he seemed a part of my own land.

Aurora, cloaked in yellow, brought us good weather:
the offshore breeze meant that we would sail soon.
A gentle wind carried us without vibration,
the sails flapped and the rigging was unstrained.
There in the sea, between Corsica and Pisa,
we saw the island, Gorgon. We shunned it
because its cliffs are monuments to disaster:
not long ago a Roman youth met there
a living death. He was of good family, wealthy,
and had the best prospects for his marriage.
For some mad reason, he left the ways of mankind
and in superstition came here to hide.
He imagined that sacred things are discovered
in a filthy place. He was crueller than
even the offended gods. Surely these beliefs
are powerful as the drugs of Circe:
in her day men's bodies were turned to something else;
now it is the minds of men that are changed.
From there we went to Triturrita which is washed
by currents that are in constant conflict.
It is a house set on a peninsula that
was built by many men carrying dirt.
The harbour which is near this place was amazing:
it is a beautiful place, completely
exposed to the wind and buffeted by the sea.
There are no piers or sea walls protecting
it, but around its wide periphery there grows
a seaweed wall that will not harm a ship.
But when the sea is high, that pulpy mass will trip
the great rollers that come in from the sea.
The harbour is congested with the merchandise
and wealth that has made Pisa powerful.

A good wind came up and it was time to sail, but
I wanted to visit Protadius.
That man is a model of goodness; no painter
could ever do justice to one like him;
his prudence and steady gaze are easily seen,
his expression denotes fairness and it
commands the respect of all. He was born in Gaul,
like me. Perhaps this sounds extravagant,
but Rome praises this man who was once her prefect.
Umbria, after Rome, gave him a home
that was humble, but his virtue accepted this
as easily as it accepted wealth.
He sees small things as significant for even
great things must have had a slight beginning.
A small farm occupies a man who conquered kings;
a few acres gave us Cincinnatus.
It seems certain that his contentment must equal
that of Serranus and Fabricius.
I gave orders that we tie up there and I drove
to Pisa. A tribune whom I had known
when I was master of the Emperor's household
offered me horses and a conveyance.
I surveyed this ancient city, which according
to legend was colonized by men who
came from Pisa in Elis, near the Alpheus.
The Arno and the Ausur surround it
and come together there with great force. Pisa was
a Greek colony before Aeneas
and his men came to Italy. There in Pisa
I saw the statue which they had put up
in memory of my father, Lachanius.
I wept when I saw the honour they gave
to my parent; tears of both joy and sadness wet
my cheeks. My father once was governor
of Etruria and exercised his power
under the symbol of the six fasces.
Though he later went on to grander offices,
he always would say, I remember, that

he enjoyed this office more than any other
  that he had been given in the Empire.
His emotions found these people more attractive
  than even the Romans; though he became
Prefect of the City, he never let his first
  love be displaced. He was not misguided
in this feeling, for these people returned his love:
  they have chiselled their affection into
verses on the base of this fine statue.
  Old men, who remember his face and times,
tell their sons how he mingled firmness with kindness.
  They were happy to welcome me because
they respected both his memory and my deeds.
  Many times when I have travelled along
the Flaminian Way, I have found the same proof
  of my father's deeds. All of Etruria
honours the fame of Lachanius as though he
  were some hero who had become a god.

This province has always been loyal; it deserves
  only the best governors as a fair reward
for its devotion to old-fashioned virtue. Such
  a man is Decius, son of Lucillus,
who governs the good people of these happy lands.
  It is no wonder that such a father,
who sees himself in his own son, should feel lucky.
  Lucillus is a satirist of such
incisive wit that he cannot be surpassed by
  Turnus or even by Juvenal: such
polished severities have restored decency
  as it was in the old days; he attacks
the evil and thereby teaches the virtuous.
  He was able to frustrate the harpies
who swarmed around the Sacred Largess in his day.
  These vultures would have torn the world to bits
and taken everything into their filthy claws.
  These men were so shrewd that Argus would seem
to have but one eye and Lynceus would be blind.

They are public thieves who pursue the men
appointed as the trustees of public moneys.
But their numberless hands did not escape
Lucillus; his one hand could deal with their thieving.
But the visit, like all good things, ended.

The sails were set to catch a gentle southern breeze
when a sudden storm fouled the sky with rain.
We stopped. Who would dare to sail a ship in a storm?
This rest was spent in a near-by forest
where we were able to stretch our legs in hunting.
Our innkeeper loaned us hunting dogs and
whatever else we might need. We tricked a wild boar
into the meshes of our nets. Flashing
his tusks, he fell. Meleager would respect us;
Hercules himself would have been impressed.
The carcass was lifted up and the distant hills
echoed again and again with the songs
we sang as we returned through the woods to our inn.
The southwest wind, with his dripping wings and
his black clouds, continued to keep us in that place.
It was the beginning of winter, when
the Hyades are setting in early morning.
This is no time to begin a voyage
because the season is much too close to the storms
of Orion. The sea turned to yellow
as the sand was disturbed and pastures were covered
with a scum that the storm had left behind.
As the sea returned again and again to flood
the lowlands, it began to seem that it
was flowing from another world to flood our world
and then returning to nourish the stars.

BOOK II

Before my book becomes too heavy on its scroll –
it could easily have been much longer –
I am quite fearful that weariness might compel

the reader to put it down. If a feast
is too long, the sweet desserts are most unpleasant.
A moderate drink of water is best
for thirst; a milestone makes the journey seem shorter.
I will divide my timidity in two parts
and spread it among the books I am composing,
though it would be simpler to do this once.

The storm finally broke and our ship left the harbour
and sailed out from Pisa. The water seemed
so tranquil in the sun that it smiled good fortune;
the waves opened and closed in a whisper.
The Apennines run down to the sea in a point
on which the wind and waves break their fury.
Anyone who wants a picture of Italy,
the queen of all the world, will see at once
that she extends like an oak leaf pinched together
by the bays along her shores. The distance
by road from north to south is just a thousand miles.
This distance is measured from Liguria
in the north to the Sicilian straits in the south.
Along her length, the Tyrrhenian and
the Adriatic Seas break the even coast line
with the fury of their raging storms. Where the land
is narrowest, at Ostia, it is only
about one hundred thirty miles in width.
The central mountains run all the way to the sea
in the south and in the east the mountains
go into the Adriatic while in the west
the granite mountains finally are washed
in the blue waters of the Tuscan Sea.
If we believe that the world has a plan
and if this great machine were designed by a god,
then we must see the Apennines as guards
placed around the outposts of Latium because
this range permits only a few footpaths.

Nature suspected that men would envy this land
  and placed the Alps for a northern defence.
In the same way, she guards the vital parts
  with limbs that are meant to be protective.
It is the way of nature to cover and hide
  every precious object that she has made.
Even then, when the world was made, Rome was worthy
  of protection by gods who cared for her.
For this reason, Stilicho's crime becomes more grave.
  He showed the barbarians how to pierce
the defences that nature had built around Rome.
  He hoped to outlive the Roman people
and left the Roman Empire naked to her foes.
  His hatred turned the world upside down and
he turned his allies loose in Italy because
  he found that he could no longer trust them
to save him from what he had so justly deserved.
  He plunged their weapons into the belly
of a defenceless land. He had no fear of war
  so long as war was not carried to him.
But not only with weapons did he attack Rome:
  before the city fell, he burned the books
of the Sibyls which were consulted when only
  the aid of the gods could save the city.
Althaea is hated because she burned the sign
  on which Meleager's life depended;
it is said that there are birds who weep for the hair
  which cost Nisus his life; but Stilicho
destroyed an eternal empire's high destiny.
  Let the torment of Nero stop at once:
here is one who deserves more than he to suffer
  within the dark glare of the Stygian torches.
Stilicho's victim was immortal while Nero's
  was mortal: one of them killed his mother
while the other one killed the mother of the world.
  But I have been loquacious in my digression,

let my verse resume the voyage we had begun.
  Set on a swift course along the coast line,
we saw white and shining cliffs of marble rising
  out of the water. That city is called Luna
after the radiant sister of the sun: its
  whiteness surpasses the lilies in spring.
Rich in marble, this land with its polished brilliance
  shines bright enough to challenge the white snows.

PAULINUS OF PELLA

(Paulinus Pellaeus)

INTRODUCTION

In the *Eucharisticos* or *Thanksgiving* by Paulinus Pellaeus, we have an ingratiating personal memoir. It is generally thought that Paulinus, a grandson of Ausonius, was born in Pella during a time when his father held the office of Prefect of Macedonia. By his own testimony, he was educated in the schools of Bordeaux. After a lifetime of misfortune (most of which he feels compelled to list), he finally turned to religion and produced in his eighty-fourth year this *Thanksgiving* which claims to discern the beneficent hand of God directing the events of a lifetime.

Though Paulinus is careful to advise the reader of his real intellectual limitations, it is obvious that he relied on a youthful reading of Virgil, Ausonius and Paulinus of Nola. In spite of his sources, however, Paulinus was writing in a relatively new tradition. Like Augustine, Paulinus couched his gratitude in the form of a confession or admission of God's goodness and mercy to one so obviously unworthy.

The reader cannot avoid being tempted to cynicism when he finds Paulinus so neatly blending the goods of the spirit with the goods of the world. Yet it is precisely this ingenuous air that is so attractive in this man's work. Apart from its value as an anecdote, the poem has particular value to the historian. The transitions and changes which were the 'fall of Rome' were not reserved to the affairs of men with political ambitions. As Rome's fortunes rose and fell, the fortunes of all – allies and enemies – also rose or fell. The fate of a few was the fate of many; the fate of Rome was an Empire's fate. With the movement of armed men throughout the countryside, there necessarily occurred economic and social disruption so that even the wine country of Bordeaux suffered the ravages of repeated invasion and retreat.

Paulinus was a single heir to many ancestral estates. In more tranquil times he would have been an extremely rich and powerful landholder. But without the stability of a strong central government, Paulinus saw his various inheritances consumed by the hazards of absentee ownership. By himself he might have more successfully maintained his wealth. But he reminds the reader that his family depended on him not only for material support but also for emotional support. Through all of this the reader has the uneasy feeling that in reality Paulinus was little more than a fairly articulate man of scanty personal resources caught up in the inexorable progress of history.

The reader might wish to seek in the narrative a recapitulation of the 'fall of princes' theme. There is at the beginning a heavy kind of arrogance which seems to remove the subject from all the tribulations of contemporary life. Abruptly this ease ends with the death of his father and the coming of barbarians almost simultaneously. In a few touching lines Paulinus identifies his idea of paternity with an awareness of place and security. When his father died, the world of legal plunder and armed deceit suddenly confronted him with an ugliness he had never before imagined. Misfortune followed misfortune until Paulinus turned to religion as his last hope. But even in this he failed because he was not permitted to abandon his family.

Early in the poem we hear of the author's educational background. In itself the brevity of his education would seem to dismiss the poem as something other than literary. But still it is most important that we see his *Thanksgiving* in all its significance. The poem is a record of a man's reaction to events so consequential that he could not possibly have understood them. His failure to perceive the magnitude of what he recounted is a failure which could not have been avoided. The fall of an Empire is necessarily a grand thing, but the grandeur can exist only for the beholder.

A SELECTED BIBLIOGRAPHY

Brandes, Wilhelm (ed.), *Poetae christiani minores*, pt 1. in *Corpus scriptorum ecclesiasticorum latinorum*, vol. XXVI, Vienna, 1888.

White, Hugh G. Evelyn (ed. and trans.), *Paulinus Pellaeus: The Eucharisticos* in *Ausonius with an English Translation*, 2 vols, London, 1961, vol. II, pp. 294–351.

Thanksgiving

(Eucharisticos)

PREFACE

I KNOW that there have been many distinguished men who have transmitted to posterity a memoir of their lives. They have done this because they were men of great achievement who wished to make their widespread renown immortal. I, however, am quite remote from men like them. Their deeds were those of another age and their fame is more than I have achieved. Though the subject of this little work is almost identical to theirs, it must be said that my reasons for writing are very different from the reasons for which they wrote. My achievements are not so brilliant as to make me famous nor have I such confidence in my ability to write that I could casually challenge the work of any author. Still – and I am not ashamed to admit this to any man – I in my long life have often lived in idleness coloured by worry. Yet I believe that even in those years the divine mercy led me to seek the pleasures proper to the conscience of an old man and his devout intention.

What I am trying to say is that I, who am convinced that my life was a gift from God, have wanted to demonstrate that all my life has been guided by him. I intended to compose a narrative trifle, this *Thanksgiving*, in his honour. I know very well that his mercy surrounded me because in my early years I lacked nothing, not even the pleasures which the body alone enjoys. In this manner I see myself always cared for by his providence. He has disciplined me with continual trouble but at the same time he has shown me first that I must not exclusively love present prosperity, which is easily lost, and secondly that I should not be greatly upset by hardships in which his mercy always assists me.

If anyone ever reads this little work, he should realize – if only from the title – that these simple reflections which I have consecrated to almighty God are intended as much for my own leisure as for another's delight. I pray that this, my little devotion, may be more acceptable in the eyes of God than in the eyes of learned men. Still, if someone with more than usual curiosity has so much leisure that he can turn his attention to the dreary progress of my life, I beg that he allow oblivion to trample what he has seen rather than commend it to the discerning eye of the future.

THANKSGIVING

As I prepare to tell the seasons of my years
and to determine the series of days through which
I have raced with the fickleness of my fortunes,
I implore you, almighty God, give me your peace
and inspire this little work so that it will be
pleasing to you. Let my writing succeed and let
my prayers be answered; let me tell of all your gifts:
each period of my life was given me by you.
Since I first drew breath in the light that is your life
I have always lived under your kind protection,
even when the storms of this world have injured me.
I am an old man and your help is with me still.
In this, my eighty-fourth year, I have seen the sun
burn the summer and I have seen the winter's frost.
It is you that renews the cycle of the years.
Permit me, I beg of you, to tell in my verse
the many gifts you have given me: may my words
pay thanks, even though my heart is open to you
and you know every thought that has ever been mine.
Choking, the voice escapes the barriers of silence
and becomes a turbulent fountain of prayer.
  When I was only an infant your great strength filled
my tiny bones so that I – born at Pella, like
Alexander, by the walls of Salonika
where my father was assistant to the prefect –
might be taken to the coast of another world.
We could not travel by sea. My nurse carried me
in her trembling arms across the snow-filled passes
and wind-swept mountain slopes. We crossed over water
and the waves of the Tyrrhenian Sea until
we came to the walls of Carthage in Africa.
This journey happened before I had seen the moon

fill herself with new light for the ninth time. Eighteen
months were spent in that place – so they tell me – under
my father's proconsulship. Then we sailed again
and took the path we had taken before until
we saw Rome gloriously rising above the world.
Though all of this passed before me, I saw nothing.
Only later did those who remembered it well
tell me what I think is important to this work.
Finally we reached the end of the journey and
I was carried into the land of my fathers
and to my grandfather's house. We came to Bordeaux
where the beautiful Garonne draws the ocean's tides
within the city's walls through a gate which opens
to a spacious harbour protected by the walls.
My grandfather, who was consul during that time,
became known to me in my third year. After this,
I grew and as strength came into my feeble limbs
and my mind, aware of itself, learned by habit
to know the nature of things, I became wiser
and older. The life that I narrate was folded
into my memory so that I can tell it.

There is so much that I can recall from this time:
the freedom, games, and cheerful youth itself suggest
that I describe their merits; still I would rather
consider and put in the verse of this small book
the role that affection, joined with my parents' pains,
played in giving me the means to live my life well.
They were adept at enticing me to learn so
that my undisciplined mind developed quickly:
almost with my first steps in the alphabet, I
learned to avoid the ten forms of ignorance and
the vices and sins that plunge the soul into Hell.
Although this kind of training is practised no more
because, I suppose, we live in such corrupt times,
still I insist that the old-fashioned Roman ways
gave me joy and make it possible to be old.
At the end of my first five years they gave me texts
of Socrates so that I would at the same time

learn to read the words and learn the doctrine he taught.
I also read the warlike stories of Homer
and the tale of the wanderings of Ulysses.
After that I travelled in the realm of Virgil
even before I knew my Latin. I had learned
Greek from the servants with whom I had always played.
Even now I must insist that I could not catch
the beauty and elegance of this foreign tongue.

Such polyglot learning is designed for strong minds
and decorates those who can do it with a twin
radiance. But for those like myself who cannot,
its wide range is destructive. Very soon it drained
dry the veins of my barren mind. I have said more
than I want to say; the page and my pen escape
my control. Unasked, I have mentioned things I hope
will not disgrace me. My parents carefully taught
me to control my thoughts so that in the future
no man could hurt my reputation with my words.
Though this reputation is still illustrious,
it would have been enhanced if my parents' desire
for my education had reached some fulfilment.
If their ambitions had always agreed with mine
and I had remained devoted to you, O Christ,
I would have given up the joys of the flesh and
desired instead the pleasures of the life to come.
But, since I believe that what has happened has gained
more than what might have been, I give my thanks to you
because your will has renewed in my sinful flesh
the gift of your own life. My sins are very great
and my thanks increase as I see your mercy.

I know very well that no matter what I did,
whether it were an unlawful act or a deed
that merits guilt, as I wandered alone among
the slippery morasses that are the times of life,
you in your mercy did forgive everything
because I repudiated myself and fled
back to you in obedience to your commands.
If I have ever avoided sins which carry

a greater guilt, this too is something you gave me.
I must return to my subject and the seasons
I went through while I was busy with my studies.
  I imagined that I was already learned
when I saw the time I had spent studying both
the Latin and Greek authors with my tutors.
Perhaps something might have been gained if I had not
suddenly become ill with a fever that burned
my body every fourth day. This malaise hindered
my willingness to learn when my fifteenth year was
just ended. This illness so alarmed my parents
that they sought the advice of every physician.
They wanted a cure for my body and forgot
about the training of my tongue in eloquence.
All kinds of gaiety and amusements were found
for my delight and my father was so concerned
that once again he took up the sport of hunting.
Indeed, he had given up those pleasures because
he had not wanted to hinder my studies by
enticing me to accompany him and he
did not wish to enjoy the hunt without me there.
For my sake, he returned to that sport with interest
sharpened by absence and the fond hope that it bring
health again to my weak body. These amusements
continued through the dreary months of my sickness
and left me with a chronic dislike for study.
This new ailment remained after the fevers left.
More than the sickness, this malady injured me
when my doting parents let me indulge myself
in a love for the falseness which the world displays:
they cared only for the state of my body's health.
  As I grew older, my self-indulgence increased
until I gave myself over to the pursuit
of a young man's desires. I wanted a fine horse
with a special harness, a tall groom, a fast hound,
a splendid hawk, and a well-made ball for my games.
I wanted to be dressed in the very best styles
and I wanted sweet perfumes from Arabia.

Now when I look back to those days and remember
how I enjoyed riding my horse at a gallop
and how often I escaped many headlong falls,
it is fitting that I attribute my safety
to the mercy of Christ. It saddens me that I,
immersed in pleasure, could not see his mercy then.
Though they were overjoyed to see my health restored,
my parents were also anxious to know that I
would father sons to continue our family name.
I felt desire burning in me at a time when
most men feel the fires of passion begin to cool.
I burst into an abandon which I had thought –
while still a boy – I could avoid when the time came.
This was a very great danger. After the first
excesses I curbed my will with a simple rule:
I would seek no unwilling victim nor would I
injure another or what was properly his.
Jealous as I was of what others thought of me,
I resolved to avoid affairs with the free born,
even voluntarily, and content myself
with the love that I could command within our house.
I could endure moral guilt but a touch of crime
would have ruined my name and my reputation.
Yet, because at this time I can have no secrets,
I must admit that a son was born in those days,
though neither he, for he shortly died, nor any
other of my bastards was ever seen by me.
Even in that, O Christ, you saved me from myself
and kept me free from the injury I deserved.
Such was the life I had lived from my eighteenth year
almost to my thirtieth year. However, my
parents' worry suddenly compelled me to stop.
They found a wife for me, a woman whose estate
had a well-known name but little prosperity.
For many years her grandfather had managed it
because her father had died and left the old man
with a child who inherited all his estate.
Once I accepted the burden she brought to me,

I settled into my responsibility
so that in a very short time I was content
to enjoy the estate while exchanging comfort
for hard work. I encouraged all the labourers
by the example of my own labour, but still
I never hesitated to show my sternness.
As I devoted myself and my energies
to this new way of life, I soon brought fallow land
under the plough and I restored the old vineyards
to something of their former state, as I had learned.
I also, and some will find this quite annoying,
voluntarily paid my tax as it fell due
so that I could have much more leisure for myself.
I always placed too great a value on leisure:
what at first was only moderate soon became
more refined and remote from what was just needed.
  Eventually my concern was for luxury
in my house and my life so that at each season
the rooms where I lived were always comfortable.
My own table was richly and handsomely set;
my servants were not only young but numerous;
the place was furnished with taste and variety;
the silver was valued more for price than for weight;
many skilled workmen were there to fill my requests;
many well-bred, well-trained horses filled my stables
and there were carriages to take me where I wished.
However, I must say that my major concern
was not so much to increase as just to preserve.
I was neither anxious to become wealthier
nor did I seek distinction as a connoisseur.
My ambitions were not complex: all I wanted
was to pursue luxury but only that kind
that could be had at little expense and without
loss of reputation. Extravagance, I thought,
should not become a reason for criticism.
While I found that all of this was quite delightful,
my love for my parents meant more to me than love
for all of these fine things. I was so drawn to them

that for almost a year I spent more time with them,
it seemed, than I spent in my own house. These visits
passed in the tranquillity that we had desired;
this joy together gave us profit together.
Would that this good life and the enjoyment of it,
which is Christ's gift to men, had continued for us;
would that those days of peace had never been ended.

My inexperience needed my father's counsel
and my maturity needed him for model.
But shortly after my thirtieth year there came
sorrow which had a double cause. The Roman world
was struck in its heart by an enemy and then
my father died, just at the time the Empire fell.
His last days came almost at the same time war came.
The invader ravaged my home but the ruin
meant little when compared to the grief that I felt
at my father's death, for it was he who had made
my home a fatherland for me and my children.
Through the kindliness that is always found with love,
we had become so close, though so remote in years,
that we were friends dearer than friends of the same age.
He was my companion and my loyal adviser
and he was taken away in my early youth.

Almost at once, as though we had not already
our share of trouble, my quarrelsome brother tried
to overturn our father's will: he hoped to halt
the special provision made for my mother's care.
Looking after her interests caused me much worry
because I desired justice out of love for her.
What is more, rumours began to spread which whispered
about my wealth so that I was again exposed
to more misfortune while the lure of ambition
made other men, strangers, more dangerous to me.
I would rather forget these past events because
remembering them even today gives me pain.
Yet, O Christ, I derive comfort from those graces
which I quickly found among my unhappiness.
When I was most oppressed by trouble, I found you

in the depths of my heart and I saw your mercy
hidden there among all the trouble I had known.
   Experience soon taught me how powerful men
and their kindnesses, which came to me through your hands,
worked to my profit when they saw my grandfather's
accomplishments revealed in me. This was before
I was old enough to claim such things for myself.
At the same time I was happy enough for this
because my own ambitions were often at odds
with what my patron sought for both me and himself.
But still it was I who suffered most at that time.
I had a home in the east and there in the place
of my birth I owned much land. Misfortune struck me
again because I was away on a journey
that was prolonged first by the slowness of my men
and also by the uncertainties of those who
were dear. Their dread of what we might find at the end
delayed the preparations already begun.
But on the other hand, my indolent nature
also delayed us while I enjoyed my repose
and the comforts of my home. Unfortunately,
it had more luxuries than the times permitted.
It was the only house to lack a Goth to care
for it. This oversight resulted in ruin
because, with no one there to protect it, the house
was looted by the enemy as he retired.
   Those Goths who had been employed served their masters well.
In addition to all of this trouble something
new was added to my concern. The cruel tyrant,
Attalus, in his vain search for regal power
conferred on me in my absence a hollow role:
he endowed me with the burden of the office
of Overseer of the Private Largesses.
While he knew that it carried with it no income
and while he even doubted his own royalty
he was forced to depend on the Goths for all things
because at that time they were preserving his life
and showed little concern indeed for his power.

He had no strength that he could call his own: neither
resources of revenue nor men aided him.
You can be sure that I did nothing to strengthen
that trembling tyrant. Rather it was peace I sought
from the Gothic masters. They themselves wanted peace
and before very long they gave to others, though
for a price, the chance to live without annoyance.
This we did not regret because we saw that they
now held power and in their favour we prospered.
Still it was not an easy thing; many endured
great suffering. I was not the least of these because
I had lost my goods and outlived my fatherland.

When the Gothic king, Ataulf, commanded his men
to leave our city they treated us as though we
had been conquered by burning the entire city.
They found me and saw that I was an official
of Attalus, a prince whose friends were not their own.
They took from me everything I owned and looted
my mother's house as well but they left us grateful
that we escaped without injury to ourselves.
Of those companions and servants travelling with us,
not a one found her virtue assaulted by them.
In all of this I was saved from greater concern
by the goodness of God, because my daughter who
had just been married was gone from that sad country.
But even this was not the end of our suffering.

When we were driven off and our ancient house burned,
we fled to Vasatis, a neighbouring city,
which had been the home of my ancestors. There too
the enemy came and again laid siege to us.
Our danger there was increased when the slaves rebelled
in a conspiracy encouraged by a few
and abandoned all care for their obligations
and armed themselves for the slaughter of their masters.
From this danger also, O just God, you kept us
so that a few of the guilty ones died and saved
our innocent blood. You commanded that the one
who had planned my assassination should be killed

by another. By this kindness you have bound me
to yourself in a renewed debt of gratitude.
In my great fear at that sudden danger I made
a new mistake: the prospect of death in that place
made me throw caution aside. I began to hope
that by appealing to their king, Ataulf, my friend,
I might escape the siege which his people had laid
around the city. And as I escaped I hoped
to take with me every one in my large household.
I hoped to accomplish this feat because I knew
that Ataulf had allowed the siege with reluctance
after the Goths demanded that he order it.
So, with that plan, I secretly left the city
and hurried to the king without any hindrance.
With great cheer and a pleasant face I spoke to him,
my supposed friend, and expected a good reply.
But then I discovered the nature of his mind.
He told me that he could not protect my life there
and that he could not permit my return unless
he himself accompanied me to the city.
He knew that the Goths were plotting against my life
and he wanted to free himself from their demands.
The terms he so easily proposed left me dumb.
In great fear at this new danger, I was aided
by the mercy of God who always assists those
who call on him. With his help I regained my speech
and, all the while trembling, I decided that I
would encourage my hesitant friend, if only
to further my own interests. I soon rejected
those terms which I could not accept while all the time
I urged him to obtain for us all that he could.
He was a wise and provident man and he did
precisely what I advised him to do. At once
he began discussions with men from the city.
He moved so quickly that it was done before dawn
by the help of God whose favour now shone on him
as it shone on us and all who were dear to us.
All his people then came from their homes: the women

of the Alans with all their soldiers and captains.
First the Romans took the king's wife as a hostage
with the king's favourite son. I myself was returned,
according to the terms of the agreement, as
though I had been saved from the Goths, our common foe.
A line of Alan men surrounded the city.
These men, who recently fought against us, were pledged
to our defence. Soon the city had a new look.
No one stood on the walls, but on every side
great crowds of men and women milled around their base.
Hordes of armed barbarians were surrounded by
wagons and more men bearing arms. When the Goths saw
that a large percentage of their army had turned
against them, they tried nothing more but retreated
from the friends who had now become their enemy.
Soon after, our new allies also left our side,
though they maintained their agreement with the Romans
wherever they went. All of this happened because
in trying to save myself with the help of God,
I saved my city. He turned my impetuous
deed into a happy end for those who were saved
along with me and mine from the terrors of siege.
All of this, O Christ, sinks me further in your debt.
I know of no way to express my thanks to you
except by insisting that I owe you my thanks.

But now I am done. It is not necessary
for me to say more about those days when I was
surrounded by the barbarians. They caused me
such pain and I suffered so much that finally
I was convinced that I must leave my own country
and go without any more delay to the east
where much of my mother's property was untouched.
Those tracts were in Greece and both parts of Epirus.
Those small estates, although they were filled with field hands,
were close together so that they could be managed
with efficiency to provide income enough,
even for a man with prodigal tastes like mine.
But not even then was hope followed by success:

I could not leave for the place I desired so much;
I could not get back even a part of that wealth
which barbarians and the laws of war destroyed
or which was taken by dishonest Romans who
acted without concern for law or decency.
Even people who were dear to me were guilty
and I suffered most because I lost my wealth through
the deceit of men bound to me by affection.
I could not fail to love them while they stole from me;
however, true wisdom insists that I rejoice
in this my fortune which you, O Christ, have approved.
You have prepared things which are far better for me
than those things I desired so strongly. When my house
was cheerful and bright with luxury and when I
was surrounded by a pleasant court of clients
crowding around my rank and the power I held,
I imagined that I lived in your good graces
and this firm conviction only strengthened my hope.
I am profoundly sorry that at that time I
loved things which would so quickly pass. As my old age
improves my vision, I see now that when I lost
all of that, the loss became a profit for me.
When those riches of the world were taken away,
I could seek those riches that never pass away.
I know, O God, that it is now late. But nothing
is ever late for you because you always know
how to lavish your mercy without end. You know
how to help those who despair of help; you answer
the prayers of men before they know what they must ask.
Even when a man prays for what cannot be his,
you refuse to give what he asks though you will give
things to those who prefer your will rather than theirs.
You know us much better than we can know ourselves.
In preventing me from attempting something at
which my strength would only fail, you proved once again
that your estimate of what I could accomplish
was far more accurate than anything I knew.
You frustrated my plans because they were more than

I could do. When I attempted to be a monk,
you in your tender mercy interfered again.
My house at the time was filled with people who had
some claim on my ability to support them –
wife, sons, mother, mother-in-law and all of those
who attended them and served them in their desires.
If I had become a monk, I would have left them
exposed like strangers in an alien land.
Neither reason, nor love, nor a divine command
could ever have permitted me to injure them.
Your powerful hand and provident strength guided
all things through the wise advice of your holy men.
They encouraged me to do as the holy men
had done in ancient times, a practice still retained
and held by the church: at once I confessed my sins.
I then gave to myself a rule and discipline
by which I proposed to live; I did not atone
for my sins by the harshness of penance so much
as I set out to live my life on the right path
always missing the side roads that lead to error.
I rejected then and still I repudiate
the false doctrines which had come to be mine along
with every other sin that I have committed.
After this period in my life, I approached
my forty-fifth year and Easter came round again.
I returned to your altar, Christ God, and received
your sacrament. This was thirty-eight years ago.
My family was still together and I found that
I could neither leave nor could I support them as
I had because the income from all my estates
in foreign places had diminished to nothing.
I wanted to travel to those countries to learn
what had happened. But my wife quite firmly refused
because she was terrified to begin the trip.
Those properties were most valuable – already
have I told of their worth – still I permitted her
to remain just as she wanted and I even
felt it right of her to stay and I decided

that I could not abandon her there with nothing,
not even children, to support her in her need.
In that manner did it happen that I was kept
from achieving the rest that I so much wanted.
After such hardships I am spending my last days
living in exile with my diminished fortune
and deprived of all those who have been dear to me.

First the old died, my mother and wife's mother
and then my wife. When she was alive her strong fears
destroyed each one of my hopes but when she was dead
I was sad because I lost her just at the time
when her life might have meant some happiness for me.
My sons left me alone. Their reasons for going
were not the same, nor did they leave at the same time.
They both, however, saw Bordeaux in the distance
and thought they could possess the freedoms they desired
among the Goths who had settled in that city.
I was sad because their desires were not my own
yet I thought that by living in Bordeaux they could
advance in my absence my neglected interests.
I hoped that they who were then young and ambitious
might recover enough of my lost property
to provide the three of us with some small support.
But this did not happen. Before long one of them,
just a youth though even then a priest, died and left
me with nothing more than sorrow. What things of mine
that he held were then taken from me by robbers.
What is more, the son who remained for my comfort
was also unlucky enough to enjoy both
the friendship and the hatred of the king. After
losing almost all of my goods, he also died.

When all my expectations of family joy
were so violently taken away from me,
I discovered, after all had been lost, that we
must seek the things we most desire in you, O God,
because in you is all power. Finally I
decided to live in Marseilles because many
holy men who had been friends were living there though

I had only a small property which was part
of my family estate. There was no new income
there to raise new hopes, there were no fields being ploughed
and no vineyards – which are that city's wealth – were mine.
All that I have is a small house in the city
with a near-by garden. It is humble indeed.
Though there are a few vines and some fruit trees, there is
no land that seems worth the care of cultivation.
Still, I was persuaded to till the fallow land
which was really quite small, and build a little house
in a rocky place so that I would not reduce
the amount of usable soil. To purchase things
that only money buys, I planned to let out land.
At that time I still had slaves to manage my house
and I still possessed the strength of my active years.
But after that, when the fickle world changed my luck,
I was finally broken both by the loss of land
and by the weakness that came on me with old age.
I was a wanderer, poor and without family.
In my destitute state any new thing seemed good:
I decided to seek my fortune in Bordeaux.
Yet in this effort, as in the others, I failed
though my needs cried at least as loudly as my prayers.
Even this, O Christ, I believe was your doing
so that my faith would be strengthened by long knowledge
of how much you give me. Though everything was gone,
there was always the kindness of a small shelter
and often providence alone fulfilled my needs.
For this luck I must give you endless thanks, O God.
Yet I wonder if I can rightly rejoice when
my house is not my own and my rich sons possess
everything that at one time I could call my own.
I am supported, however modestly, by
the kindness of others; still I am helped by faith
which tells me that nothing belongs to us; all things
are given men to be shared with one another.
Yet you did not permit me to endure this state
for long. Without my asking – I had already

asked for so much – you hurried to give me comfort.
You have always been anxious to ease my old age
with niceties which combat all my weaknesses.
In your mercy, you restored something of my youth.
You showed me the folly of expecting support
from the estates that my grandfather had once owned.
Finally all my property still in Marseilles
had been placed under a mortgage. Though I owned it,
the benefits of ownership were another's.
Then you, in your kindness, found for me a buyer,
indeed he was a Goth, who wanted the small farm.
Without my asking, he sent a sum of money
which, though not an equitable price, was enough.
This cash came to me as a gift comes from Heaven
because it meant that once again I could manage
to keep the feeble remnants of my broken wealth
while still avoiding any new embarrassment.

I rejoice in my new wealth and I offer thanks
to you, almighty God; may this new gratitude
exceed the gratitude I have written before.
Although my continuous devotions, which are
now prolonged, beg me to put aside my writing,
I still find that I have not the skill to compose
a conclusion to this list, O Christ, of the gifts
you have given me and the thanks that must be yours.
I seek nothing more, I desire only this good:
with all of my strength I tell you, all that I want
is in every place and at every time to tell
about your mercy and how you have dealt with me.
When I must become silent I will remember.
Since all that I am has come from you, O my God,
and since it was you who began this little work,
so must it end in your name. I have needed you
before; now I have need of you more than I did.

With the coming of age all fears, but one, have left;
the remaining terror will be my last: I fear
death and in that one fear I call on your mercy.
Beyond that, there is little enough that I ask.

Let my heart resist any sorrows that remain,
may the strength of your grace always remain in me.
I have lived many years obedient to your laws;
may I be saved as you promised, may I not fear
too greatly the moment of death which is nearer
now because I have grown old. May I remember
that every time of life is subject to your law.
As my life takes its fateful turn, may I avoid
the last threat to my salvation, may I be safe
with your guidance, O God. May I, at last, be safe
from that terror which comes with death and forces men
to doubt that you will save them as they have believed.
But whatever comes, let my hope of seeing you
ease my final pains, O Christ. May my fears and doubts
be put away by the knowledge that while I live
I am yours because everything that lives is yours
and when I have died I will become part of you.

ANICIUS MANLIUS SEVERINUS BOETHIUS

INTRODUCTION

BOETHIUS, who was descended from the Anicii, a very ancient family which had become Christian at the time of Constantine, was born about A.D. 480 and died under torture in about A.D. 524. As a young man he studied literature, philosophy and science in Athens where he gained a reputation for learning and scholarship. This fame, coupled with that of his family, brought him into the favour of Theodoric when he returned to Rome. He was first named consul in A.D. 510 and again in 522.

Unfortunately Theodoric was an Arian who was most suspicious of the relations between the papacy and the eastern Empire. So far as Theodoric was concerned, any Roman favouring such a liaison was necessarily a traitor. Boethius had with brilliance defended a senator who had been so accused with the result that he too was denounced as an enemy of Rome. He was imprisoned at Pavia and died sometime between A.D. 524 and A.D. 526.

While imprisoned Boethius composed his masterpiece, the *De consolatione philosophiae* or *Consolation of Philosophy*. The five books of the work are a dialogue in which the speaker plainly seeks happiness until the person of Philosophy comforts him by showing that happiness is to be found in philosophy. In book III, the source of the passage here translated, Philosophy defines beatitude as 'that state of good which is perfected by all that is good'. Philosophy demonstrates that no man can escape the desire for beatitude. However, she notes that most men go astray in seeking it in externals – riches, honour, power, glory and pleasures. The final hymn of the third book, here translated, is the aria-like statement which sees in God the source of beatitude, the source which once found must never be lost.

In using the story of Orpheus and Eurydice to illustrate this point, Boethius put himself squarely in the mainstream of two traditions – classical pagan myth and, because of the nature of his argument, Christianity. By using Orpheus to illustrate his insistence that the pursuit of beatitude is single-minded and uncompromising, Boethius was reiterating rather subtly the sensual metaphors that were the usual vehicle for stating the teachings of ascetical theology. It is interesting to note that he could have drawn his figure from the Old Testament story of Lot's wife. However, for his purpose, the story of Orpheus and Eurydice was not only much richer in figurative content, but was also more interesting as a story. Lot's wife was nothing more than curious. Orpheus, on the other hand, was a being clearly superior whose love and desire were much grander than a simple itch to know.

It is interesting also to note that in the opening lines of the first book the poet perceives the inadequacy of the traditional muses. As Philosophy enters the prisoner's cell she speaks: 'Who has let these whores of tragedy enter this sickroom? Not only will they fail to ease his grief with good remedies, they will actually prolong the sickness with their sweetened poisons. It is they who kill the rich crop of reason with the sterile thorns of emotion while making men love disease rather than health' (*De consolatione philosophiae*, I, 1).

The Lady Philosophy – literally, love of wisdom – befriends him and becomes his succour and guide to beatitude. With her guidance all things are turned to good, and ultimately wisdom is found resident in every kind of beatitude. As she leads him to distinguish the kinds of goodness, he finds himself freed from the oppression of fear. The story of Orpheus and Eurydice is clearly a story proper to the classic muses. They, however, lack that perspective which is found only in a hope transcending all fears and limitations. By turning the fate of Orpheus to another purpose, Boethius breathed into the creaking machinery of literary antiquity a new life which would carry it through the Middle Ages into the Renaissance.

A SELECTED BIBLIOGRAPHY

Bieler, L. (ed.), *Philosophiae consolatio*, in the *Corpus christianorum: Series Latina*, vol. XCIV, 1. Turnhout, Belgium, 1957.

Green, Richard H. (trans.), *Consolation of Philosophy*, New York, 1962.

Pieper, Rudolph (ed.), *De consolatione philosophiae*, in the *Bibliotheca scriptorum graecorum et latinorum teubneriana*; Leipzig, 1871.

Stewart, H. F. (ed.), *The Consolation of Philosophy with the English Translation of 'I.T.' (1609)*, in *Boethius*, London, 1968.

Watts, V. E. (trans.), *Boethius: The Consolation of Philosophy*, Harmondsworth, 1969.

Weinberger, Wilhelm (ed.), *Philosophiae consolatio*, in the *Corpus scriptorum ecclesiasticorum latinorum*, vol. LXVI, Vienna, 1934.

Philosophy's Warning

(From *De consolatione philosophiae*, III, 12)

Happy the man who sees
the fountains of goodness;
happy the man who breaks
the cord which binds
all men to the dull earth.

*

The Thracian poet
wept for his wife
with songs so sweet
that even the woods were moved.
When he played in a mournful mode
the music was so strong
that rivers stopped and
a deer was brave enough
to stand by a lion's side;
the melodies soothed the hound
and the rabbit lost his fear.
But when grief returned
and squeezed his heart in its burning
grip the music was powerless and
the gods above seemed hard and cruel.
He sought the underworld. He made
pleasant verses and mingled them with
the music of his harp: all that Calliope
gave him, all that his grief taught
him, all that love
could offer was in his song
and even Hell was moved.
An act without precedent,
he entered and begged forgiveness
for his beloved.

The three-headed doorman
had no reply to such eloquence.
The furies, who torture the guilty,
began to weep when they heard his song;
Ixion's wheel ceased to turn
and Tantalus forgot his thirst;
the vulture was sated by music
and ignored the liver of Tityus.
The Lord of the shadows spoke:
'We are conquered. We will give him
the wife that his song has won.
But we cannot give too freely.
There must be one condition: he cannot
turn back when he leaves our world.'
Who can make laws for lovers? Love itself
is a greater law. Orpheus stood
between night and day and destroyed
Eurydice and himself
with his foolish pride.

*

Consider this story before you
turn your mind to higher things.
If you escape the flesh but
even once look back to that hell,
you will be lost.

COLUMBA

INTRODUCTION

COLUMBA, who is traditionally thought to have been the author of this poem, was born in Donegal in northwest Ireland, on 7 December 521 and died in the monastery chapel on Iona on 5 June 597. If the poem is the work of Columba, it must be said that its author, apart from references to Cocytus, Charybdis and Scylla, had virtually no reliance on the works of the classical period. The poem does recall Jerome's translation of the Old Testament Book of Sophonias, particularly in its last stanza, which also anticipates the 'Dies Irąe' composed by Thomas of Celano in the thirteenth century.

According to an Irish gloss on the text of the poem, there are many divine graces attendant upon a recitation of the work. For example, angels are present, the demons will avoid whoever recites it daily, no foe will defeat him on a day when it is recited, the house where it is said will be free from discord, violent death will be prevented and famine and nakedness will not touch the place of its recitation.

According to the traditions of the period, it was composed by Columba as a hymn of thanks and praise while he was grinding grain in the mill on Iona. Shortly after, emissaries came with rich gifts from Gregory. In return Columba gave them the text of the poem as a gift for Gregory. As they returned they altered three of Columba's verses which they thought defective. When the emissaries read the hymn to Gregory, he stood surrounded by angels until the spurious verses were recited. At this point everyone, Gregory as well as the angels, sat down. The messengers confessed, the forgery was rectified, and Gregory expressed his pleasure and gratitude.

It must be said, however, that Gregory himself found it difficult to avoid criticizing the poem. He found fault with Columba for allowing what he considered an improper or inadequate distinction between the persons of the Trinity. Columba responded almost at once by composing a hymn in praise of the Second Person.

A SELECTED BIBLIOGRAPHY

Bute, John Marquess of (ed. and trans.), *The Altus of St Columba*, Edinburgh, 1882.

Gaselee, Stephen (ed.), 'St Columba: Altus Prosator' in *The Oxford Book of Medieval Latin Verse*, pp. 25–34, Oxford, 1952.

Raby, F. J. E. (ed.), 'St Columba: Altus Prosator' in *The Oxford Book of Medieval Latin Verse Newly Selected and Edited*, pp. 59–68, Oxford, 1959.

Todd, James Henthorn (ed. and trans.), *The Book of Hymns of the Ancient Church of Ireland*, 2 vols., Dublin, 1855–9.

[1–26]

In Praise of the Father
(Altus Prosator)

The Most High, First Begetter,
Ancient of Days, Unbegotten:
he was without source,
primordial, unbounded;
throughout the span of ages
unending he is and will be.
With him is the only-begotten
Christ and the Holy Spirit
together eternal in the
unbroken glory of the godhead.
We do not present three gods,
rather we say that God is one
while we preserve our faith
in three most glorious persons.

In perfection did he create
the angels – orders and archangels
of every dominion and throne
and of every power and strength –
so that the goodness and
majesty of the Trinity
would not be idle
in any gift but
rather be surrounded
by heavenly beings who reveal
gifts greater than anything
words can ever describe.

From the apex of the Kingdom
of Heaven, from the paramount

brightness of the angelic ranks,
from the comeliness of his form
there fell, by excessive pride,
Lucifer, whom God had made.
In the same mournful fall
of the author of vanity
and persistent envy
there went the apostate angels
while all the others remained
in the dignity of their dominions.

The great, most hideous dragon,
who was both terrible and old,
was also the slippery serpent
more knowing than all
the ferocious beasts and things
living on the earth.
He took with himself
into the pit of infernal life
and imprisonment, a third of the stars
who had given up the true light
and were evicted
by force from paradise.

The Most High, because he foresaw
the design and harmony of the world,
made the heavens and the earth.
He fashioned water and the sea,
as well as herbs producing seed;
the trees growing in groves,
the sun, the moon and the stars,
fire and all things needed;
birds, fish, cattle,
beasts and all living things.
Finally, as he had planned, he made
the first man to rule creation.

When this was done, the stars,
the lights of the heavens,
and the angels all together
praised the wonderful acts
performed by the Lord
of marvellous deeds,
the architect of Heaven.
Out of love and freedom
and without compulsion
the heavenly voices gave
thanks from their own natures
in harmonious concert to the Lord.

When our two first parents had been
assaulted and seduced,
the devil and his sycophants fell
a second time. These are the ones who
by the ugliness of their faces
and the clattering of their wings
would be quite pleased to frighten
fearful men whose fleshly eyes
are unable to gaze upon
beings of such a nature;
these are the ones bound in bundles
by the chains of their prison.

But that one was taken
from their midst and thrown
down by the Lord. Though his
rebellious followers remain
invisible to men, still like a storm
they clutter the airy spaces.
If men could see them
their foul deeds and evil
example would pollute
and then entice
the flesh to defile itself
before the eyes of all.

On the year's shortest day
a span of clouds drives out of
the ocean's three deeper sources,
the three regions of the sea,
through dark blue columns
of water into the skies.
In time this water
will fall to the fields,
the vines, and the bursting seeds.
The stirring of the wind
as it comes from its treasury
empties the shallow places.

When the transient and tyrannical glory
of kings, which lasts but a moment in the world,
has been deposed by God's command,
the giants themselves will testify
that they groan under the waters
where they are burned by ulcers
in much heat and humiliation.
They are strangled by the raging
whirlpools of Cocytus which are worse than
Charybdis. They are pressed down
by rocks like Scylla and the flood
dashes them against the stones.

The waters held aloft in the clouds
are frequently sifted out by the Lord
so that they do not break their dikes
and fall out all at once.
This heavenly water which flows
as though flowing from breasts
pours across the great land masses
of the earth so that whether
the changing seasons are cold or hot,
the rivers of water always run
along in rich streams
and never fail to be in movement.

The globe of the earth
and the circle of the great abyss
depend upon the divine power
of the great God to be their support.
The hand of God
is under them like
a pillar upholding the bars,
promontories and cliffs.
All the earth
is immovably fixed
on that strong foundation,
the base of all that exists.

No one seems to doubt
the presence of an inferno somewhere
deep in the earth. In that place
there are darkness, worms,
and terrible beasts. There is burning
sulphur glowing with the hungry flames.
There are the bestial screams of men,
the weeping and gnashing of teeth.
There is the wailing of Gehenna,
that terrible and ancient noise.
There is the flamelike burning
of a horrible hunger and thirst.

From our reading we know
that under the earth there dwell
those whose knees often bend
to the Lord. Among them there was
no one able to unroll the book
of the seven seals. But Christ,
according to prophecy,
alone released those seals and
opened the book. In this way
there was fulfilled all
that the prophets had announced
concerning his coming.

In those most noble opening lines
of Genesis we read that the Lord
began by planting a garden.
From the sweet springs in this place
there flowed four rivers.
Among the flowers
was set the tree of life
whose undying leaves were
for the health of all men.
He made this garden
a place of unspeakable and
abundant delights.

Who has climbed to the heights
of Sinai, the mountain chosen by the Lord?
Who has heard the thunder
echo across the rocky cliffs?
Who has heard the enormity
of the trumpet's blast?
Who has seen the lightning
flash like a circlet around the peak?
Who has seen the barbs of lightning,
the meteors and the rocks colliding?
What man has seen these things? Only
Moses, the judge of the Israelites.

The day of the Lord,
the most righteous King of kings,
is near. That will be
a day of wrath and revenge,
a day of clouds and darkness,
a day of marvellous thundering
and a day of distress,
of mourning and of sadness.
It will be a day on which will stop
the love and desire for women,
the contentions of all men
and the cupidity of this world.

We will stand in fear
before the tribunal of the Lord
and we will render to him
an accounting of all we have done.
Then will we see
all of our evil deeds.
At this time the records
of our consciences
will be opened in front of our eyes.
Then will we weep the bitterest tears
because no longer will we have
the materials needed for work.

When the first archangel sounds
that wonderful, deafening trumpet,
every common burial place and even the most
securely built tombs will burst open.
The cold which penetrates
the bodies of men will thaw and
then, wherever they are scattered,
bones will return to their sockets
and the spirits from Heaven
will come to meet these bones
so that everyone will enter
again his proper dwelling place.

Let Orion wander from the peak
of the heavens, the hinge of the sky,
leaving behind the Pleiades,
the brightest of all the stars.
Let him cross the edges of the sea
and the unknown eastern paths
so that in time as he turns
in his roundabout way he will come
again to the place he held before.
After two years he will replace
Hesperus as the evening star.
We see a sacred meaning in this.

When Christ the Lord, the Most High,
finally comes down from Heaven,
the cross, the most radiant sign
and banner, will cast its beams.
The two heavenly lights will be covered
and stars will fall to earth
like unripe fruit dropping from a fig tree.
The lengths of the world
will become a blazing furnace
and at that time bands of men
will go into hiding in the cavities
of the mountains.

By the constant ringing
of hymns of praise
and by the thousands
of angels in their glittering
ritual dance and by the four
living creatures covered with eyes
and by the blissful twenty-four
old men who threw their crowns
beneath the feet of the Lamb of God,
the Trinity is praised
by an eternal repeating
of the three times sacred hymn.

The raging fury of fire
will consume those adversaries
who prefer to believe that Christ
has not come from the Father.
We, on the other hand, will be taken
up to meet him in the heavens
and we will enter, as we deserve,
the various unending ranks
of dignity and exaltation
with the Lord, our eternal reward.
We will remain with him
in glory through all the ages.

ALCUIN

INTRODUCTION

THOUGH the *Conflictus Veris et Hiemis* or *The Dispute Between Winter and Spring* has been traditionally attributed to Alcuin (about A.D. 735–804), one recent critic (P. von Winterfeld in 1905) has argued that a supposed Horatian allusion,

may the goats
approach their milking with udders full

militates against Alcuin's authorship because Horace presumably was unknown in York and at Charlemagne's court during Alcuin's lifetime. Winterfeld argues that the poem must be assigned to an Irish poet of the tenth century (necessarily anonymous) because it was not until that late date that Horace was known in that area. Helen Waddell handles the objection rather well by noting that the particular 'line, however reminiscent of Horace (which was Alcuin's self-chosen nickname), is not beyond the range of any countryman's imagination' (*Medieval Latin Lyrics*, Harmondsworth, 1968, p. 317).

The poem, regardless of who might have written it, is a debate between Spring and Winter. In the north of Europe the arrival of the cuckoo is almost universally the mark of Spring's arrival. As a literary form, the debate or dialogue goes back into antiquity and was clearly a popular and widely used form. The debate is set before a tribunal composed of the two shepherds, Daphnis and Palaemon, surrounded by their pastoral retinue.

The work is in three sections. In the first, the author's prologue, the scene is set and the characters are introduced. In the second, which records the debate, we hear the litigants present their cases. In the third, after hearing Winter concede victory to Spring, Palaemon addresses the assemblage and terminates the debate by commanding that the cuckoo be allowed to enter so that the vitality of Spring can renew all the land.

A SELECTED BIBLIOGRAPHY

Dümmler, E. (ed.), *Monumenta Germaniae historica: poetae latini aevi carolini*, Hanover and Berlin, 1881, vol. I.

Raby, F. J. E. (ed.), 'Contention of Winter and Spring', in *The Oxford Book of Medieval Latin Verse Newly Selected and Edited*, Oxford, 1959, pp. 99–101.

Waddell, Helen (ed. and trans.), *Medieval Latin Lyrics*, Harmondsworth, reprinted 1968, pp. 92–7.

[1–24]

The Dispute between Winter and Spring

(Conflictus Veris et Hiemis)

From the high mountain retreats the shepherds
came in the light of Spring to gather beneath
the spreading trees. All together, they will
make merry by making songs. Young Daphnis
and old Palaemon also came to that place
and everyone prepared to sing the cuckoo's praise.
Spring arrived richly adorned with flowers
while frosty Winter, his long hair frozen,
met them there. An argument arose between them
before the cuckoo sang. Spring spoke first
folding her thought within three verses:

Spring: I wish the cuckoo, most beloved bird,
were here. The favoured guest of every roof,
his bright red beak would measure out fine songs.

Winter: Frozen Winter answered in a harsh voice:
May the cuckoo not come; may he sleep on
in his dark hole for hunger follows him.

Spring: I would that he might come with those cheerful
new plants that mark the end of frost. Phoebus,
his comrade, brings long days and serene light.

Winter: May the cuckoo not come. He brings hard work
and the outbreak of strife. Rest is ended,
all things are upset, earth and sea suffer.

Spring: Who are you to speak so contentiously?
Your feasts of Venus, your drafts of Bacchus,
leave you torpid within your dim caverns.

Winter: Conviviality and wealth are mine.
My rest is as sweet as the blazing hearth.
The cuckoo destroys what he does not know.

Spring: But he brings flowers and also honey.
Nests are built for him; the sea is tranquil
for his coming; the herds and fields are rich.

Winter: What seems to give you such joy is my foe.
I prefer to count out my wealth,
relish my food, and then sleep the long sleep.

Spring: Lazy Winter, always ready to sleep,
who would have won such riches for you if
the time of the cuckoo had never come?

Winter: You speak the truth. Everyone works for me:
all are slaves and subject to my command;
each of them works for me as for his lord.

Spring: Not a lord but poor, mendicant and proud.
You could not be full for a single day
unless the cuckoo brought his gifts to you.

Then old Palaemon spoke from his lofty seat
while Daphnis and the pious shepherds concurred:
'We have heard enough of Winter's prodigal words.
Let the cuckoo, the shepherd's friend, enter.
May the joyous new growth come to our hills;
may the grazing be plentiful. May there be peace
in the new ploughed fields. May the green branches
give shade to men wearied by labour, may the goats
approach their milking with udders full.
May the birds, each in his song, call to Phoebus.
For all of this, cuckoo, come now to us.
You are Love himself, our dearest and sweetest guest,
and all things – earth, sea and sky – await your advent.
All hail to you, cuckoo, sweet splendour;
through all the ages may your glory be revered.'

GLOSSARY AND INDEX OF NAMES

Aaron: brother of Moses and descendant of Jacob (4th generation); after the death of Moses, Aaron led the Jews into the Promised Land. 143, 151

Abraham: originally, Abram of Ur; migrated with his brother, Lot, and all their families to Canaan; Abraham was promised that from his numberless progeny would come the Messiah. 127, 209

Abram: Abraham's original name; the change was made to signify the covenant between Yahweh and Abram. 127

Achan: member of Joshuah's party; brought disaster by his sin against God's mysterious law; after his death divine wrath was turned aside. 143

Acheron: a river in Epirus; also one of the mythical rivers of the underworld. 78, 94, 176

Achilles: the Greek hero of the Trojan War who was widely acclaimed for his physical prowess; son of Peleus and Thetis. 107f

Acis: a river in Sicily that flows from Aetna to the sea. 103

Adam: literally, 'first man'; father of the human race. 135, 203

Adonis: son of Cinyras, King of Cyprus; loved by Venus for his unusual attractiveness. 65, 67

Adour: anc. 'Aturrus'; river flowing through Aquitanian Gaul. 64

Adriatic Sea: Mediterranean E of Italy; also Gulf of Venice. 29, 239

Aeas: a tragic figure. 65

Aegaeon: a giant, one of the mythical sons of Earth and Tartarus; also known as Briareus, the hundred-armed. 76, 103

Aegean Sea: Mediterranean between Asia Minor and Greece. 75, 111f

Aegeon: v. Aegaeon

Aeneas: son of Venus and Anchises; hero of the Aeneid; legendary father of the Roman people. 223, 226, 236

Aeneid: Virgil's epic about the journey of Aeneas from Troy to Rome. 65

Aeolus: son of Jupiter and Menalippa; god of the winds; ruler of the islands between Italy and Sicily. 77, 89

Aethon: literally, 'burning'; one of Pluto's horses. 83

Aetna: volcano on the island of Sicily. 79f, 85, 95, 99, 103, 105

Africa: for the Roman world, the northern coastal area of the continent and land mass surrounded by Mediterranean on the N, Atlantic on the W, Indian Ocean on the E. 11, 34, 79, 103, 106, 222, 225, 246

Aganippe: a fountain on Mt Helicon; sacred to the muses of poetical inspiration. 63

Agylla: Etrurian town; later called 'Caere'; modern Cervetri. 227

Aisne: anc. 'Axona'; river in NW France. 64

Alans: Scythian tribe that migrated into N Italy, Gaul and Spain. 256

Alaric: a Gothic king. 11, 72, 217

Alastor: one of Pluto's horses. 83

Glossary and Index of Names

Albinus: a friend of Rutilius Namatianus. 225, 233
Alcuin: A.D. *c.* 735–804; scholar and poet. 278–81
Alcyoneus: daughter of Aeolus; wife of Ceyx; changed to a bird. 99
Alexander the Great: 356–323 B.C.; son of Philip and Olympia. 223, 246
Alexandria: Egyptian port city at the mouth of the Nile; founded 332 B.C. by Alexander the Great; centre for the Hellenistic culture. 72
Allecto: one of the furies. 82
Allia: river in the Sabine territories N of Rome. 224
Alpha and Omega: first and last letters of the Greek alphabet; hence a divine title to indicate unity or omnipotence. 194
Alpheus: principal river in Peloponnesus; mod. Rufia. 86, 236
Alps: mountain range in S of Europe. 89, 103, 112, 240
Alsium: coastal town west of Rome on the Aurelian Highway. 227
Althaea: mother of Meleager; daughter of Thestius; wife of Oeneus, King of Calydon. 240
Amalek: leader of the Amalekites, hereditary enemies of the Israelites. 213
Amazons: ancient tribe of warrior women. 84, 86
Ambrose, Saint: A.D. *c.* 340–97; Bishop of Milan; author of Latin hymns. 122f
Amphitrite: goddess of the sea; wife of Neptune. 112
Amsanctus: also 'Ampsanctus;' lake in Italy which releases dangerous vapours; hence the mythical entrance to the Netherworld; v. 'Avernus.' 93
Amyclae: town in Sparta; residence of Tyndarus; birthplace of Castor and Pollux; renowned for its temple and Colossus of Apollo. 43, 79, 88
Andronicus, Livius: 3rd Century B.C.; first Roman epic and dramatic poet. 12, 16, 17
Angels: immaterial beings who serve as divine attendants. 128, 170, 268, 270f, 272, 277
Anicius: very ancient Roman surname. 263
Antaeus: Libyan giant; slain by Hercules. 84
Antichrist: personage prophesied in the New Testament as a sign of the imminent end of the world. 181
Antigone: daughter of Oedipus, King of Thebes. 29
Antiphates: Laestrygonian king who sank the Greek fleet and ate a companion of Odysseus. 231
Aonian Maids: the muses, i.e., frequenters of Aganippe and Mt Helicon. 63
Apennines: mountain range in central Italy. 239
Aphrodite: Venus.
Apollo: also Phoebus and Phoebus Apollo; son of Jupiter and Latona; twin brother of Diana; god of the sun. 28, 43, 57, 83, 102, 110
Apuleius, Lucius: 2nd century A.D.; Roman philosopher and satirist. 120
Arabia: land mass E of Africa; generally, the mysterious east. 113, 249
Arar: also Araris; river in Gaul; mod. Saone. 29
Arcadia: central Peloponnesus; traditional setting for the literary pastoral. 77
Arcadius: son of Theodosius; became Augustus in A.D. 382. 72
Archangel: member of an angelic rank. 270, 276

Archimedes: renowned mathematician who focused the sun's rays to burn the Roman fleet besieging Syracuse. 60

Arethusa: renowned spring (fountain) near Syracuse in Sicily; v. Alpheus. 86

Argentarius: point on the Etrurian coast. 230

Argos: capital of Peloponnesian Argolis; hence sometimes refers to all of Greece. 83

Argus: the hundred-eyed; became Juno's guardian after Jupiter turned her to a heifer; hence, the epitome of watchfulness. 237

Ariadne: daughter of Minos, King of Crete; saved Theseus from the Labyrinth. 66, 115

Arian: follower of Arius. 263

Aristides: an Athenian of renowned integrity; a rival of Themistocles; also, a distinguished sculptor. 62

Aristotle: 384–322 B.C.; student of Plato; most distinguished Athenian philosopher. 17, 18, 22

Arius: A.D. 256–336; prominent Christian heresiarch; taught that Christ was not the eternal Son of God. 149

Armenia: mountainous Asian area; part of Persia. 113

Arno: Tuscan river flowing through Florence W to the Ligurian Sea. 236

Asia: continent and land mass to the E of Europe. 11, 59

Asia Minor: peninsula, W edge of Asia; Turkey. 16

Assyria; ancient empire; E of the Tigris. 223

Ataulf: Alaric's brother-in-law; became King of the Visigoths in A.D. 410. 254f

Athens: capital of Attica in Greece. 49, 85

Atlas: mythical king transformed into Mt Athos upon seeing Medusa's head; father, by Pleione, of the seven Pleiades and, by Aethra, of the seven Hyades. 77, 89, 103

Atropos: one of the three *parcae* or fates. 81

Attalus: became a puppet emperor under the Goths. 253f

Augustine, St: A.D. 354–430; Bishop of Hippo; Church Father. 17, 19f, 21f, 118, 123, 242

Augustus: surname of Octavius Caesar (63 B.C.–A.D. 14) taken upon consolidation of his authority as emperor; later extended to every emperor. 57

Aurelian Way: Roman highway running W and NW from Rome along the Ligurian Sea. 222

Aurora: goddess of the dawn; daughter of Hyperion and Tithonus. 70, 235

Ausonius, Decius Magnus: A.D. *c.*310–*c.*95; Latin poet and rhetorician. 44–68, 69

Ausur: river in N Etruria. 236

Avernus: literally, 'without birds'; lake near Cumae thought to be the entrance to Hades; v. Amsanctus. 57, 76, 93

Baal: literally, 'lord'; ancient semitic deity of soil and flocks; name later used as source for Beelzebub,' literally, 'lord of flies', the chief devil. 214

Babylon: famous ancient city; 55 miles S of Baghdad on Euphrates River. 30, 169

Bacchus: god of wine and poets; son of Jupiter and Semele, a Theban woman. 28, 41, 56f, 76, 86, 113, 115, 223, 280

Bears: *Ursa Major*, The Great Bear, a constellation; and *Ursa Minor*, The Little Bear, a constellation; also Big Dipper and Little Dipper. 89, 208

Belgium: area in N Gaul inhabited by warlike people. 52, 60, 63

Belial: principal evil spirit. 147

Bellerophon: son of Glaucus; grandson of Sisyphus; carried a message requesting his own death. 233

Bellona: Roman goddess of war. 144

Bethlehem: village in Palestine; birthplace of Jesus Christ. 183

Biblis: daughter of Miletus and Cyane; fell in love with her brother but was repulsed and then became a fountain. 28

Bissula: barbarian servant girl in the household of Ausonius. 47–9

Bituriges: people in Aquitanian Gaul. 231

Boethius, Anicius Manlius Severinus: c. A.D. 480–c. 524; statesman, poet and theologian. 263–7

Boötes: the Bear-Keeper; a nearly unmoving constellation of stars. 89, 115

Bordeaux: city in SW of France; the surrounding countryside. 44, 52, 64, 242, 247, 259f

Boreas: the north wind. 35, 77, 103

Brennus: a leader of the Gauls who defeated the Romans. 224

Briareus: v. Aegaeon. 99

Britain: islands N-NW of continental Europe. 33, 62

Busiris: Egyptian king who killed travellers; killed by Hercules. 84

Cacus: giant of tremendous physical strength; son of Vulcan; killed by Hercules. 84

Cadmus: brother of Europa; husband of Harmonia; father of Polydorus, Ino, Semele, Antonoë and Agave; according to legend, invented the alphabet. 28, 104, 112

Caenis: later Caeneus; born a girl, she was violated by Poseidon who promised whatever she might wish; she desired to become a man and thereby invulnerable. 66

Caere: Etrurian town originally called Agylla; mod. Cervetri. 227

Caesar, Caius Julius: 100–44 B.C.; very successful Roman general; the name was taken by each of the emperors. 15, 42

Caesarea: important Palestinian town. 15

Calliope: principal muse; goddess of epic poetry; mother of Orpheus by Oeagrus; mother of the sirens by Acheloüs. 28, 266

Calpe: mod. Gibraltar; one of the Pillars of Hercules. 34

Camerina: mod. Camerino; town on the border of Picenum. 86

Canace: daughter of Aeolus; killed herself after giving birth to her brother's (Macareus) child. 66

Cannae: village in Apulia where Hannibal defeated the Romans. 52

Cappadocia: country in Asia Minor N of Cilicia between the Taurus and the Pontus. 34

Capraria: island N of Corsica in the Tuscan Sea; known for its wild goats. 233

Carinus: son of Carus; a western Emperor. 26, 29, 30
Carpathian: mountains between Poland and Czechoslovakia; Carpathian Sea = Black Sea, Pontus Euxinus. 111
Carthage: port city in N Africa. 11, 26, 225, 246
Carus, Marcus Aurelius: emperor after Probus. 26, 29
Caspia: area on the Caspian Sea. 97
Castrum: ancient city on the coast of Etruria; Castrum Inui may have been the same place; its name suggests an association with the cult of Pan. 227
Cato, Marcus Porcius: Cato the Elder; most distinguished of that family. 12
Cato; Valerius: a grammarian in Gaul. 62
Catulus, Quintus Lutatius: responsible for the defeat of the rebel, Marcus Aemilius Lepidus in 77 B.C. 229
Cecrops: most ancient Attic king; founder of Athens i.e., Cecropia. 75
Celano, Thomas of: medieval biographer of Francis of Assisi and reputed author of the *Dies irae*. 268
Centaurs: Thessalian monsters half man and half horse; sons of Ixion. 84, 107
Centumcellae: mod. Civita Vecchia; port city in Etruria. 227
Cephalus: grandson of Aeolus; husband of Procris. 66
Cephisus: river in Phocis and Boeotia; hence a river god and father of Narcissus. 88
Ceres: daughter of Saturn and Ops; sister of Jupiter and Pluto; mother of Proserpine; goddess of agriculture. 32, 41, 76, 78f, 80f, 85, 92, 94, 96f, 98f, 101f, 104
Chaos: the void that came into being at the beginning of the universe. 82, 85
Charante: anc. Carantonus; river in France flowing W to Bay of Biscay. 64
Charlemagne: A.D. 742–814; Frankish king and Emperor of the West. 278
Charon: ferryman of Hades. 94
Charybdis: deadly whirlpool between Italy and Sicily, opposite Syclla. 181, 268, 273
Chaucer, Geoffrey: A.D. *c.* 1340–1400; prominent English poet. 119
Cherubim: a rank of angels. 168
Chiron: a centaur; son of Saturn; famous for his knowledge of herbs, medicine and divination. 107
Christ: literally, 'the anointed one'; a title of Jesus of Nazareth. 123, 128f, 130f, 136, 139f, 143, 146, 148f, 150, 152f, 154f, 156f, 158, 161, 163, 166f, 169, 171f, 174f, 177f, 180f, 182f, 184, 189, 191, 193f, 195, 200, 202, 204, 205, 208, 212f, 214f, 216, 248, 250, 252, 256f, 258, 260f, 262, 270, 274, 277
Christian: adherent to the teaching of Jesus Christ. 14, 19f, 21f, 23, 44f, 131, 143, 218, 263
Christianity: the teaching of Jesus Christ as understood by his followers. 14, 44, 120, 263
Cicero, Marcus Tullius: 106–43 B.C.; renowned Roman orator, rhetorician and statesman. 12, 13, 14, 17, 19, 20
Cincinnatus, Lucius Quinctius: 5th century B.C.; Roman farmer who became dictator and then saved Rome. 236

Circe: daughter of the Sun and Perse; sea nymph known for her magic. 29, 235
Claros: village near Colophon in Ionia; famous for its oracle and temple of Apollo. 79
Claudianus, Claudis: A.D. *c.*370–*c.*405; Roman poet. 72–117
Cocytus: literally, 'river of lamentation'; river in Hades. 78, 83, 94, 268, 273
Coeus: a titan; father of Latona. 103
Columba: A.D. 521–97; poet and apostle to Scotland. 268–77
Comforter: title given to the third person of the Trinity. 177
Constantine: A.D. 306–37; Roman Emperor who legalized the practice of Christianity. 22, 52, 263
Corinth: Peloponnesian city famous as a commercial centre. 11, 230
Corsica: Mediterranean island off Etruria. 232, 235
Corybantes: priests of Cybele. 81
Cos: island on the Carian coast; famous for wine and clothmaking. 188
Cosa: ancient Etrurian town near the coast. 229
Crates of Mallos: a grammarian mentioned by Suetonius. 12
Crete: Mediterranean island; site of a very ancient civilization. 60, 66, 84f, 173
Crimisus: river on the SW coast of Sicily. 86
Crocus: a youth who became a saffron blossom. 65
Cumae: ancient Campanian coastal town; famous for its Sibyl. 57, 61, 227
Cupid: son of Venus; god of love and desire. 40, 57, 65f, 67f, 109f
Curetes: ancient residents of Crete; worshipped Cybele with much noise. 92
Cyane: nymph; daughter of Meander; mother of Caunus and Biblis; also a fountain on Sicily near Syracuse. 86, 99, 101
Cybele: originally a Phrygian goddess; later worshipped at Rome by priests called *galli*. 80f, 97f, 101, 105
Cyclops: race of one-eyed Sicilian giants. 77, 81, 89, 98, 103
Cymothoe: nereid; also a spring in Achaia. 111f
Cynthus: mountain in Delos; birthplace of Diana and Apollo. 91
Cyprus: Mediterranean island off Asia Minor. 40, 85, 109, 111
Cytherea: i.e., Venus; according to myth, Aphrodite or Venus was born on Cythera, an island off the Pelopennesus. 111
Daedalus: v. Dedalus.
Danaus: twin brother of Aegyptus; son of Belus; emigrated from Egypt to Greece where he founded Argos; father of fifty daughters. 28
Daniel: a Hebrew prophet. 170
Danube: river central Europe; flows from Baden to the Black Sea. 48, 54, 115, 234
Daphnis: son of Mercury and a Sicilian shepherdess; inventor of the pastoral. 278, 280f
David: second of the Israelite kings and author of the Book of Psalms. 139, 209, 211
Decius: son of Lucillus; Consul for Tuscany and Umbria in A.D. 416. 237
Dedalus: literally, 'skilful' or 'clever'; mythical Athenian architect who designed the Labyrinth for Minos; father of Icarus. 60

Deidamia; daughter of Lycomedes; mother of Pyrrhus. 108
Delos: Aegean island; birthplace of Apollo and Diana. 41, 79, 85, 88
Delphi: city in Phocis; famous for its oracle of Apollo. 91
Demi-god: being with one divine and one mortal parent. 231
Despérier of Lyons: A.D. *c.* 1500–1544; French poet and writer. 69
Devil: non-human, angelic inhabitant of the Hebraic and Christian Hell. 133, 272
Diana: daughter of Jupiter and Latona; sister of Apollo; under the name of Luna, she was goddess of the moon; under the name of Lucina, she was patroness of virginity and protector of women in childbirth. 30, 41, 81, 84f, 88, 90f, 100, 102, 110, 114f
Dindymus: mountain in Mysia sacred to Cybele. 92
Dinochares: builder of a pyramid which, according to Ammianus Marcellinus, dwindled like a flame to a point. 60
Diomede: Greek hero at the siege of Troy. 83
Dione: mother of Venus. 39, 41, 42
Dirce: a spring in Boeotia; also a Theban princess who, for her cruelty, was killed and thrown into the spring. 28
Dis: god of the lower regions; Pluto. 81f, 83, 85, 94
Don: river in SE Russia. 86
Donegal: area in the NW of Ireland; mod. Ulster. 268
Dordogne: anc. Duranius; river in SW France flowing to the Garonne. 64
Doto: v. nymph. 112
Drome: anc. Druna; river flowing W to the Rhone. 64
Dryads: wood nymphs. 30, 96, 101
Dumnisus: probably modern Densen, near Kirchberg. 52
Durance: anc. Druentia; tributary of the Rhone. 64
Ebro: river in NE Spain flowing into the Mediterranean. 109
Echo: a nymph who fell in love with Narcissus but was repulsed; she could neither initiate discourse nor fail to respond to discourse. 30
Eden: the primal garden in which Adam and Eve were placed. 135
Egypt: African country around the Nile. 16, 57, 174
Elbe: river flowing through Germany and Czechoslovakia to the North Sea. 115
Electra: daughter of Pleione and Atlas; mother of Dardanus by Jupiter; one of the seven Pleiades; Proserpine's nurse. 99
Eleusis: Attic town NW of Athens. 75
Elias: Hebrew prophet. 184
Elis: area in the Peloponnesus where Olympia was located. 236
Elissa: Dido; legendary wife of Sychaeus; brother of Pygmalion who killed Sychaeus for his very great wealth; she fled to Africa where she founded Carthage; later fell in love with Aeneas. 66
Elysium: the islands of the blessed; the afterlife reserved for the good. 92f, 115
Elz: anc. Alisontia; river in Belgic Gaul; tributary of the Moselle. 61
Emmanuel: literally, 'God with us'; name given in prophecy to the Messiah. 189

Enceladus: one of the giants; after the giants were defeated by the gods, he was imprisoned under Mt Aetna. 79, 88, 98f, 103
Endymion: son of Calyce and Aethlios; he was loved by Selena, the Moon. 66
Ennius: 239–169 B.C.; one of the most renowned of the early Roman poets. 12, 17
Ephesus: Ionian city on the coast of Asia Minor. 60
Ephraim: an area whose inhabitants were enemies of the Israelites; known for its haughtiness. 214
Epirus: province in N Greece. 256
Erebus: primal darkness born of Chaos and Night. 76, 83, 93
Eriphyle: wife of Amphiraüs whom she betrayed to Polynices; slain by her son, Alcmaeon. 66
Erymanthus: mountain in Arcadia. 84
Eryx: mountain in NW Sicily where Aphrodite was worshipped; according to myth, he was a son of Venus (Aphrodite) and Poseidon. 68
Etruria: area in central Italy. 234, 236f
Europa: daughter of Agenor; seduced by Zeus (Jupiter) in the form of a bull; bore Minos and Rhadamanthus. 228
Europe: continent bordered on S by Mediterranean; on E by Asian land mass; on N by North Atlantic and North Sea; on W by Atlantic. 11, 59, 122, 278
Eurydice: dryad; wife of Orpheus. 263f, 267
Exuperantius: a governor in Gaul; known to Rutilius Namatianus; father of Palladius, a 4th century A.D. author. 227
Fabricius Luscinus, Gaius: fl. early 3rd century B.C.; typical of Roman honesty and frugality; ambassador to Pyrrhus 280–279 B.C. 236
Faleria: mod. Falese in Italy. 231
Falernian: wine of exceptional quality grown in Falese. 195
Fates: i.e., *parcae*; three offspring of Zeus and Themis; together they spin the great realities around men; Lachesis, Clotho and Atropos. 92
Father: divine title, as in Father of the gods; in Hebrew and Christian tradition, the first person of the Trinity. 78, 82, 92, 95, 102f, 105, 129, 146, 148, 161, 164f, 168, 170f, 173, 177f, 181, 183, 185, 192, 197, 200, 202, 204f, 210, 215f, 277
Faun: a woodland deity, sometimes Pan. 56, 95, 107
Festus: Roman surname; a Roman governor assigned to Jerusalem. 15
Fiends: devils. 93, 131
Flaminian Way: ancient highway N from Rome to Rimini. 237
Florentinus: Prefect of the City, A.D. 395–7; patron of Claudian. 74, 84
Furies: i.e., *erinyes*; avengers of crime, especially crimes against relatives. 76, 90, 93, 207, 224, 267
Galataea: a nereid with whom Polyphemus fell in love. 103, 112
Galli: castrated priests of Cybele. 92
Gargara: peak of Mt Ida in S Phrygia. 81
Garonne: river in SW France; principal river of Bordeaux. 56, 64, 247
Gaul: i.e., Transalpine Gaul; modern France. 23, 45, 52, 63, 111f, 217f, 221, 226f, 231, 236

Gaurus: a mountain in Campania. 56f
Gehenna: Valley of Hinnom near Jerusalem; served as the city's refuse area; hence synonymous with Hell in the Bible. 274
Gela: city on S coast of Sicily. 86
Genesis: literally 'beginnings'; first book of the Bible. 275
Gentiles: literally the 'nations' or 'tribes'; all non-Jews. 14
Geryon: three-headed monster. 84
Getes: tribe on the Danube. 86
Gibbon, Edward: 1737–94; British historian; author of *History of the Decline and Fall of the Roman Empire*. 44
Glaucus: sea god whose immortality was derived from a herb. 59, 94, 112
God: in Hebrew and Christian monotheism, the name assigned to the deity. 126f, 128f, 130f, 132, 136, 139, 143, 145f, 147f, 149f, 152, 154, 157, 159, 161f, 163, 165f, 167f, 169f, 173, 175f, 178, 182f, 184, 186, 188f, 192f, 194, 197f, 200, 202, 205, 207f, 209f, 212, 215f, 242, 244, 246, 254f, 256f, 258f, 260f, 262, 270, 274
Goliath: gigantic opponent of David. 136
Gomorrah: with Sodom, an ancient city on the Jordanian plain; synonymous with unnatural vices. 127
Gorgias of Leontini: a renowned sophist and teacher of rhetoric. 17, 18
Gorgon: i.e., the Gorgon's head; generally, Medusa, whose severed head was so ugly as to turn men to stone. 90
Gortyn: ancient Cretan city famous for its laws. 85
Goths: a Teutonic tribe. 72, 222, 225, 234, 253f, 255f, 259, 261
Graces: divine personifications of loveliness or grace; generally subordinate to another deity of higher rank. 110
Gratian, Flavius: son of Valentinian; pupil and patron of Ausonius; co-regent A.D. 367–83. 44, 62,
Graviscae: small Etrurian town. 229
Greece: area SE Europe in the SW of the Balkan Peninsula; includes Ionian Islands and Crete. 11, 16, 34, 55, 163, 214, 256
Habakkuk: Hebrew prophet. 170
Hadas, Moses: American classicist and writer. 37
Hadrianus, Publius Aelius: A.D. 76–138; succeeded Trajan as emperor in 117. 37
Haemus: range of mountains in Thrace. 83
Hannibal: Carthaginian general in the Second Punic War; invaded Italy. 224
Harmonia: daughter of Mars and Venus; wife of Cadmus who gave her an ill-fated necklace forged by Hephaestus. 66
Heaven: the divine abode, usually above the skies. 39, 77f, 81, 90f, 100f, 102f, 105, 110, 115, 137, 144f, 146, 162, 165, 167f, 170, 173, 176, 181, 185f, 189, 191, 194, 198, 201, 209f, 222, 225, 261, 270f, 276f
Hebrew: one of a group of semitic tribes; the Jews or the Chosen People. 16, 123, 174
Hebrus: principal Thracian river. 83
Hecate: daughter of Perses and Asteria; a goddess of the lower world. 76

Helicon: mountain in Boeotia sacred to the muses. 28, 88, 228

Hell: the underworld; Hades; a place of suffering in the after-life. 76, 78, 81, 84, 90f, 93, 97, 131, 142f, 155, 176, 181, 194, 196, 201, 205, 207, 210, 247, 266

Henna: ancient city on Sicily from which Pluto carried off Proserpine. 78, 80, 86, 92

Hephaestus: god of fire and the fiery arts; the gods' blacksmith. 101

Hercules: also Heracles; most famous of the ancient heroes; won immortality by accomplishing the 'labours' imposed by Eurystheus. 28, 83f, 84, 223, 238

Hermaphroditus: son of Hermes; was loved by Salmacis who endowed him with her sex, hence 'hermaphrodite'. 68

Hermus: river in Aeolis. 86

Hero: priestess of Aphrodite at Sestos; loved by Leander. 66

Herod: name of several Judaean kings who reigned from 37 B.C. 211f

Herrick, Robert: A.D. 1591–1674; English poet. 69

Hesperus: the evening star. 107, 276

Hippodamia: daughter of Oenomaus; wife of Pirithous; at her wedding the centaurs tried to kidnap her. 28

Hippolyte: a queen of the Amazons whose girdle was taken by Hercules. 86

Holofernes: Nebuchadnezzar's general; slain by Judith. 130

Homer: Greek epic poet; author of the *Iliad* and the *Odyssey*. 114, 226, 233, 248

Honorius: son of Theodosius; brother of Arcadius; father of Honorius II. 72, 107–17, 217

Horace: Quintus Horatius Flaccus; 65–8 B.C.; Roman writer. 278

Huns: barbarian Asiatic tribe that invaded Europe. 72

Hyacinth: Spartan youth loved both by Apollo and Zephyr; slain by the jealous Zephyr. 65, 88

Hyades: literally, 'the raining ones'; daughters of Atlas by Pleione or daughters of Oceanus and Tethys; a constellation of stars. 238

Hybla: mountain and town on Sicily. 41, 86

Hydra: poisonous water snake with many heads; beheaded by Hercules. 84

Hymen: god of weddings and marriage. 113

Hyperion: a titan; either the sun or its father. 57, 86

Iberia: area of Spain and Portugal; SW Europe. 34,

Icarus: son of Dedalus; died by flying close to the sun and thereby melting the wings made for him by his father. 60

Ictinus: one of the architects (the other was Callicrates) who designed the Parthenon. 60

Ida: range of mountains in S of Phrygia .80f, 92, 108

Igilium: small island in the Tyrrhenian Sea. 230

Ilva: island in the Mediterranean; mod. Elba. 231

India: area E of Africa; subcontinent to S of Asia. 86

Io: daughter of Inachus, King of Argos; Zeus fell in love with her and changed her to a heifer so as to avoid Hera's jealousy. 28

Iona: island of the Inner Hebrides off the Scottish coast; site of an ancient foundation of the Celtic Church. 268
Ionia: country in Asia Minor on the Aegean Sea. 84
Ionian Sea: Mediterranean between SE Italy and W Greece. 75, 79
Iscariot: literally, 'man from Kerioth'; surname of Judas who betrayed Christ. 143
Ischia: island in the Tyrrhenian Sea. 99
Israel: literally, 'contender with God'; Jacob; the descendants of Jacob (Jews); the northern kingdom. 211
Israelite: one of God's chosen people; a descendant of Jacob. 146, 246
Italy: peninsula in the Mediterranean; site of Rome. 11, 16, 79, 89, 106, 111, 218, 236, 239f
Ixion: punished in Hell by being tied to a wheel; murdered his father-in-law and then fathered the centaurs. 93, 267
Jacob: Hebrew patriarch; son of Isaac; father of the twelve tribes of Israel. 159, 213
Jaeger, Werner: German cultural historian, 12, 121
Janus: male counterpart of Diana; god of beginnings. 30
Jericho: ancient village N of the Dead Sea; defeated by Joshuah. 143
Jerome: A.D. *c.*340–420; a Church Father; translated the Bible into Latin. 17, 268
Jerusalem: holy city of the Jews and the Christians in Palestine. 14, 15, 16, 150
Jesse: father of King David. 209
Jesus: founder of Christianity. 155, 189
Jew: Judean, one belonging to the tribe of Judah; an Israelite. 14, 143, 209, 218, 231
Job: a biblical hero exemplary for his suffering. 133
John the Baptist: cousin of Jesus; announced the coming of the Messiah. 184f
John the Evangelist: one of the apostles; author of the fourth gospel, three epistles and the Book of Revelations. 181
Jonah: a prophet who was swallowed by a whale. 186f
Jonathan: friend of David and son of Saul. 139
Jordan: Palestinian river flowing S to the Dead Sea. 131, 159
Joseph: Hebrew patriarch; Jacob's son; saved his family in time of famine. 179
Joshuah: Hebrew general at the fall of Jericho. 213
Jove: god of the sky; also Jupiter; Roman counterpart of the Greek god, Zeus. 76f, 79, 86f, 99, 103, 107
Judah, Sons of: Israelites; descendants of Judah; the tribe of Judah was the largest and most prominent of the twelve tribes. 139, 143
Judea: area settled by the Israelites. 207, 214
Judge: a title for the Jewish and Christian God. 153, 186f, 197
Judges: those who governed Israel after Joshuah's death; also a book of the Bible. 213
Judith: a Biblical heroine who killed Holofernes to defend her people. 130
Juno: the feminine counterpart of Jupiter; Hera, goddess of women. 78f, 87, 94, 103, 105

Jupiter: in war, the god of victory; in peace, the god of public morals and justice; the chief god; corresponds to the Greek god, Zeus. 81, 90, 94, 103, 112, 228
Justice: a divine title. 186
Juvenal, Decimus Junius: A.D. *c*.65–*c*.128; Roman satirist. 237
Kyll: anc. Celbis; river in Belgic Gaul; tributary of the Moselle. 61
Labriolle, Pierre de: French scholar. 25
Lachanius: father of Rutilius Namatianus. 236f
Lachesis: one of the fates. 76, 94, 105
Ladenburg: anc. Lupodunum; German town near the source of the Danube. 63
Lamb: title given to Jesus Christ. 166, 180, 277
Laodamia: wife of Protesilaus; daughter of Bellerophon; mother of Sarpedon. 66
Latin: language of the Roman Republic and people; also, Roman. 11, 16f, 23f, 42, 48, 63, 73, 123, 221, 248
Latium: area around Rome. 225, 239
Lato: v. Latona.
Latona: daughter of the titans, Coeus and Phoebe; by Zeus she conceived but was rejected out of fear of Hera's jealousy; bore Artemis and Apollo; also Leto. 30, 78f, 102, 114
Laurentine: i.e., Laurentum, a coastal town in Latium. 42
Lazarus: a brother of Martha and Mary; restored to life by Jesus. 195
Lazarus: beggar in the gospel parable of the rich man (*dives*) and the beggar. 203
Leo, Sign of: sign of the Zodiac; associated with the heat of summer. 33
Lepidus: a prominent Roman surname; v. Catulus. 229
Lethe: river in Hades whose water conferred forgetfulness. 83, 92, 178
Leucas: a high place on the island of Leucadia. 66
Leucothoe: a goddess of the sea. 112
Levi: literally, 'joining'; one of the twelve sons of Jacob; the priestly tribe. 142
Lewis, C. S.: British scholar and novelist. 18, 122
Liber: an ancient Italian god of creativity; later, Bacchus. 57
Libya: area on the N African coast. 33, 84, 111
Lieser: anc. Lesura; river in Belgic Gaul; tributary of the Moselle. 61
Liguria: area of NW Italy. 112, 239
Lilybaeum: seaport NW Sicily. 79
Livia, Drusilla: the second wife of Augustus Caesar (i.e., Octavian). 108 brought the ways of Greek poetry to Rome.
Loire: anc. Liger; French river flowing into Bay of Biscay. 64
Lord: a divine title to emphasize omnipotence. 142, 145, 152, 154, 161, 168, 170f, 173, 177, 184, 203, 207, 213f, 272f, 274f, 276f
Lot: Abraham's nephew who escaped Sodom. 127, 264
Love: Cupid; also Eros. 40–42, 66f, 85, 110, 281
Loves: deities attendant on Cupid. 39

Lowell, Robert: American poet. 23
Lucifer: literally, 'Light-bearer'; morning star, Venus; in Hebrew and Christian tradition, the Prince of the Devils. 87, 271
Lucillus: father of Decius, a Roman hero and statesman; a satirist. 237f
Luna: moon goddess; also an Etrurian city. 66, 241
Lynceus: one of the Argonauts whose vision was so keen that he could see through the earth. 237
Macedonia: area in Balkan Peninsula including parts of modern Greece, Yugoslavia and Bulgaria. 72, 242
Maenalus: Arcadian mountain sacred to Pan. 91
Maia: daughter of Atlas; mother of Hermes. 77
Manasseh: a king of Judah. 214
Manes: the hostile spirits of the dead. 93
Mantua: town in Cisalpine Gaul; reputed birthplace of Virgil. 61
Maria: wife of Stilicho; also, Stilicho's daughter. 72, 107–17
Marne: anc. Matrona; river NE France flowing W to the Seine. 64
Mars: god of war. 42, 67, 79, 135, 223
Marseilles: anc. Massillia; port city SE France. 259, 261
Mary: wife of Joseph; mother of Jesus; sister of Elizabeth. 131
Massillia: v. Marseilles. 83
Mauritania: area of N Africa to the W of Numidia. 34
Medea: daughter of Aeotes, King of Colchis; had magical powers; wife of Jason. 29
Medes: people of ancient Media in NW Persia. 114
Medusa: v. Gorgon. 90
Megaera: one of the furies. 104
Meleager: son of Oeneus, King of Calydon, and Althaea; his life depended on the preservation of a brand of wood; when he killed his uncles, Althaea in anger threw the brand into the fire. 238, 240
Menocrates: a renowned architect. 60
Mercury: god of commerce. 77
Messalla: Roman aristocrat; minor poet. 228
Messiah: literally, 'the anointed'; the anticipated king and saviour of the Jews. 150
Milan: anc. Mediolanum; founded *c.*396 B.C.; an important crossroads, it later became capital of the west. 112
Milan, Edict of: Constantine's edict giving Christianity legal status. 22
Milton, John: 1608–74; English poet. 119
Mimas: an Ionian mountain range. 103
Minerva: goddess of guilds and artisans. 100, 223
Minos: ancient king of Crete; married Pasiphae; father of Ariadne and Phaedra. 66, 93
Mnemosyne: a titaness; mother of the muses. 114
Molossis: country in E Epirus; also Molossus. 31, 33, 83
Moors: natives of N Africa. 113
Moses: Hebrew prophet and lawmaker; led the Jews out of Egypt. 14, 173f, 175, 184, 212f, 275

Moselle: river in NE France; flows to the Rhine. 52–64
Mulciber: literally, 'the smelter'; a name for Vulcan. 109
Munio: Italian river S of Graviscae; mod. Mignone. 229
Muses: goddesses of literature and the arts; daughters of Mnemosyne; nine in number. 28, 43, 62, 264
Mycenae: ancient Peloponnesian city; N of Argos. 29, 104
Mylae: port city NE Sicily; scene of naval battles 260 and 36 B.C. 57
Myrrha: mother of Adonis. 28, 67
Naiads: nymphs of the waters – lakes, springs and rivers. 30, 86
Namatianus, Rutilius Claudius: Roman poet; author of *De reditu suo*. 23, 217–41
Narcissus: son of Cephisus; because he rejected Echo's love, he was so enamoured of his own reflection that he was drowned. 65, 88
Nature: generic term; principle of life and motion. 82, 95
Nava: German river; flows into the Rhine; mod. Nahe. 52
Nazarene: Jesus of Nazareth. 183
Neckar: anc. Nicer; river in Germany. 63
Nemea: valley W of Corinth. 84
Nemesianus, Marcus Aurelius Olympius: Roman poet; author of *Cynegetica*. 26–36, 37
Neptune: god of the sea. 54, 78, 89, 112
Nereids: daughters of Nereus. 29, 35, 111f, 115
Nereus: benevolent ocean deity. 35, 78f, 94, 107, 112
Nero Claudius Caesar: Roman Emperor A.D. 54–68. 240
Neumagen: anc. Noviomagus or Nivomagus; a city of the Treveri on the Moselle. 52
Nile: principal river of Egypt; flows N to Mediterranean. 29, 84, 109, 113, 146, 173, 225
Nims: anc. Nemesa; river in Belgic Gaul; flows into the Sauer. 61
Nineveh: ancient Assyrian capital on the Tigris. 187f
Niobe: daughter of Tantalus; after she boasted of her many children, they were killed by Apollo and Artemis; she wept until she turned to stone. 28
Niphates: part of the Mt Taurus mountain range in Armenia. 101
Nisus: King of Megara; father of Scylla; his kingdom depended on his hair; in order that she might win the love of Minos, Scylla cut his hair. 29, 240
Noricum: province south of the Danube; mod. Austria. 230
Notos: south wind; also Auster. 75
Numerianus: i.e., Numerianum; a son of Carus. 26, 29, 30
Numidia: area of N Africa; mod. Algeria. 34
Nycteus: one of Pluto's horses. 83
Nymph: a feminine personification of a natural object. 30, 39f, 54, 56, 83, 86, 90, 94f, 99f, 101, 109
Ocean: the river and its god; flowed from the underworld and encircled the flat earth; also Oceanus. 82, 86, 112
Odyssey: epic poem attributed to Homer; tells the wandersings of Odysseus. 12

Oeta: mountain range between Thessaly and Aetolia. 107
Olympus: mountain on the boundary between Thessaly and Greece; its summit was the residence of the gods. 89, 101, 107
Ophion: obscure deity; defeated by Cronus and Rhea. 103
Orders: a rank of angels. 270
Orion: a gigantic hunter in Boeotia; a constellation. 89, 238, 276
Orontes: principal Syrian river. 104
Orpheus: legendary pre-homeric poet of fantastic abilities; married Eurydice; often called the Thracian. 83f, 263f, 267
Orphnaeus: one of Pluto's horses. 82
Osiris: most prominent Egyptian god; god of the dead and father of life. 231
Ossa: prominent Thessalian mountain. 83, 89, 107
Ostia: port town in Latium at the mouth of the Tiber; Rome's seaport. 239
Othrys: a Thessalian mountain. 107
Pachynum: SE point of Sicily. 79
Padus: v. Po.
Paean: god of healing. 223
Paestum: city on the Gulf of Salerno; W Lucania. 70
Palaemon: a character in Virgil's *Eclogues* (III:50ff) who calls for the praise of spring. 278, 280f
Palladius, Publius Rutilius Taurus Aemilianus: 4th century A.D. author of an agricultural treatise; friend of Rutilius Namatianus. 226
Pallas: Pallas Athene; daughter of Zeus and Metis; patroness of Athens and the arts of spinning and weaving. 81, 85, 88, 90
Palmer, Robert B.: translator of Strecker's *Einführing in das Mittellatein.* 25
Pan: Greek god of shepherds and flocks; also Faunus. 56, 227
Panchaia: a fabled island of immense wealth in the Erythraean Sea E of Arabia. 86
Pangaea: a Thracian mountain near Philippi. 56
Pannonia: area between Dacia, Noricum and Illyria. 33
Panope: sea nymph. 56
Pantagias: stream E Sicily. 86
Paphos: city on Cyprus; sacred to Venus. 114
Paphos, Queen of: Venus. 70, 88
Paradise: literally, 'garden'; place of rest and repose; Heaven; Eden. 203
Parrhasia: Arcadian town. 85
Parthenius: Arcadian mountain. 88, 91
Parthenon: literally, 'the maiden's temple'; temple of Athene on the Acropolis at Athens. 60
Parthia: home of a Sycthian people; NE of the Caspian passes, S of Hyrcania. 30, 76, 87, 89
Pasiphae: wife of Minos; daughter of the Sun; mother of Ariadne and Phaedra; seduced by Poseidon's bull, she bore the Minotaur. 66
Patriarch: a son of Jacob, hence a founder of one of the twelve tribes of Israel; generally, an old man who leads a tribe. 143

Paulinus of Nola: Meropius Pontius Anicius Paulinus; AD. 353–431; patrician student of Ausonius who left the world to seek his salvation. 44f, 242

Paulinus of Pella: Paulinus Pellaeus; A.D. 376–c.459; grandson of Ausonius; author of *Eucharisticos*. 242–62

Paul of Tarsus: originally Saul; Apostle to the Gentiles; author of epistles. 14, 16

Pavia: anc. Ticinum; city in Lombardy S of Milan. 263

Pegasus: winged horse. 228

Pelion: forested mountain near the Thessalian coast; home of the centaurs. 107

Pella: city in Macedonia near Salonika. 242, 246

Pelops: son of Tantalus. 113

Pelorus: point on NE Sicilian coast. 79, 101

Peneus: primary Thessalian river. 107

Pergus: Sicilian lake. 87

Persia: area in SW Asia; mod. Iran. 30, 208, 214, 223

Peter: one of the twelve apostles; also Simon. 154

Phaedra: daughter of Minos and Pasiphae; wife of Theseus; fell in love with Hippolytus, son of Theseus. 66

Phaethon: son of the Sun (Helion) and Clymene. 28, 104

Phaon: boatman who received youth and beauty from Aphrodite (Venus) when he carried her without demanding payment. 66

Pharaoh: title of the kings of Egypt. 173, 179, 212

Pharos: island near Alexandria; site of a famous lighthouse. 60, 109, 232

Philo of Athens: a famous architect. 60

Philomela: daughter of the Athenian king, Pandion; seduced by Tereus, King of Thrace, who cut out her tongue to silence her; turned to a swallow. 28

Phlegethon: one of the rivers intersecting Hades. 76, 78, 93, 104, 167

Phlegra: area of Macedonia; habitat of the giants. 91, 103

Phoebe: literally, 'the bright one;' a titaness; later associated with the moon. 31

Phoebus: Phoebus Apollo; v. Apollo. 32, 75, 79, 85, 107, 280f

Phoenix: son of Amyntor; nurtured Achilles. 86

Pholoë: forested Arcadian mountain. 84

Phorcus: a sea god. 94

Photinus: Christian heresiarch. 149

Phrygia: area of Asia Minor famous for its goldsmiths and indolence. 80, 97, 105

Pierian mountain or spring: dwelling place of the muses; source of poetic inspiration. 228

Pillars of Hercules: Gibraltar (anc. Calpe) and Jebel Musa (anc. Abila); straits of Gibraltar. 34

Pisa: ancient Etrurian city. 235f, 239

Plato: c.429–327 B.C.; student of Socrates; great Athenian philosopher. 120

Pleiades: seven daughters of Atlas and Pleione; became a constellation of stars; also Pleiad. 226, 276

Pluto: literally 'wealth'; god of the underworld from whom comes all earthly wealth; husband of Proserpine; brother of Jupiter and Neptune. 77, 80, 82, 89f, 92, 94

Po: anc. Padus; river in N Italy flowing to the Adriatic. 29, 89

Polybius: *c.*202–120 B.C.; renowned Greek historian. 13, 16, 17

Polyphemus: a cyclops; son of Poseidon. 103

Pompey: Gnaeus Pompeius Magnus, 106–48 B.C.; Roman military genius; expanded the empire in the east. 231

Populonia: Etrurian coastal town. 232

Priapus: grotesquely phallic god of fertility. 67

Procris: daughter of Erechtheus; husband of Cephalus. 66

Prophet: literally, 'fore-teller'; one who reveals that which is secret; one of a number of Old Testament Biblical figures. 143

Proserpine: also Persephone; an earth goddess; daughter of Zeus and Demeter (Ceres); kidnapped by Pluto to become his bride and Queen of Hades. 67, 73, 75–106

Protadius: associated with Symmachus; born at Trier; son of a public official. 236

Proteus: sea god; escapes detection by assuming many different shapes. 94

Prudentius Clemens, Aurelius: A.D. 348–*c.*405; a Christian Latin poet. 18, 19, 118–216

Prüm: anc. Promea; river in Belgic Gaul; flows into the Sauer. 61

Psamathe: a spring or fountain; a sea nymph. 112

Ptolemy: surname of the Macedonian rulers of Egypt; Ptolemy XIII (r.63–47 B.C.) married his sister, Cleopatra VII, in 51 B.C. 60

Pyraemon: a cyclops; servant of Vulcan. 81

Pyrgi: Etrurian colony. 227

Pyrrhus: *c.*318–272 B.C.; King of Epirus who found his victory against Rome more costly than defeat; hence, Pyrrhic victory. 224

Quintilian, Marcus Fabius: A.D. *c.*35–*c.*95; famous rhetorician. 62

Quirites: oldest inhabitants of Rome; applied to Romans as citizens. 42

Raby, F. J. E.: British scholar. 17, 21, 24, 25, 37, 73

Rahner, Hugo: German scholar. 24

Ramnes: one of the three tribes of ancient Rome. 42

Rand, E. K.: American medievalist. 24

Red Sea: anc. Sinus Arabicus; waterway between Arabia and Africa; probably not the Red Sea crossed by Moses and the Israelites. 102, 112, 146, 174

Rhine: anc. Rhenus; German river; flows N to the North Sea. 29, 48, 63, 102, 115, 225

Rhodope: Thessalian mountain range; part of the Haemus. 56, 79, 83

Rhone: anc. Rhodanus; river flowing S and W to Gulf of Lyons in S France. 64

Roman de la rose: medieval love allegory. 122

Rome: principal Italian city; capital of the Empire. 11–16, 30, 37, 42, 44f, 52, 57, 63, 72, 123, 126, 214, 217f, 219, 221f, 223f, 225f, 229f, 234, 236, 240, 242, 247, 252, 263

Romulus (and Remus): twin brothers; sons of the Vestal Virgin, Rhea Silvia and Mars; founders of Rome. 42, 223
Ronsard, Pierre de: 1524–85; French poet. 69
Rufius: son of Albinus; friend of Rutilius Namatianus. 225, 232
Ruwar: anc. Erubris; tributary of the Moselle. 61
Saar: anc. Saravus; river NE France flowing N–NW to Moselle. 54, 65
Saba: i.e., Sheba; country SW Arabia; noted for its production of aromatic resins. 199
Sabine: a people of the Apennines NE of Latium. 42, 227
Salia: consul at the birth of Prudentius. 125
Salm: anc. Salmona; river in Belgic Gaul flowing S to the Moselle. 61
Salonika: anc. Therma then Thessalonica; port city NE Greece. 246
Samuel: literally, 'he whose name is God'; Hebrew judge and prophet. 139, 141
Sappho: poetess of Lesbos; born at Mitylene *c.* middle 7th century B.C. 66, 114
Sara: later, Sarah; wife of Abraham; mother of Isaac. 128
Sardinia: Mediterranean island S of Corsica. 229, 231
Saturn: literally, 'the sower'; god of agriculture; later identified with Cronus. 78, 89, 92, 95, 101
Satyrs: attendants of Dionysus; wood and hill spirits; lustful and grotesque. 56
Sauer: anc. Sura; river flowing S then E to Moselle. 61
Saviour: title of Jesus Christ. 154, 197
Saxons: a Germanic tribe. 113
Scorpion: a sign of the zodiac. 226
Scotland: N of England. 54
Scylla: daughter of Phorcus and Hecate; loved by Poseidon but turned to a monster who devoured men near the whirlpool of Cocytus. 106, 268, 273
Scyros: island in the Aegean Sea. 108
Scythia: area beyond the Black Sea. 214
Semele: daughter of Cadmus; begged Zeus to reveal his divinity to her and then died; mother of Dionysus. 28, 66
Senate: Rome's legislative body. 30, 221
Seneca, Lucius Annaeus: A.D. *c.*1–65; Stoic philosopher and statesman. 119
Seraphim: an order of angelic beings. 168
Serena – wife of Stilicho; also called Maria. 108, 111
Serranus, Gaius Atilius Regulus: a ploughman who became consul. 236
Shepherd: i.e., Jesus Christ, the Good Shepherd. 192
Sibyl, Books of the: collection of oracular statements used to determine the causes of divine anger. 240
Sicily: largest Mediterranean island; SW of Italian Peninsula. 79, 81, 86, 89, 96, 98, 100, 102
Sidon: coast city in Phoenicia. 113
Sigambri: very powerful Germanic tribe. 115
Simois: a stream in Troas. 61, 104
Sinai: peninsula at N end of Red Sea; probable location of the Biblical Mt Sinai. 275

Sirius: literally, 'scorching'; the Dog Star; brightest star in the heavens; found in the constellation Canis Major. 208
Smyrna: port city W Turkey; legendary home of Homer. 61
Socrates: Athenian philosopher; Plato's teacher. 247
Sodom: with Gomorrah an ancient Jordanian city; notorious for its vices. 127, 130
Solomon: son of David; King of Israel and Judah 10th century B.C.; proverbially wise. 149f
Son: second person of the Trinity; also, Jesus Christ. 128, 131, 148, 150, 168, 170, 177, 184f, 194
Sophonias, Book of: Biblical book of doom and desolation. 268
Spain: anc. Hispania; country on the Iberian Peninsula. 33, 102, 118
Sparta: capital of Laconia in the Peloponnesus; also Lacedaemon. 31, 33
Spenser, Edmund: *c.*1552–99; English poet. 69
Spirit: third person of the Trinity. 128, 131, 149f, 178, 185, 189, 194, 270
Statius, Publius Papinius: A.D. *c.*45–96; Roman poet. 120
Steropes: a cyclops; son of Uranus and Ge. 81
Stilicho: a successful Roman general; advisor to Honorius and father of his wife, Maria; effectively ruled the Western Empire A.D. 395–408. 72, 107–17, 240
Strecker, Karl: German scholar and bibliographer. 25
Stymphalus: lake in N Arcadia. 84
Styx: literally, 'the abhorrent'; primary river of the underworld. 76, 78, 143
Swabia: area of Germany. 47
Symplegades: two rocks at N end of the Bosporus; thought to clash together and hence crush passing ships. 233
Syria: country at E end of the Mediterranean. 16
Syrtian: refers to the land along the coast of N Africa near Tunis and Tripoli. 184
Taberna: town E of the Moselle; mod. Berncastel. 52
Tantalus: father of Niobe and Pelops; for his sin, which is variously given, punished in Hades by immersion in water which receded when he attempted to drink; and by being near fruit trees which leapt up when he attempted to pick their fruit. 29, 93, 267
Tarn: anc. Tarbellicus; river in Gaul; tributary of the Garonne. 64
Tartarus: area of the underworld reserved for the wicked, 92f, 96
Tartessus: coastal town in Spain; mod. El Rocadillo. 112
Taygetus: mountain range in Laconia. 91
Tereus: King of Thrace; husband of Procne. 28, 43
Tereus, maid of: Philomela; seduced and held captive by Tereus. 43
Terpsichore: muse of dancing. 107
Tertullian: A.D. *c.*155–*c.*230; early Christian writer. 17, 45, 120
Tethys: titaness; wife of Oceanus. 84, 86
Thalia: muse of comedy. 114
Thaumantis: Iris, the daughter of Thaumas. 94
Themis: titaness; mother of Prometheus, the seasons and the fates. 78, 81

Theodoric: A.D. *c*.454–526; King of the Ostrogoths, 474–526. 263
Theodosius: A.D. *c*.346–95; became Augustus of the East in 379. 72, 115, 118
Thessally: area of E central Greece. 72, 89
Thetis: nereid; wife of Peleus; mother of Achilles. 112
Thisbe: a Babylonian girl; loved by Pyramus. 66
Thrace: area E of Macedonia on the Black Sea, Propontis and N Aegean; legendary home of Orpheus. 72, 83f, 214
Thron: anc. Drahonus; river flowing into the Moselle at Neumagen. 61
Thunderer: title applied usually to Jupiter or Zeus; occasionally used in Christian literature as a divine title. 76, 96, 98f, 107, 110, 146, 180, 210
Tiber: river flowing through Rome W to the Mediterranean. 11, 62, 89, 225f
Tiberianus: Latin poet of the 4th century A.D. 37
Tigris: eastern of the two Mesopotamian rivers (other, Euphrates); SE Turkey. 29, 114
Tisiphone: a fury. 76
Titans: (feminine: titaness); children of Uranus and Ge, the life source; associated with the various forces of nature. 76f, 86, 99
Titus: a Roman general who laid siege to and finally destroyed Jerusalem in A.D. 70; Emperor A.D. 79–81. 16, 231
Tityus: giant; slain by Apollo and Artemis. 93, 267
Tobias: a Biblical figure noted for his fidelity. 200
Toulouse: anc. Tolosa; city in S of France on the Garonne; SE Bordeaux. 217, 234
Trier: city on the Moselle; mod. Treves. 53, 65
Trinity: union of three persons in one God as in Christian theology. 128, 178, 268, 270, 277
Triptolemus: son of Celeus and Metaneira; favorite of Ceres. 75, 223
Triton: son of Poseidon and Amphitrite; a minor sea god. 111f
Triturrita: coastal town in Etruria. 235
Troy: ancient city S of the Hellespont; defeated by the Greeks; according to legend and the *Aeneid*, the Roman people were descended from refugee Trojans led by Aeneas. 42, 62, 107
Truth: a divine title. 184
Turnus: Roman satirist during the time of Domitian (first century A.D.). 237
Tuscany: area in Italy on the Tyrrhenian and Ligurian Seas between Liguria and Latium. 33, 222
Twins: the Dioscuri, Castor and Pollux; twin sons of Zeus and Leda; inseparable in death as in life, they became identified with the constellation, Gemini; a sign of the zodiac. 225
Typhon: monster with a hundred serpents' heads; son of Tartarus and Ge. 85, 99
Tyre: anc. Phoenicia; coastal town in S Lebanon. 87, 226
Tyrrhenian Sea: part of the Mediterranean SW of Italy, N of Sicily. 79, 239, 246
Ukraine: area in E Europe, N of the Black Sea. 113

Ulysses: also, Odysseus; son of Laertes, King of Ithaca, and Anticlea, daughter of Autolycus; husband of Penelope; father of Telemachus; hero of the *Odyssey*. 248
Umbria: area in NE Italy on the Adriatic Sea. 236
Umbro: Etrurian river. 230
Vada: Ligurian town; mod. Savona. 233
Vandals: a Germanic tribe. 72
Vasatis: Aquitanian city. 254
Venus: goddess of love and fertility; also Aphrodite. 37, 41, 42, 57, 67f, 70, 81, 85, 87f, 91, 99f, 101, 105, 109f, 111f, 113f, 223, 225, 280
Vesuvius: volcano in Campania. 57, 99
Victorinus: friend of Rutilius Namatianus. 234
Vincum: city W of Mainz in Germany; mod. Bingen. 52
Virgil: Publius Vergilius Maro; 70–19 B.C.; Roman poet; author of *Aeneid*. 65, 69, 225, 242, 248
Visigoths: literally, 'the good goths'; later, the western Gothic tribes. 72
Volaterra: Etrurian town; mod. Volterra. 233
Volusus: leader of the Rutilians in the *Aeneid*. 225
Vulcan: god of fire and the smithy; also Hephaestus. 61, 81, 85, 89, 104, 105
Waddell, Helen: British scholar and translator. 278
Wilson, Herbert: translator of de Labriolle's *Histoire de la litterature latine chrétienne*. 25
Winterfeld, P. von: German classicist and critic. 278
Wisdom: a divine attribute; hence, a divine title. 151f, 202, 204
Word: i.e., Logos; second person of the Trinity. 131, 178, 183f, 204f, 210
Xerxes: famous Persian king 486–65 B.C. 59
Zephyr: the west wind. 86f, 109

MORE ABOUT PENGUINS

Penguinews, which appears every month, contains details of all the new books issued by Penguins as they are published. From time to time it is supplemented by *Penguins in Print*, which is a complete list of all books published by Penguins which are in print. (There are well over three thousand of these.)

A specimen copy of *Penguinews* will be sent to you free on request, and you can become a subscriber for the price of the postage. For a year's issues (including the complete lists) please send 30p if you live in the United Kingdom, or 60p if you live elsewhere. Just write to Dept EP, Penguin Books Ltd, Harmondsworth, Middlesex, enclosing a cheque or postal order, and your name will be added to the mailing list.

Note: *Penguinews* and *Penguins in Print* are not available in the U.S.A. or Canada